What People Are Saying about
Kaydie by Penny Zeller...

This story is well worth reading, with wonderfully crafted characters and plenty of love and inspiration. It's guaranteed to steal readers' hearts.

—*Shirley Kiger Connolly*
Author, *Flame from Within* and
the I See God nonfiction series

This tender prairie romance shows how God works in all circumstances, even horrible ones. Kaydie and Jonah's budding relationship teaches them how to trust one another and to believe in a love that goes beyond their safe friendship. Readers will enjoy the pulse-pounding romantic moments between them when painful memories are broken down and shattered hearts are mended.

—*Michelle Sutton*
Author of more than a dozen inspirational novels,
including *Never without Hope* and *Letting Go*

A compelling and, at times, humorous read, with characters fighting against the lies they believe and the fears they have learned, to find joy in discovering that life isn't what they expected.

—*Diana Lesire Brandmeyer*
Author, *Wyoming Weddings* and *Hearts on the Road*

Well-drawn characters, a dysfunctional relationship between a hurting Kaydie and her parents, and a hero who is heartbreakingly compassionate make this a winning historical romance.

—*Laura V. Hilton*
Author, *Patchwork Dreams*

Penny Zeller has a sweet way with words. She presents *Kaydie* as a story of healing and shows that, though her characters go through difficulties, God's love heals. Life in the Montana Territory is a full of hazards and hard work, but so are relationships. Readers who like good historical love stories will enjoy Zeller's tale of healing hearts on the frontier.

—*Angela Breidenbach*
Inspirational speaker and author

Penny Zeller is a fresh new voice in Christian fiction, and her stories touch and inspire. After reading *McKenzie*, the first book in the Montana Skies series, I knew I had to read *Kaydie*, as well. What a wonderful addition to the series. Don't miss out on this heartwarming, exciting, and adventurous series.

—*Sharlene MacLaren*
Award-winning author of three series:
Little Hickman Creek, The Daughters of Jacob
Kane, and River of Hope (book one, *Livvie's Song*,
releasing in spring 2011)

For a charming tale of love and faith in the Montana Territory, look no further than Penny Zeller's *Kaydie*.

—*Amanda Cabot*
Author, *Tomorrow's Garden*

Yet another sweet story from an up-and-coming author.

—*Cathy Bryant*
Author, *A Path Less Traveled*

Kaydie

Penny
ZELLER

WHITAKER
HOUSE

Publisher's Note:
This novel is a work of fiction. References to real events, organizations, or places are used in a fictional context. Any resemblances to actual persons, living or dead, are entirely coincidental.

All Scripture quotations are taken from the King James Version of the Holy Bible.

KAYDIE
Book Two in the Montana Skies Series

Penny Zeller
www.pennyzeller.com

ISBN: 978-1-60374-217-7
Printed in the United States of America
© 2011 by Penny Zeller

Whitaker House
1030 Hunt Valley Circle
New Kensington, PA 15068
www.whitakerhouse.com

Library of Congress Cataloging-in-Publication Data

Zeller, Penny, 1973–
Kaydie / by Penny Zeller.
    p. cm. — (Montana skies ; bk. 2)
  ISBN 978-1-60374-217-7 (trade pbk.)
1. Single women—Fiction. 2. Montana—Fiction. I. Title.
PS3626.E3565M33 2010
813'.6—dc22

                                    2010050377

1 2 3 4 5 6 7 8 9 10 ⨆⨆ 17 16 15 14 13 12 11

To Makay

CHAPTER ONE

"No, Darius, I'm not going with you!" Kaydie Kraemer winced in pain as her husband, Darius, grabbed her arm and pulled her out the door of her sister's house toward his waiting horse. She tried to pull her arm loose from his tight grasp, but her efforts were futile.

Darius then reached around and grabbed her other arm, squeezing it so hard that Kaydie could already see the bruises he would leave behind. "You don't have a choice, Kaydie. You're my wife, remember?"

"No, Darius. I'm staying here. I don't want to be married to you anymore." Kaydie fought back her tears, hating that they would be sign of weakness to her callous husband.

"You don't have a choice," he snarled. "Now, you can either come willingly, or I can carry you. Which will it be? Because I ain't leavin' without you." He turned his head to the side and spit on the front porch.

"I thought—I thought you were dead," Kaydie stammered.

Darius threw back his head with an evil laugh, which caused the nostrils on his prominent nose to flare in and out. His mouth was open wide, revealing more missing teeth than Kaydie remembered. His stringy brown curls bounced from his collar, and he removed a hand from Kaydie only long enough to slick back the few strands of greasy hair that had fallen over his forehead. He narrowed his eyes, which were already too small for his large face, making them appear even smaller. "I had you fooled, didn't I? You're a foolish woman, Kaydie. Ain't no way I'm gonna die and let you go free! When you said 'I do,' it meant that you were bound to me forever!" He gritted his teeth and gripped her arm even tighter.

"No, Darius! No!"

Kaydie's eyes popped open, and she stared into the darkness. She could hear her heart thumping in her ears, a sound loud enough to rival cannon fire. She placed her hand over her heart and felt it thudding wildly. Sweat poured down her neck; her hands were damp with moisture, and her forehead was covered in beads of perspiration. *It was just a nightmare*, she told herself, still breathless with terror. The vision had seemed so real.

Her heart continued to pound as she reached with her other hand and rubbed her belly. "I think it was only a nightmare, little one." She sat up, swung her legs over the side of the bed, and stood to her feet. Groping in the dark, she made her way to the window and looked outside. The moon and the stars were the only things she could see. Darius and his horse were nowhere in sight.

"Thank You, Lord, that it was just a dream," Kaydie whispered, then turned around and went back to her bed. Burying her face in her pillow, she whimpered softly, not wanting to wake McKenzie, Zach, and Davey. "Thank You, God, that Darius is not coming back," she prayed, her voice muffled by the pillow. "Thank You that You are my *'refuge and strength, a very present help in trouble.'*"

You are safe here, My child, she felt the Lord say to her.

"I know, Lord, but I don't feel safe—not with the memory of Darius," she whispered. Turning over on her back, she gazed up at the ceiling, and the words of Psalm 91 filled her heart: *"He shall cover thee with his feathers, and under his wings shalt thou trust: his truth shall be thy shield and buckler. Thou shalt not be afraid for the terror by night; nor for the arrow that flieth by day; nor for the pestilence that walketh in darkness; nor for the destruction that wasteth at noonday. A thousand shall fall at thy side, and ten thousand at thy right hand; but it shall not come nigh thee."*

Tears of joy slid down Kaydie's face and onto the pillow. "We're going to be all right, little one," she whispered to the baby within her. "We're going to be all right, because the Lord will keep us safe." She gently rubbed her belly again, thankful that God had been there when her husband had been tormenting her and had delivered her from him.

Darius was dead, and he wasn't coming back to take her away. Kaydie had been there. She'd seen it happen. Now, here she was, staying with her beloved sister McKenzie, McKenzie's husband, Zach

Sawyer, and their young son, Davey. Never would Kaydie have guessed that McKenzie would move to the Montana Territory and marry a rancher. For one thing, McKenzie had always despised hard work; for another, she'd had her eye on a wealthy doctor from Boston for years. Yet, from everything Kaydie had seen in her first month at the Sawyer Ranch, McKenzie was happy and wouldn't trade her life there for anything.

McKenzie had told her that God had changed her heart. Kaydie smiled at the memory because He had changed her heart, as well. She had learned about the Lord from Ethel, the woman who had taken her in after Darius's death and given her a steady dose of God's Word. That solid foundation had stayed with Kaydie, and she yearned to know more about her Creator day by day. Yes, she had grown up knowing there was a God, but she hadn't truly experienced Him until Ethel had helped her begin a relationship with Him.

Kaydie turned from one side to the other, unable to fall asleep. In a few short hours, it would be dawn, and she would join the Sawyer family and their hired help at the kitchen table for breakfast. The day she'd met each of the members of McKenzie's new family filled her mind, and she recalled asking McKenzie in private about each one of them. Fearful of placing herself and her unborn baby in danger again, Kaydie had felt it necessary to find out as much as she could about the people with whom she would be living as long as she stayed with her sister. She felt safe around Zach—and, of course, precious Davey. But the others she wasn't so sure about, especially the hired man named Jonah, who had met her in downtown Pine Haven and driven her to the Sawyer Ranch the day she'd found McKenzie....

⤲

"Thank you, McKenzie, for taking me in like this," Kaydie said as she sat with her sister on the front porch, sipping tea. The late September air was chilly, but the fresh breeze felt good.

"I wouldn't have it any other way," McKenzie said. She leaned over and put her arm around her sister. "I have missed you something horrible, Kaydie. I thought for a while that I might never see you again."

"I thought the same thing, myself," said Kaydie. "I never dreamed you would go to all that trouble to find me. I hoped that you would, but I knew better than to count on it."

"It happened thanks only to the Lord," McKenzie said. "Montana Territory is a huge place. I could not have imagined how big it is until I arrived here, and I've seen barely a fraction of it. To have found you within its borders is a miracle, indeed."

"Yes, it is," Kaydie agreed. "I must have thanked the Lord more times than I can count for rescuing me through you."

"And I must have thanked the Lord more times than I can count for rescuing you and bringing you to me," McKenzie said with a giggle.

Kaydie giggled then, too—something she hadn't done for a long time. Oh, how she had missed her sister! "I think you were the only one in our family who didn't give up on me," she said, growing serious again.

"Well, Mother did come out here to take me back to Boston—"

"Thank you, McKenzie."

"You are more than welcome. Besides, I couldn't let 'my baby' stay lost somewhere in the uncivilized Montana Territory forever!"

Kaydie giggled again. "I think Mother feared you would call me 'my baby' as long as you lived!"

"Mother feared a lot of things," said McKenzie. "However, I don't think she ever counted on my leaving our home in Boston to become a wife on the wild frontier and then falling in love with a rancher!"

Kaydie smiled and shook her head. "No, I don't believe she did, or her worst fear would have come true."

"I think the worst thing, though, would have been for Peyton to have done the same thing we did—follow a man to the ends of the earth and forsake our privileged upbringing."

"Oh, Peyton never would have done such a thing." Kaydie rolled her eyes. "Perhaps she isn't our true sister. She's so different from us."

"She's our true sister, just unique. I pray for her daily that she will someday find true joy."

"It would take a completely different outlook on her part—as well as the part of Maxwell—for that to happen," Kaydie said. She thought of her oldest sister's uppity, prudish husband. "Speaking of husbands, Zach seems like a good one," she said, choosing to change the subject to something more positive.

"He is. I'm blessed beyond belief, Kaydie. It took me so long to see the gem that he is. Someday, I'll have to share the entire story with you. To think that

I could have missed out on him because of my own pride and stubbornness...." She shivered.

"I'm happy for you, McKenzie."

"Someday, God will give you a love like that, Kaydie."

"Oh, I think the days of courtship and marriage are over for me. I have my little one to think about now."

"I know marriage is the furthest thing from your mind right now, especially in light of the horrid circumstances in which you found yourself while married to Darius. Still, I have faith that someday God will bless you with the husband He's planned for you all along."

"I suppose I might reconsider marriage—when I'm forty-five," Kaydie said, laughing. But she wasn't kidding. Never again would she trust a man, especially with her heart. She now had not only herself to consider, but also—and more important—her baby. How many times had she thanked the Lord that her baby hadn't been born while Darius was alive? She shuddered at the realization that her survival—and her baby's survival—would have been unlikely, at best, if she had remained with Darius. No, never again would Kaydie be so foolish as to fall in love. Things like true love happened only to others, like McKenzie, and not to her. Such a thought might have in the past bothered her, but not now. She was content in the thought of being reunited with the sister she loved and of soon becoming a mother.

"I will tell you whose marriage is a wonderful model: Asa and Rosemary's," McKenzie said. "They both have taught me so much about a marriage that's

centered on God, and they've been married pretty close to forever."

"Yes, it was so nice to meet them yesterday," Kaydie said. "They seemed quite friendly and charitable."

"They are. I wasn't fond of Rosemary at first, and I didn't really know Asa, since he works with Zach outside most of the time, but once I became acquainted with them, I realized the treasures they are. They have both taught me so much—especially Rosemary. She's like the mother we never had. No offense to Mother, for I know she tried the best she knew how to raise us, but Rosemary...she's different. She has always been so accepting of me, even when I didn't accept her. She taught me how to cook and stitch and how to survive in a home so different from anything I had ever known. She and Asa are like grandparents to Davey, and I believe Zach has all but adopted them as a second set of parents, even though he speaks very well of his parents, who, as I told you, are deceased."

"I think I shall like Rosemary, too," Kaydie said. "And Asa does seem like a good father figure."

"That he is. His Irish accent makes him unique in these parts. I think Rosemary confided to me once that was one of the things that drew her to him when they began courting so many years ago."

"They live just down the road, right?" Kaydie asked.

"Yes, they do. It's nice having them so close. I know you'll come to love Rosemary as much as I do." McKenzie paused. "And then there's Jonah Dickenson, the other hired man. He's a hard worker, always willing to help. He lives alone in the bunkhouse."

"He makes me nervous," Kaydie admitted.

"Jonah?" McKenzie asked. "Why do you say that?"

"When he brought me here from town yesterday, there was just something about him...I can't place my finger on it, exactly, but it was odd."

"I'm not sure what it could be, Kaydie. He's never been anything but polite, and Zach doesn't know what he would do without him. I think the two of them have become brothers, in a way. When Davey's father, Will, died, I think Jonah slipped into the spot he'd had in Zach's heart."

"I think it's wonderful that Zach adopted Davey after his parents died," Kaydie said.

"Yes. A man who accepts another's child as his own is a special man, indeed. Of course, who wouldn't want Davey for a son? I loved him almost immediately."

"So, you don't think I need to be afraid of Jonah?"

"I honestly don't, Kaydie, but if he makes you uncomfortable, you are within your rights to keep your distance. If he ever does anything...." McKenzie paused. "If he ever lays a hand on you or anything else, tell Zach or me right away. Promise?"

"I promise," said Kaydie.

"But, again, I don't see any reason to fear him. He's a godly man with a heart the size of the Montana Territory. I think you'll discover that for yourself once you get to know him."

Kaydie nodded but still wasn't convinced....

CHAPTER TWO

$\mathcal{J}$onah Dickenson walked into Granger Mercantile to retrieve the supplies for Zach. He pulled out his list and eyed the requested items.

"Well, hello, Jonah," said Lucille Granger, who owned the mercantile with her husband, Fred. She waved to him from the counter, behind which was displayed a large quilt stitched with the words "Lucille's Love Connections." Since her success with finding a mail-order bride for Zach, she had launched a matchmaking business, but Jonah didn't think she had many customers.

"Hello, Lucille." Jonah removed his hat and searched the far wall of the store for the coffee Zach had requested and the tea McKenzie had asked for.

"What brings you in to town on this cold October day?"

Jonah turned to face Lucille. She always looked the same—her gray hair pulled into a tight bun on top of her head, her short, plump, apple-shaped body bulging in her gingham dress, the front of which was covered by a white apron. "I needed to pick up some supplies for the ranch."

"Anything I can help you find?" Lucille prided herself in being helpful.

"Uh, yes—actually, there is something you can help me with, Lucille. McKenzie mentioned something about some special-order fabric. She wanted me to ask you if it had arrived."

"Why, yes, it did! I had forgotten about that. I'll be right back." With short, quick strides on equally short legs, Lucille sprang through the door toward the back room. A minute later, she returned. "Here it is. Isn't it just the loveliest print you've ever seen?"

Jonah arched an eyebrow. Didn't Lucille realize that fabric prints, lovely or not, mattered nothing in the least to him, a member of the male species? He thought of her husband, Fred, to whom Lucille had been married probably for more years than Jonah had been alive. Did Lucille often ask him whether or not he found a piece of cloth to be "lovely"? Likely so, Jonah thought. "It's fine, Lucille," Jonah answered, trying to sound sincere.

"Well, it's more than fine, Jonah. This fabric came all the way from back East! It's my understanding that McKenzie wanted it so she could sew Kaydie a dress." Lucille, ever the town busybody, leaned forward over the counter as if the next thing she was to say was strictly between the two of them. "I hear that she's getting quite large in the belly."

"I wouldn't know about that, ma'am," said Jonah, feeling himself blush. Why did Lucille insist on gossiping with him as if he were some townswoman?

"Now, Jonah, you tell McKenzie that I said this is the best fabric this side of the Mississippi." Lucille unfolded the piece of cloth on the counter and repeatedly ran her chubby hand across it. "And the color, too—won't it just make Kaydie's brown eyes stand out? I mean, not everyone can wear yellow gingham. For one, it just doesn't complement some women's features. For instance, it makes some women appear extremely pale, sallow, and unhealthy. Complexion has everything to do with choosing just the right fabric for a new dress." Lucille leaned over the counter, again as if to insinuate that her conversation with Jonah was private, even though they were the only ones in the mercantile. "But with Kaydie's big, brown eyes and her long, blonde hair, it should go quite well."

Jonah shook his head and silently thanked the Lord that he wasn't a woman. Each morning, he pulled on one of the three shirts he owned, neither knowing nor caring whether it complemented his complexion. What's more, he cared little whether the fabric came from back East or from the nearby Dakota Territory. All he cared about was that the item of clothing did its job. "I have a few more things to get, Lucille," Jonah said, placing several sacks of coffee and tea on the counter. "I'll need three pounds of sugar and some kerosene."

"Of course—we have everything you need here at Granger Mercantile," Lucille said, pride raising the pitch of her voice. She retrieved the items and added them to the growing pile on the counter. "Will that be all for you today?"

"Yes. Please add it to the bill."

"Certainly," said Lucille. Reaching for a pencil, she carefully recorded the items and their prices in her journal. "You know, Jonah," she began when she had put down her pencil, "I've been giving a lot of thought to your predicament."

"My predicament?"

"Well, yes, your predicament." Lucille looked baffled that he didn't know what she was talking about.

"I wasn't aware that I had a predicament," said Jonah, bracing himself for her answer.

"*You* know," said Lucille, her eyes widening.

"I honestly don't know, Lucille. Last time I checked, I was happy and healthy."

"Now, now, you may be healthy, but you don't really believe you're happy, do you?"

Jonah looked around to be sure no one else had walked into the mercantile. Zach, his employer and best friend, had so much more patience with Lucille than he did. Jonah thought she was a gossipy nuisance, albeit a good-hearted one. Of course, Zach had every reason to think highly of Lucille. She and her husband had treated him like their own son and had given him a job when he'd first come to Pine Haven. That, and Lucille was the reason Zach had found McKenzie; she'd helped him place an advertisement for a mail-order bride in several Boston newspapers. "I am happy, Lucille," Jonah insisted.

"You might think you're happy, but you're really not," Lucille stated with a decisive nod of her head. "You're not one hundred percent happy because you don't have a wife."

Jonah was taken aback. "Now, wait a minute here, Lucille. With all due respect—"

"Oh, fiddlesticks," said Lucille. "Don't even try to argue with me, Jonah Dickenson. Besides, I know what you're going to say. You may hide it well, but inside, your heart is broken, like a piece of fine china that has fallen from its high place on the hutch in the kitchen...." Lucille held her hand to her heart and closed her eyes.

Then, her eyes popped open again, wide with fervor. "But don't despair, Jonah," she said, her voice deepening in seriousness. "I can help you.

"Lucille—"

"Lucille's Love Connections, at your service." She pulled a tablet from under the counter and reached again for her pencil. In her neat, large printing, she wrote "Jonah Dickenson" at the top of the page.

"Lucille, really." Although Jonah knew Lucille, he was still shocked at how domineering she could be.

"Please don't interrupt me. That will do you no good. Now, let's see here. How old are you?"

Jonah sighed. "Twenty-five." He acquiesced to play along with Lucille's game but dreaded the outcome.

"Very well. You're twenty-five, and you have... let's see, how should we describe that hair?" Lucille reached up and patted him on the head. "Hmm. Let's say you have hair the color of a dark-orange pumpkin."

"A dark-orange pumpkin?" That was the farthest thing from a compliment Jonah had ever received. He'd always rather liked the color of his hair but had never considered it to resemble an autumn squash; the word *rust* or *copper* seemed more appropriate to describe it. A dark-orange pumpkin? Really? Jonah shook his head. Not even close. He thought of his pa's hair, which was the color of a bright-orange pumpkin. His pa had a collection of freckles dotting his face, whereas Jonah had not a one.

"Well, it is kind of an orange hue," Lucille said, her tone defensive.

"Kind of orange, yes. Pumpkin-colored, no," said Jonah.

"Well, anyway, let's see those peepers," Lucille said, changing the subject as she leaned toward him and stared into his eyes.

"Lucille, really...." Jonah took a step back.

"I think we could say that your eyes are the color of...hmm." Lucille put her hand on her chin. "What's something gray? A rock, perhaps?"

"Couldn't you just say that my eyes are gray?" Jonah suggested.

"You're so right, Jonah. You see, even though I have much experience in this matter, and although I have had some formal schooling, to say that your eyes are the color of a rock is just not becoming, especially to a potential bride."

"You're writing this down to find me a wife?" Jonah asked.

"Why, yes," Lucille replied as she jotted down the information.

"I've told you before, Lucille, I don't need or want a wife."

"But I found one for Zach—a mighty good one, at that."

"Yes, and he's grateful to you, Lucille. But I'm not Zach."

"Oh, you'll thank me someday. Every man tries to argue, but in the end, they see that I was right all along. Now, let's see. Here's what I've written so far: 'Kindhearted Montana Territory ranch hand, twenty-five years of age, with handsome gray eyes and hair the color of a dark-orange pumpkin, seeks a wife.' How does that sound?"

Jonah knew he was in a losing battle and once again thought of Lucille's husband, Fred. Poor man, he probably never won an argument with her. That likely explained why he almost always worked in the back room of the store instead of in the front with Lucille. Fewer opportunities for arguments. How could Jonah persuade Lucille that he didn't need a wife? She'd already refused to listen to him when he'd stated it plainly.

Then, an idea came to him. "Lucille?"

"Yes, Jonah?" Lucille said distractedly, her eyes still on the paper.

"I have an idea."

"Now, Jonah, if you really are opposed to seeking a mail-order bride, I have an alternate plan in mind. Do you know that new family who recently moved here, the Grouards? Well, they have a daughter—she must be close to twenty—named Gillian. I could arrange for the two of you to meet. That way, we could keep the whole affair in Pine Haven."

"No, thank you, Lucille. That's not what I was thinking of at all. Besides, I hear that there's someone else who has his eye on Gillian. No, what I'm thinking is far better than that." This time, Jonah leaned toward Lucille to privatize their conversation. He motioned at her to do the same.

"Yes?"

"I don't know. I probably shouldn't say—"

"What do you mean, you shouldn't say?" asked Lucille. The quickest way to pique her curiosity was to make her think you were privy to information about which she was yet ignorant.

"All right, I suppose I can tell you. It's Mr. Victor."

"Mr. Victor at the post office?"

"Yes, he's the one," Jonah said, trying to muffle a chuckle at the thought of there being more than one Mr. Victor in the small town of Pine Haven.

"Well, of course, I know Mr. Victor," said Lucille. "Who doesn't? He's worked at the post office forever."

"He is the one in desperate need of a wife," said Jonah, shaking his head. "Poor man, he would like to have a wife, but the years are passing him by faster than a wild pony runs from a cowboy."

Lucille looked pensive for a moment.

"I would feel horrible, Lucille, if you found a wife for me before you found one for Mr. Victor," Jonah went on. "I mean, I'm still young. I can wait. Mr. Victor...." He shrugged. "Mr. Victor isn't so young."

"Oh, poor, poor Mr. Victor," Lucille lamented. "I had forgotten about him." She shook her head. "Yes, you are right. I must find him a wife first." She tore the page she'd written about Jonah from her notebook and, at the top of the next page, wrote "Mr. Victor."

"Let's keep this between us, Lucille," Jonah said, meanwhile knowing that would never be the case if Lucille was involved. She was far too nosy and excited to share the newest piece of gossip to keep anything to herself.

"But of course we will," she said, patting Jonah's arm. "Whatever would I have done if you hadn't stopped by today? My goal is to use Lucille's Love Connections to benefit others in the best way possible. You have made that a reality by suggesting Mr. Victor. I'm forever indebted to you."

"I best be going now, Lucille. I think a storm is coming in, but you keep me posted on the progress with Mr. Victor."

"I will, Jonah. You tell everyone at the ranch I said hello."

Jonah nodded and grabbed the box of items. As he loaded it into his wagon, he heaved a huge sigh of relief. Never had he been so thankful to be released from the clutches of Lucille Granger.

After covering the box, Jonah walked to the post office, which doubled as a telegraph office, as the first raindrops began to fall. "Hello, Mr. Victor," he greeted the man at the counter.

"Good afternoon, Jonah. Let's see here...I do have a letter for McKenzie and a parcel for Davey." He handed Jonah the items.

Jonah studied Mr. Victor. He estimated the man to be in his late forties. His face was heavily wrinkled, especially at the corners of his eyes—*Probably on account of his constant smile*, Jonah mused. Come to think of it, Jonah couldn't remember ever seeing Mr. Victor with a frown on his face.

"Is there something else I can do for you?" the postman asked.

"No, this is fine," Jonah said, holding up the parcel.

"I hear there's a storm coming in," said Mr. Victor.

"Yes. It's raining now, but if the weather turns even a slight bit colder, I reckon it'll turn to snow," Jonah said.

Mr. Victor nodded, then narrowed his eyes in concern. "Are you all right, son?"

Jonah was surprised at his question, but then he realized he'd been staring at Mr. Victor for the past several minutes. No wonder Mr. Victor thought that something might be wrong with him. "Yes, I'm fine, thanks."

"Well, good, then. Everything going all right at the ranch?"

"Yes, sir."

"How is McKenzie's sister? Is she settling in all right?"

"Kaydie? Yes, she's fine," said Jonah. He hadn't given much thought lately to Kaydie or how she was doing. She seemed to avoid him on purpose, and he knew very little about her, other than what McKenzie and Zach had shared with him. "Mr. Victor?" Jonah finally said.

"Yes?"

"I'm sorry."

"You're sorry? What for, son?" Mr. Victor leaned over the counter, his forehead creased with lines of worry.

Jonah shifted his feet. How could he tell Mr. Victor he was sorry for suggesting that Lucille find him a wife? Would Mr. Victor be angry with him? Did Mr. Victor even want a wife? Jonah regretted bringing up the subject with Lucille in the first place. But it had been the only way to divert her attention from her unshakable goal to find him a bride.

"What are you sorry for, Jonah? Whatever it is, I assure you, I will forgive you," said Mr. Victor.

"I—I think Lucille is trying to find you a wife." There. He'd said it. And with his words came the huge breath of air he'd been holding in.

"Lucille is trying to find me a wife?" Mr. Victor asked, then chortled a deep and loud chuckle that, had it not been for the rain, which fell heavily now, could have been heard out on the streets of Pine Haven.

"You're not mad, then?" said Jonah, relieved that Mr. Victor had taken the news so well.

"No, I'm not mad, Jonah. I'm not at all surprised, either. Best of luck to her, because I've been searching for a wife for over thirty years, and I haven't had any success. Perhaps she will."

"If I know Lucille like I think I know Lucille, you'll be experiencing wedded bliss very soon," Jonah said with a laugh.

"You know, son, I've never been married. I had a chance once, when I was twenty-seven and living in Kansas. Her name was Celia. I should have taken the chance, and I regret it to this day that I didn't."

"Maybe it's not too late," said Jonah, shocked that for the second time today, he was conversing about a subject that seemed an exclusive interest of womenfolk.

"Oh, it's far too late," Mr. Victor said with a sigh. "Celia married another man and had three children—two sons and a daughter. And...Celia passed away a year ago." He shook his head mournfully.

"I'm sorry to hear about Celia, Mr. Victor."

"Thank you, Jonah. I appreciate that. I suppose it taught me a lesson—one that I share with others when the occasion arises, and that I'm going to share with you now. If you should ever experience true love for someone, grab on to her and don't let her go. Otherwise, you'll probably be haunted by regret forever."

"I'm really not one for marriage, Mr. Victor," Jonah said quietly.

"Not one for marriage?" Mr. Victor paused for a moment. "Did you know that marriage was God's idea? Now, not everyone will marry. Look at the apostle Paul. He wasn't married, and he was used by God to spread the gospel in an amazing way. So, no, marriage isn't for everyone, but it was God's idea, and a man would be a fool to pass up someone the way I passed up Celia."

"I'll remember that," said Jonah. Although he appreciated Mr. Victor's insight, Jonah wasn't about to change his mind on marriage because of it. No, as far as Jonah was concerned, he would be content living eighty years without ever marrying.

By the time Jonah arrived back at the Sawyer Ranch, the temperature had dropped several degrees, and he knew it was only a matter of time before the rain turned to snow. He grabbed the box of goods from the back of the wagon and walked toward the house. He could hear laughter coming from the barn and figured Davey was jumping from the loft into the soft pile of hay below, as he did so often, and he grinned. *Ah, to have had a childhood like that boy has*, he thought to himself.

Jonah opened the door and stepped inside the house, and that's when he saw her. Sleeping peacefully with a baby quilt-in-progress spread across her lap was Kaydie. Her head rested against the back of the fancy blue chair McKenzie had ordered from Boston; her long, wavy blonde hair cascaded over her right shoulder; and her petite, stocking-clad feet were propped on the bottom rung of a nearby chair.

Her slender arms were folded across her belly, and her rosy lips were parted slightly as she breathed with a soft, feminine snore. Jonah stopped for a moment to take in the sight, struck by the beauty before him.

Jonah knew something of Kaydie's past and of her marriage to a cruel husband named Darius. He knew she had suffered at his hands, and that he had died in a bank robbery gone awry. From what McKenzie had told him, Kaydie's married life had been anything but peaceful. However, reclined in the chair, which looked completely out of place in the otherwise rustic, sparsely decorated living room, she had an aura of peace about her that tugged at the deep recesses of Jonah's heart.

He glanced at the fireplace and saw that the fire had gone out, save for the small glow of an ember hidden in one of the black logs. Kaydie must have been sleeping for some time. Was she cold? Should he cover her up with a blanket? Jonah gulped at the unexpected concern he felt, and he debated whether to go back outside and return later so as not to continue violating Kaydie's privacy. Where was everyone else? His mind returned to the noises he'd heard in the barn. No doubt Zach and McKenzie were out there with Davey. McKenzie took as much delight in swinging from the rope in the barn and falling into the hay pile as Davey did.

As quietly as he could, Jonah walked over to the table and set down the box of goods. He then turned and tiptoed toward Kaydie, pausing for a moment to pick up the large crocheted blanket from the wooden chair next to the fireplace.

When he reached Kaydie's chair, he carefully lifted the small baby quilt she had been working on and replaced it with the larger, much warmer, crocheted blanket. He spread it gently over her shoulders, hoping not to disturb her, and made sure it covered them completely. Next, he would stoke the fire, he thought as he smoothed out the blanket. He knew next to nothing about pregnant women but figured it was important to keep them warm.

He had nearly covered Kaydie's legs with the blanket when she opened her eyes and gasped. "What are you doing?" she exclaimed.

Jonah stood up straight and held up his arms defensively. "Kaydie! Uh, you were sleeping, and I... uh—"

"Get away from me, please," she said, her voice trembling.

"I...uh, all right." Jonah took a step back from her and watched as she leaned back as far as the chair would allow and pulled the blanket tightly around her. "Kaydie..." he began, intending to explain himself.

"I don't know what you were doing, but please leave," she said.

"I walked in and saw you sleeping. The fire had almost burned out, so I thought I'd cover you with a warmer blanket. I—I didn't want you to be cold."

"I wasn't cold," Kaydie insisted.

"That's good," said Jonah. "I was going to get the fire going again, too."

"Do you make a habit of sneaking up on people, Mr. Dickenson?" Kaydie demanded.

"No, ma'am, I don't. I never meant to scare you. I just—I just didn't want you to be cold."

Kaydie eyed him warily.

"I just returned from picking up a few items from Granger's Mercantile," Jonah said, attempting to change the subject. He added several logs to the fire and gave them a stir, then backed away from Kaydie, making sure there was sufficient distance between them. Since her arrival at Sawyer Ranch, he'd noticed how she seemed to avoid him. He'd even changed seats with Rosemary at the dinner table so that she wouldn't have to sit right next to him, which, he could tell, made her uncomfortable. Yet, even seated across from him with the table in between, Kaydie still seemed to cower from him.

"Please don't sneak up on me again," Kaydie said, her voice barely above a whisper.

"I promise, I won't," said Jonah. The last thing he wanted to do was make a frightened woman even more frightened. "Kaydie?"

"Yes, Mr. Dickenson?"

"I'm truly sorry. I wasn't trying to scare you." Jonah took off his hat and stared at the wood floor.

"All right," Kaydie said hesitantly.

"And you can call me Jonah, if you'd like," he drawled.

"I don't know about that," Kaydie said, not looking at him.

"Kaydie, I don't know you very well, but I do know a little bit about Darius and how he treated you. I've heard McKenzie and Zach speak of it." Jonah cleared his throat. "I just want you to know that I would never hurt you."

Kaydie finally looked at him. "You have to understand, Mr. Dickenson, that I don't believe what men say anymore."

"That's fine, Kaydie. I respect that. You don't know me very well, and you probably figure me to be lying, but it's the truth, just the same. I'm a God-fearing man of honor, and I intend to stay that way."

Kaydie gave a half smile and nodded.

It didn't seem that he had convinced her, so Jonah decided to drop the subject for a while. "Do you know where Zach and McKenzie are?" he asked her.

"In the barn, I think," she replied.

Jonah nodded. "I reckon I'll go out there and see what's going on."

"Uh, Mr. Dickenson?"

"Yes?"

"Did you say you picked up some items in town?"

"Yes, I did, ma'am. I had a whole list of things, and I pretty near got them all," Jonah said.

"Did there happen to be any fabric for me?" Kaydie asked, her soft voice hopeful.

"Yes—yes, there was." Jonah chuckled at the memory of Lucille and the piece of cloth.

"What's so funny?" Kaydie asked.

"Lucille is what's so funny," said Jonah. "She tried to get me to admit that it was the loveliest piece of cloth I'd ever seen, and that only certain womenfolk could wear that color because of their complexion, and so on."

Kaydie giggled softly. "I've met Lucille only twice, but I can imagine how she sounded."

"I couldn't believe she would ask my opinion of a piece of cloth. Now, if she had asked my opinion on a gun or a horse, I could have given my earnest approval, but a piece of cloth? No—"

"Is it in the box?" Kaydie interrupted him.

"It is. Can I get it for you?"

"That would be fine, thank you."

Jonah walked over to the table and rifled through the box until he found the fabric wrapped in brown paper. "Here it is," he said, then made his way back over to Kaydie. Maintaining what he figured was a safe distance, he handed the package to her.

"I can't wait to see it," Kaydie exclaimed. Her face lit up with a smile as she pulled off the brown paper. "Oh, it is lovely!" She held it to up her chest and smiled. "Lucille was right."

Jonah watched her hug the cloth. He was thankful she no longer seemed angry with him.

"McKenzie and Rosemary are going to help me sew a new dress. This one is getting a bit small," Kaydie said, grabbing a handful of the dress she was wearing. "The nice thing is that after the baby comes, I can take the dress in again. With this beautiful fabric, it would be a shame to wear it for only a short time."

Jonah nodded, amused by how Kaydie talked softly, even when excited. Of course, when he'd first met her in the post office, where she'd cowered against the wall, he hadn't figured her to be boisterous and loud. He wanted to ask her when she would be having the baby, just to make polite conversation, but decided against it. It wasn't proper to speak of such things, even if he was trying to help her to trust him.

"Well, I best be heading outside," said Jonah.

Kaydie nodded, then turned and gazed at the fireplace.

"Again, Kaydie, I am sorry about—about the blanket."

Kaydie nodded again, keeping her eyes on the fire. "Thank you for picking up the fabric."

"Anytime you need something from town, just let me know. I'll see you at dinner, then." Jonah turned on his heel and left the house, hoping that Kaydie trusted him at least a little more than she had before.

CHAPTER THREE

Kaydie was pleased with how quickly she settled in to life at the Sawyer Ranch. Although she was extremely tired due to her pregnancy, she took great pleasure in helping McKenzie around the house whenever she could muster the energy. Her life was busy yet fulfilling. She enjoyed the cooking and baking lessons Rosemary gave to her and McKenzie, and in her spare time, she continued to work on the baby's quilt, which she hoped to finish before January, when the doctor had said she was due to give birth. Together with McKenzie, she'd visited Rosemary's house three times, where they had sewn gifts they would be giving for Christmas, now a little over a month away. Kaydie had attended Sunday services at Pine Haven Chapel with McKenzie, Zach, Davey, Asa, Rosemary, and Jonah. There, she had met many friendly townsfolk, whose kind words and welcoming ways were helping her heal, bit by bit, from the horrors of being married to an abusive man.

Despite the many changes that had occurred in her life in recent months, there was one thing that hadn't changed: Kaydie's parents. Kaydie thought about this as she reached into the pocket of her apron and pulled out the letter she'd received from her mother the day before. She unfolded the floral stationery and reread the letter, line by line.

My dearest Kaydence,

Your father and I hope this letter finds you well. A blessing it was to find out that Darius has passed on. His character was utterly reprehensible. We are thankful that you are now staying with McKenzie, although I have visited her new home and cannot say I am completely pleased with the uncivilized town and surroundings. Still, I suppose it is better than nothing.

This brings me to another important issue: your father and I are making plans for your return to Boston next summer. We are eager to have you home once again and away from the crude, unsophisticated Montana Territory. Prolonged exposure to that area is sure to cause irreversible damage, even though you had a proper upbringing. Besides, losing one daughter to the primitive West has taken its toll on our health. Losing two would be unspeakable. I am thankful that your eldest sister, Peyton, kept her wits about her, married well, and remained in the civilized East.

Finding a suitable husband for you in the Boston area is sure to prove effortless, inasmuch as the Worthington family has one of the most up-standing reputations in the State of Massachusetts, despite your unseemly elopement with Darius and McKenzie's reckless marriage to a rancher. We have already told the other families in our social circle that you married Darius, but we altered the details in order to protect your reputation. We did this from the moment you made the egregious error of choosing him as a husband. What else could we say? Our disappointment in you, as you know full well, was profound. Had our peers been privy to the frustrations you placed on your family by your foolhardy choice of a husband, the damage to our family's good name would have been immeasurable.

The other families in our social circle believe Darius to have been a successful young doctor from an upstanding New York family who took you to the Montana Territory to open his new practice with the hopes of bringing medical care to the barbaric folks of that area. Sadly, an intestinal illness claimed his life and left you a widow. This was even more heartbreaking for you since you had discovered shortly before your husband's death that you were with child. The discovery did your heart good in one way— it gave you something of Darius's to keep with you, since he was a loving, caring husband who unfortunately met with an untimely death.

Please begin to ingrain this story in your memory so that your account will align with it and not contradict it when you return to Boston

*next year. Nothing would be worse than a fail-
ure to effectively memorize the aforementioned,
as it would put a conspicuous mark on the reputation of the Worthington family. I fear such
an instance would make your father's already
fragile heart fail.*

*Hearing of your loving husband's death, a
suitable bachelor is sure to want to woo you
and give you and your child a home. Finding
a man of wealth and status is important, for
he must be willing and able to support your
child. Your father has been hard at work locat-
ing such a man. We will continue to inform you
by post of our progress.*

*I recently sent a box of books to Davey, pur-
suant to McKenzie's request. It is my hope that
the boy has received them by now. Please inform McKenzie that I will be mailing an addi-
tional parcel in the coming weeks with more of
her books for him.*

*Also express to McKenzie, if you would, that
it is not too late for her to change her mind and
return to Boston. While she has assured me
time and time again that she is pleased with
her current circumstances, I find that difficult
to believe. My hope is to one day have all three
of my daughters living presentable lives in Boston once again.*

Yours truly,
Mother

Kaydie refolded the letter and tucked it back inside her pocket. Wiping a tear from the corner of her
eye with the back of her hand, she thought of the

words her mother had written. Wealth, status, and propriety had always been of paramount importance to Florence Worthington. And Kaydie couldn't help but notice that while her mother had gone to great lengths to express her disapproval of Kaydie's choice in matrimony, she'd offered no words to affirm Kaydie or to write what she longed to be told: "I love you." No, it was clear that, even though her parents had never been openly affectionate, Kaydie had fallen out of their good graces, and it was doubtful that their arranging a respectable union for her would restore their esteem for her.

It was for the sake of their own names that Kaydie's parents were set on bringing her back to Boston and marrying her off to a man who was suitable in their eyes—not a man like the real Darius, whom Kaydie had chosen to marry, but a man of status and wealth. Kaydie had made her own choice—and she had suffered the consequences. Now, her parents would plot out her destiny, since they presumably knew better.

Kaydie thought of her sisters, Peyton and McKenzie, and how each of them responded to their overbearing parents. Peyton was almost an exact copy of their mother in appearance and in personality. She had done everything right in the eyes of her parents from the time she was born. She had married well—her husband was a lawyer in their father's law firm—had had a child, and spent her time attending fancy galas or volunteering at charitable organizations. Peyton was the perfect Worthington daughter and easily their mother's favorite.

McKenzie, on the other hand, was their father's favorite. Bright and brave, she would have made an excellent partner in his law firm, he often said, if it were proper for ladies to practice law. Yet she had taken a path in life that had led her far away from the expectations that her parents, especially her father, held for her.

And then, there was Kaydie. Neither perfect nor brave, she had never held a favorite place in either parent's heart. Named Kaydence Louise Worthington after her mother's dearest brother, Kayde Dudley, Kaydie much preferred her shortened name to the more formal Kaydence. Reserved, soft-spoken, and submissive, she had caused quite a shock when she had firmly announced her decision to marry Darius. "Well, Mother and Father, I'm afraid I can't do as you wish this time, either," Kaydie said aloud, thankful that no one else was in the house. "The reason is that I have decided never to marry again. That way, I will never be in danger of making the mistake of choosing someone like Darius a second time."

Kaydie wiped another tear from her eye and knew she needed to do something to take her mind off of the upsetting letter. While she had told McKenzie about it the previous evening, the words her mother had penned still disturbed her. She didn't want to spread falsehoods about the man she had married. Instead, she wanted to share with others the grace the Lord had bestowed upon her, even though she was completely undeserving of such grace. She wanted to tell others how God had rescued her and opened her eyes to His truth through the love of a woman named Ethel, who had taken Kaydie in, even though she was a stranger.

Looking around, Kaydie spied the stove. She could bake, she thought. She'd wanted to make gingerbread cookies for some time now and hadn't yet had the chance. She had fond memories of eating them as a child when Cook would make them for her and her sisters during the Christmas holidays. It was a good thing she'd asked McKenzie to purchase some ginger and molasses during her trip to town last week. Thankful for a task to take her mind off the letter, Kaydie went about baking the cookies, humming happily as she measured the ingredients.

Once she had mixed the dough, Kaydie rolled it out and fashioned round cookies using a teacup as a makeshift cookie cutter. She wished she had one in the shape of a gingerbread man. Perhaps Lucille Granger could order her one. *No matter*, thought Kaydie. Round gingerbread cookies were just as much a delicacy as gingerbread men. What frightened Kaydie was the realization that in her present state, she could probably eat the entire batch. The odd assortment of food cravings she had experienced ever since the Lord had blessed her with a child in her womb had been unreal. Sometimes, the cravings even came in the middle of the night. Still, despite the drastic changes to her body, her food habits, and her emotions due to pregnancy, Kaydie wouldn't trade it for the world.

When she had filled one baking sheet with the rounded portions of dough, Kaydie opened the door of the cast-iron stove and placed the sheet inside. While the cookies baked, she whipped some icing. Wouldn't Davey be thrilled when he returned home from an afternoon of sliding down hills on the toboggan with his parents to the aroma of fresh gingerbread? Kaydie patted her stomach with a gentle hand. "Someday, little one, I'll bake gingerbread cookies for you," she said.

After she had finished baking and icing the cookies, Kaydie felt fatigued and knew it was time to take a rest. She returned to the out-of-place, overstuffed blue chair near the fireplace and sat down, then reached for her Bible on the table beside the chair. She turned to the book of 1 Samuel and began to read, glancing up after every few lines to look out the window. Large snowflakes had begun to fall, and Kaydie marveled at the beauty of the setting around her.

A few minutes later, she heard footsteps on the porch and paused to see who would enter the house. It was too soon for McKenzie, Zach, and Davey to return from their toboggan outing, so perhaps it was Rosemary stopping by for a visit. Much to Kaydie's surprise, it wasn't Rosemary who entered the house seconds later but Jonah.

"Hello, Kaydie," Jonah said as he stomped the snow off his boots. "Are you all right today?"

"I'm just fine, Mr. Dickenson. Why wouldn't I be?" Kaydie still felt uneasy around Jonah, although less so than when she had first met him.

"Mmm, what's that I smell?" Jonah closed his eyes and inhaled. "Did you bake something?"

"Gingerbread cookies," Kaydie replied in a matter-of-fact way.

"I love gingerbread," said Jonah, his gaze roving toward the kitchen. When he spied the plate of cookies on the kitchen table, he grinned. "May I have one?"

Kaydie nodded and watched as Jonah walked over to the table and helped himself to one of the frosted cookies. All the while, she wondered about the purpose of his visit, so she decided to find out. "What brings you in here, Mr. Dickenson?"

Cookie in hand, Jonah returned to the living room and sat down in the wooden chair across from Kaydie. "McKenzie asked if I would keep an eye on you while she and Zach were away," he answered.

"Keep an eye on me?" Kaydie asked incredulously.

"Yes—you know, because of your condition."

My condition? "You must mean because of the baby," she said.

"Yes," Jonah said. "I know it'll be your time soon, and McKenzie was concerned about you being in here all by yourself." He paused and eyed the cookie in his hand. Raising it to his mouth, he took a bite, closed his eyes, and chewed slowly. It appeared that he found her cookies as delicious as everyone else who had tried them.

"I take it the cookie meets with your approval?" she said.

The look on Jonah's face almost made her laugh. It was as if he were a young boy eating his very first cookie.

Jonah swallowed, then smiled broadly. "These are delicious, Kaydie. I can't tell you the last time I had gingerbread cookies, and they're my favorite!" He took another bite, chewed, and swallowed.

"They're my favorite, too," said Kaydie. "It's very odd—since being with child, I have had some of the most powerful cravings for food. I'd had a hankering for gingerbread for a while, and—" Kaydie stopped then, amazed that she had spoken of something so personal to him. After all, he was basically a stranger, even though she'd known him for several months.

"Can I get one for you?" Jonah asked as he stood to his feet.

"Yes, thank you," Kaydie said. She had planned to wait until the cookies cooled but could not pass up Jonah's offer.

When Jonah walked back with three cookies in hand and held out two of them for her, Kaydie tried not to cower as she accepted them. She nibbled on one as Jonah took a giant bite of his second cookie. "They are quite good, if I do say so, myself," she said. "When I was a little girl, Cook would allow me to help her make cookies every now and then. Gingerbread was the type we made the most often, so I memorized the recipe."

"Your family had a cook?" Jonah asked, finishing off his cookie.

"Yes, and we had a nanny, too. My mother's job was not to raise us but to find worthwhile ways to contribute to Boston society." Kaydie allowed a bit of sarcasm to seep through.

"Quite different from the way I grew up," Jonah said with a shake of his head. "We were poor, and I was fortunate to have anything to eat some days. Not that it mattered; I was fine."

"I actually know what it feels like not to have any food," said Kaydie. She focused her gaze on the flame in the fireplace. "There were times when I would make Darius dinner, and he would eat it in front of me, saving me only a tiny morsel, if that. It was as though he enjoyed seeing me go hungry."

"That's awful, Kaydie. I'm sorry about that," said Jonah.

"I don't know why he changed. He wasn't that way when I met him. Then, after we got married, he spent all of my inheritance and began robbing banks to support himself. Once in a while, he would allow me to buy a piece of fabric for a new dress or some sugar to bake something, but that usually wasn't the case. He hoarded the money for himself and spent most of it on alcohol. While I did eat, I never had as much as a healthy person needs to survive. I know I was pretty close to skin and bones when my friend in Wheeler found me. Her name was Ethel. When she took me in, I couldn't remember a time when I had eaten so well. And now, the Lord has blessed me with a home here where food isn't scarce."

"I know what you mean when you speak of a man spending most of his money on alcohol," Jonah reflected. "My pa was that way. Anything extra he earned went into the Saloon Fund, as I called it."

Kaydie saw a look of melancholy cross Jonah's face, but he quickly plastered on a smile. "So, were you reading?" He nodded toward the Bible lying face-down on Kaydie's lap.

"Yes, I was reading aloud to the baby from First Samuel. I love the story that tells of Hannah wanting a child so badly and the Lord blessing her with one. She then dedicated her son Samuel to the Lord."

"That is one of the many great stories in the Bible," Jonah agreed.

"Have you been a believer all your life?" Kaydie asked. Seated at a safe distance from Jonah, she found herself relaxing a bit. She also felt sorry for the man whose childhood had been less than ideal.

"Since I was seventeen," Jonah said. "A man on the cotton farm in Mississippi where I worked intro-duced me to the Lord. That man's name was Jamal

Winthrop. I'll never forget him. He was an elderly man and had been a slave once, and he loved the Lord with all his being. I'd never even heard of God before I met Jamal. My pa certainly never told me anything about Him."

"What about your mother?"

Jonah swallowed hard. "My ma left when I was just a young'un. I don't remember much about her."

"I'm so sorry, Mr. Dickenson. I had no idea." Kaydie thought of the letter she'd recently received from her mother. While her mother's mannerisms and priorities seldom agreed with Kaydie's, at least she hadn't left her or her sisters behind. She did care for them, even if it was not always easy to see. Jonah hadn't been so privileged. His mother had turned away from him and likely had never looked back.

"It was a long time ago," said Jonah. "I always wondered why she did it, and why she didn't take me with her. I asked my pa a couple of times and was shown with the back of his hand why I shouldn't speak of it further. I do wonder, though, when I see you here with your baby, doing things...." Jonah hesitated and cleared his throat.

"I'm sure she loved you, Mr. Dickenson," Kaydie said, not knowing what else to say. Her heart ached for him, and also at the thought of leaving a child behind. That was something she could never imagine doing.

"I'm not sure of that fact, Kaydie. If my ma loved me, she shouldn't have left me." He swallowed again and seemed to be fighting back tears. "I do wonder, though, if she ever read to me from the Bible or craved gingerbread cookies or patted her stomach and called me 'little one,' like you do."

Kaydie felt the warmth of a blush on her face. Had he heard her address the baby as "little one"? She met his gaze, then quickly averted her eyes and slouched in the chair, wishing she could disappear and escape her embarrassment.

"Your baby will be greatly blessed," Jonah added. Was that a blush on his face, too?

"I already love her and can't wait to meet her," Kaydie said, gently rubbing the roundness of her belly.

Jonah chuckled. "So, it's a 'her'? What if the baby's a boy?"

Kaydie cocked her head and reflected on his question. Until now, she hadn't given much thought to the baby's gender. "I've always called the baby a 'her.' I don't know why for sure; I just always have. Promise me, Mr. Dickenson, that if the baby is really a 'he,' you won't say a word about my calling him a 'her.'"

"For another cookie, I may be persuaded to make that promise," said Jonah, his eyes twinkling in a way Kaydie had never seen before.

"Please, have another cookie." Kaydie waved her hand toward the kitchen table.

"Do you care for another?" Jonah asked.

Kaydie nodded. She could have eaten the entire plate of cookies and still craved more. She feared for a moment that her baby would be born with a sweet tooth.

Jonah picked up the plate and carried it over to Kaydie. "We might as well finish these off, as there's only five left," he said with a boyish grin.

"Oh, let's leave one for Davey," Kaydie suggested as she took two cookies from the plate.

"Good idea. I know he would appreciate that." Jonah claimed two for himself, leaving one lone cookie on the plate, which he put back on the kitchen table.

"I can't believe we're eating almost an entire plate of cookies!" Kaydie exclaimed.

"Promise me you'll make them again soon," said Jonah.

"I promise."

"Oh, and Kaydie?"

"Yes?"

"Would you please call me Jonah? When you call me Mr. Dickenson, half the time I don't know who you're talking to."

Kaydie raised her eyebrows at him. "For one of your cookies, I might be persuaded to make that promise," she teased.

Jonah looked down at his last cookie, then up at Kaydie again. "Oh, all right."

"I'm just teasing, Mr.—uh, Jonah. I've had more than my fill today. You keep it."

"Are you sure? I'd gladly spare it, especially for a woman in your condition, who's not just eating for herself."

"I'm sure. You go ahead."

Without arguing, Jonah ate the cookie, then brushed the crumbs from his fingers.

For a moment, the two of them sat in companionable silence, contentedly stuffed full of gingerbread cookies. Finally, Jonah broke the quiet. "Kaydie?"

"Yes?" Kaydie looked at him.

"I want you to know that I would never hurt you."

She quickly turned her head away from him. How had he made the switch to that subject from a discussion about names and cookies? And why did he keep insisting that he wouldn't hurt her? She gulped. How could she be sure that Jonah was even safe to be around? Just because McKenzie had entrusted her care to him didn't mean Kaydie would trust him.

"I mean it, Kaydie," Jonah continued. He leaned forward in his chair and looked at her, his expression serious. "I just want to be your friend."

Kaydie turned to face Jonah again. There was something about the tenderness in his eyes and the warmth in his voice that gave her little reason to doubt the sincerity of his words. However, no man could be fully trusted, Kaydie reminded herself. They pretended to be one way and proved with time to be another, just as Darius had done. He had swept her off her feet with gifts and promises of a delightful future together, only to change into an abusive monster once they were married and he had access to Kaydie's inheritance. Jonah was likely the same way. Still, if all he wanted was to be her friend, was there any harm in agreeing to that? After all, Zach was a gentleman. He treated McKenzie well, and he was kind to her, too. "I suppose that would be fine," she squeaked.

"As your friend, I'm here for you. If you ever need anything, just let me know," Jonah said, then stood to his feet. "I reckon I should head out to the barn and feed the livestock. Zach and McKenzie should be back soon."

"Thank you, Mr.—uh, Jonah."

"And thank you for the cookies. I've never tasted a finer gingerbread cookie in all my life. Hopefully,

Zach and McKenzie won't be too cross with us for not saving them one." He chuckled.

"I'll make another batch tomorrow," Kaydie assured him.

"Be sure to save me at least six cookies," Jonah teased.

Kaydie giggled. "All right."

"I'll see you at supper, Kaydie." With that, Jonah left, and Kaydie found herself suddenly missing his company. It was nice to have a friend, she decided.

CHAPTER FOUR

One afternoon several weeks later, Jonah hitched the horses to the wagon. A recent snowstorm had cleared, and the ground, while frozen, was free of snow. He wanted to take advantage of the favorable weather and make a trip to town for the supplies needed at the ranch. Jonah enjoyed making these trips to town. They gave him a break from his day-to-day chores, and he found himself offering to take on the task every time it was necessary.

When the wagon was ready, Jonah headed back inside to ask McKenzie for the list of supplies she needed him to pick up. She was seated at the kitchen table, scribbling away on a piece of paper, and she paused to look up when he came in.

"Oh, Jonah—good. Thank you again for offering to make a trip to town." She added one more thing to the list, then handed it to him. "Oh, and would you mind checking to see whether a parcel arrived from my mother for Davey? She mentioned she would be sending it soon. I've been reading to Davey from the books I had as a girl, and if Mother doesn't send me some fresh reading material, we'll have to read the same books a second time around!"

"I'll certainly stop by the post office," Jonah assured her.

The stairs creaked, and Kaydie came slowly down, taking each step more gingerly than the previous one. "Jonah, did I hear that you were going to town?" she asked.

"Yes, I am. I have some supplies to pick up for Zach and McKenzie. Is there anything I can get for you?"

"Well, I...uh, I was actually wondering if I might accompany you," Kaydie said shyly.

"That would be just fine with me," Jonah said, "but are you sure you want to in...in your condition?"

"Yes, I'm sure. After all, the doctor said I could travel to town and back, provided the speed is slower than usual and every effort is made to avoid bumps in the road," Kaydie explained.

"All right, then."

"Kaydie, are you sure?" McKenzie put in. "Maybe Jonah could pick up whatever it is that you need. I know what the doctor said, but I would prefer taking every precaution to protect you and the baby."

"It isn't just a matter of picking up something I need—although there is a special order from Lucille that I am hoping has arrived—but that I would very much like to do some Christmas shopping and get some fresh air," Kaydie said, her voice quiet yet enthusiastic. "Oh, and I also need to stop by the doctor's office for a quick visit."

McKenzie looked at Kaydie and smiled. "Well, when you put it that way, I think that sounds like a good idea."

～∞～

With her sister's help, Kaydie put on her coat, pushing one arm through an armhole and then the other. As if that wasn't hard enough, Kaydie tried to fasten the buttons, but to no avail. The buttons and buttonholes could hardly meet, thanks to her protruding stomach, and she gave an exasperated sigh. "I can't even button my coat!"

McKenzie giggled, and rather than get annoyed, Kaydie gave in to the giggles, as well. She had always been petite, and now, viewed from the back, she had noticed when looking over her shoulder in the mirror, she still gave no sign that she was with child. Yet her abdomen was quite rounded, and here she was, for the first time in her life, unable to close the gap in the front of her coat. McKenzie began to laugh even harder, which prompted Kaydie to do the same. Before long, they both had tears streaming down their faces. "I must—I must be quite the sight!" Kaydie managed between fits of laughter and gasps for breath.

Poor Jonah stood there, motionless, watching the two of them laugh uncontrollably. He looked rather confused, or perturbed, or both. Then he rolled his eyes, and Kaydie couldn't resist scolding him. "Oh, Jonah, really!"

"Pardon?"

"You are so—so *solemn* about the whole thing, and McKenzie and I are so...are so...." She found it impossible to continue because she and McKenzie had begun a new round of giggling. Kaydie tried time and time again to pull the front of her coat closed and to pull at least one button into the corresponding hole on the opposite side, but each attempt was futile and succeeded only in prompting more giggles from her and McKenzie.

"You two sound like a bunch of cackling hens," Jonah said, shaking his head. "If I stay here and listen much longer, I might not leave a normal man. I have to go." With that, he turned toward the door.

"No, Jonah, wait!" Kaydie retrieved a handkerchief from her coat pocket and dabbed at her eyes. "I would like to come, too."

"You could just stay and laugh all day with McKenzie," Jonah suggested.

Kaydie giggled. "As much as I would like to do that, I would really like to go to Pine Haven."

"Are you sure about that?" Jonah asked.

"Quite sure, sir."

McKenzie burst out laughing. "I never thought of Jonah as a 'sir.'" She puffed out her chest and deepened her voice to announce, "Ladies and gentlemen, I now present to you Sir Jonah!"

"All right, that's it," said Jonah, sternly but good-naturedly. "I have a job to do. I'll be back later."

"Wait, Jonah, I'm ready." Kaydie wiped her eyes with her handkerchief once more and followed him to the door, holding the front of her coat closed. "So long," she said, turning to wave at McKenzie.

"So long," McKenzie echoed as she dabbed at her eyes with her own handkerchief.

As Kaydie followed Jonah to the wagon, she thought of how the episode of laughter reminded her of when she and McKenzie had been children. In the presence of their parents, they were forbidden from speaking above hushed tones, but whenever they were playing by themselves and Mother and Father were away, they relished many a comical moment by laughing out loud. *Thank You, Lord*, she prayed silently. *Thank You for the blessing of my sister McKenzie and for bringing me here to be with her.*

⁂

Jonah assisted Kaydie into the wagon and handed her the blanket he kept in the wagon for particularly cold rides, saying a silent prayer of thanks that the humorous interlude between the sisters was over. At least, he thought it was. Yet Kaydie still snickered to herself from time to time as they set out on their journey.

He was careful to take the ride slower than usual and to avoid any obvious bumps in the road for Kaydie's sake. Out of the corner of his eye, he could see her head turn from left to right, then right to left, as she watched the scenery pass. She looked beautiful today, as she always did. A tortoiseshell comb at the back of her head held some of her hair, which otherwise flowed down her shoulders. Her face was glowing, and her brown eyes were bright. Jonah noticed she was wearing the new yellow gingham dress that she had sewn with McKenzie's help. There was something about Kaydie that had put her on his mind in the recent weeks, and Jonah tried to stop himself from thinking too much about her, even as he dwelled on her unmatched features.

"Did you say you were from Mississippi?" Kaydie asked, interrupting his thoughts with an attempt at small talk.

"Yes," Jonah said, nodding. "I was born in Jackson, and I lived there until I was seventeen. Then I moved to the Montana Territory."

"Before I knew you were from Mississippi, I wondered about your accent," said Kaydie.

"Everyone says I have an accent, but it sounds to me like it's y'all who have the accents," Jonah said with a grin.

Kaydie smiled. "And it was in Mississippi that you worked on a cotton farm?"

"I did. It was completely different from ranching, and I much prefer ranching. However, as I mentioned before, it was on that cotton farm that I met Jamal Winthrop, who introduced me to God."

"I didn't really know about God growing up, either," Kaydie said. "I mean, we attended church most Sundays, but it was more of a social activity than a spiritual exercise, and I never really knew the Lord. I'm so thankful Ethel told me about Him. Of course, when I was going through some difficulties with Darius, I did pray a lot. I don't know what I would have done if the Lord hadn't rescued me from the life I lived."

"I've often been amazed at His grace, as well," Jonah agreed. "When I was fourteen, I left home. I doubt my pa even noticed. I found odd jobs here and there, and then, when I was sixteen, I started working at the cotton farm. I was beginning to head down the wrong path, spending a lot of time drinking in the saloon and wasting all the money I'd earned on liquor. They didn't mind me coming in, even though I was young, because the saloon owner knew it meant more money for him. I went there mainly to escape the pain I felt at the thought that neither of my parents wanted much to do with me. It was an easy escape of sorts. I also didn't care much for others. My thinking was, why should I be nice to them when I've had such a rough life? God really showed me how the choices I was making weren't the right ones, and He helped me grow in compassion and kindness, because I didn't come by those things naturally."

Jonah hoped he hadn't shared too much. He also hoped that the fact he'd had problems with alcohol would not scare her off because of her experience with Darius.

To his relief, Kaydie nodded emphatically. "He is a gracious and merciful God." But then, after a few moments, she spoke again. "Do you still drink liquor?"

He should have known she'd ask, "No. I haven't touched the stuff since those years in Mississippi, when I was young and didn't know the Lord."

Kaydie nodded. "Darius, he drank a lot."

Jonah turned and looked steadily into her eyes. "I have no desire to step foot inside a saloon again, Kaydie."

They rode along in silence for a few minutes, and Jonah was starting to feel awkward, when Kaydie shrieked, "Oh!"

"Are you all right?" Jonah asked as he pulled on the reins, slowing the horses to a stop.

"Oh!" Kaydie shrieked again, pressing her hands to the upper right of her stomach.

Jonah turned and faced her, ready to take whatever action was necessary. "Is it time?" he asked, trying to keep the concern out of his voice. He glanced at the vacant road ahead. They were halfway there. He could get them to the doctor rather quickly if Kaydie rode in the back of the wagon, where she would not have to worry about falling out. "Kaydie, please answer me. Is it your time?"

"No, Jonah, it's not my time," she said, sounding strangely calm.

"Then, what is it?" Jonah asked.

"I'm so sorry I alarmed you, Jonah. It's not my time, and I'm perfectly fine." Kaydie smiled, then winced. "Oh! There it is again!"

"There *what* is again?" he asked, still not convinced.

"It's the little one. She's kicking up a storm."

"Pardon?"

"Here, feel." To Jonah's shock, Kaydie reached over and took his calloused hand in hers, then placed it high on her stomach. "Do you feel her kicking? You can almost feel the exact shape of her little foot."

It took all of Jonah's control to leave his hand on her belly as he waited for the baby to kick again. Finally, he felt the tiny outline of a foot. "I feel it!" he said.

"Isn't that the most amazing thing in the world?" Kaydie asked, her eyes beginning to tear.

"It is amazing," Jonah agreed. It was true—he had never felt anything like it before and wondered if he ever would again. He stared at Kaydie in disbelief that she would allow—even invite—him to be this close to her. His face was only a few inches from hers, and at this range, he found her to be even more beautiful than he'd first thought. He sucked in his breath and held it for fear that even the slightest movement would cause her to wake up from this oblivious state and recoil. Looking down at his hand, he watched as she placed her palm on top and waited for the next kick.

"I always praise the Lord when my little one kicks," Kaydie said, closing her eyes as if in prayer. "That means she's all right. She's done it many times, but it always feels like a new experience to me."

Jonah didn't say anything but stared at Kaydie in awe as questions overwhelmed his mind. How many men had the privilege of feeling an unborn baby kick? Had his own pa ever felt him kicking inside his mother's womb? Had his mother been overjoyed when she'd felt him kick for the first time? His thoughts turned to Kaydie again. Did she realize that the man of whom she was afraid was touching her stomach? Did she realize she had shared something so tender with him that it had melted his heart beyond repair? As he continued to stare at her, he realized he was close enough to kiss her. Immediately angry at himself for entertaining such a crazy notion, he forced the thought from his mind. There was no room in his heart or his life for a woman. He wasn't interested in falling in love, even with someone as beautiful as Kaydie, of whom he'd grown rather fond in the past several weeks. Besides, he had worked so hard to earn her trust, to erase her fear of his mere presence, that to even consider pursuing something beyond friendship was out of the question.

Kaydie opened her eyes, then opened them even wider in a look of surprise. Jonah heard her gulp. Hastily he pulled his hand away from her stomach and shifted in his seat, trying to look natural, to pretend that the unexpected moment of closeness had never happened.

"Kaydie—," he began.

"Jonah—," Kaydie said at the same time.

"You go first," Jonah said.

"I...I'm sorry I alarmed you. That wasn't my intent. I just find myself so overjoyed when my little one kicks. And I apologize if you were uncomfortable when I made you feel her kick."

"I didn't mind feeling the baby kick," Jonah said. "It's something I've never experienced before and never really expected to."

"I know you must think me odd for making such a to-do about the baby, but she is so precious to me, and I can't help reveling in every stage of her life."

"I don't think you odd at all, Kaydie," Jonah said, his voice low. How could he think of her as odd? That was the farthest thing from his mind.

"I wonder what she'll look like, whom she'll favor in features," Kaydie mused.

"I think she'll be beautiful, just like—" Jonah cut himself off, afraid that if he told her she was beautiful, she'd shudder and shrink further from him. He turned his gaze to the vacant road ahead.

"You really think she'll be beautiful?" Kaydie asked hopefully.

"I do think she'll be beautiful, just like her ma." There. He had said it. If she recoiled from him, so be it. It was the honest truth, and he wouldn't allow himself to sway from it.

"Well, thank you, Jonah. That's the nicest thing I've heard in a long time." Kaydie sniffled, and Jonah hoped she wasn't about to cry. He could not deal with an overly emotional woman, not when his own emotions were more volatile than they had ever been.

"I reckon we should be on our way," Jonah said. As much as he hated the thought of leaving this moment behind, he also knew that if he remained this close to Kaydie for much longer, he would kiss her. And if he kissed her, all that he had worked for in earning her trust and convincing her not to be afraid of him would have been for naught. Granted, he knew that Kaydie was not yet fully comfortable around him, but she had made great strides, and he wanted to do nothing to hamper that. Besides, the last thing she needed was a man telling her she was beautiful and showering her with compliments after what she'd been through with her husband. Healing didn't happen overnight—that much Jonah knew from personal experience. Yet, more than anything, he wanted to help her heal from the pain that was within her. To let her know that he was beginning to develop feelings for her was not the way to go about it.

Kaydie nodded. "Yes, we should get going, or McKenzie will start to wonder about us."

Jonah saw her shiver slightly. "You're not cold, are you?" he asked.

"No, I'm fine," said Kaydie. "The sun is shining, and little one is kicking. This is the perfect winter day."

⌥

"Well, aren't you looking lovely today, Kaydie," Lucille Granger gushed when Kaydie and Jonah entered the mercantile.

"Thank you, Lucille," said Kaydie.

"I just knew that color would look good against your rosy complexion. I was telling Jonah just that when he picked up the fabric several weeks ago."

Kaydie exchanged glances with Jonah, who rolled his eyes and headed toward the shelves in the back of the store.

"I was wondering if the cookie cutters I ordered had arrived," Kaydie said as she approached the counter. In Boston, it took only a quick trip downtown to find most anything. In Pine Haven, however, weeks often passed before a desired item appeared on the shelves of Granger Mercantile.

"Yes, they have," Lucille announced. She reached under the counter and pulled out a large, round tin.

Kaydie gasped with delight. Carefully, she opened the lid, then peered inside at the contents: six small, metal cookie cutters, all neatly fitted inside the tin. Kaydie pulled out each one—a gingerbread man, a circle, a half moon, a horseshoe, a heart, and a star. "These are perfect, Lucille. Thank you for ordering them for me."

"You're most welcome. Here at Granger Mercantile, we do our best to satisfy our customers' needs."

"I can't wait to bake cookies with these!" Kaydie exclaimed, inspecting each shape more closely. "I would like to make some ornaments for the tree and, of course, to make more cookies, gingerbread and sugar, for eating."

"I had no idea you were a woman who knows her way around the kitchen," said Lucille. "I figured you and McKenzie were accustomed to hired help and didn't know a thing about baking."

"I never learned to cook as a young girl, as my parents employed someone to do that—although I did watch our cook bake cookies. But I had to teach myself when I got married, or we never would have eaten! Then, when I arrived at the ranch, Rosemary taught me a lot more," Kaydie explained.

"Well, that is grand." Lucille beamed.

Kaydie nodded. "Do you mind if I have a look around?" In Boston, she had frequented many dry goods stores and other boutiques. But during her marriage to Darius, she had rarely been permitted to set foot inside any such establishment. Now she embraced the chance to see all that Granger Mercantile had to offer, even though she had been in the store twice before.

"Please, go ahead! Be sure to let me know if you have any questions or need assistance," Lucille told her.

Kaydie thanked her and began moving about the aisles, her eyes lapping up every item. She eyed a fancy hat on one of the shelves and picked it up for a closer look. It was made of peach felt and boasted a large, wispy white ribbon around the brim that was tied in a bow at the back. A larger peach-hued bow was affixed in the center of the hat, surrounded by tiny, cranberry-colored flowers with small green leaves. Kaydie placed the hat on her head and, for a moment, relived the years she'd spent wearing fancy hats in Boston.

Spotting a mirror on the wall, Kaydie moved in front of it and did a twirl, watching her reflection with delight. She stopped twirling when she saw Jonah's reflection and realized he was watching her from several aisles over. With feigned nonchalance, she removed the hat from her head and returned it to the display, putting on her ladylike composure lest Jonah think her childish. She continued to browse as she worked her way back to the front counter, where Jonah met her several minutes later.

"Would you add these to the bill, Lucille?" he asked the older woman, who was eyeing his merchandise with rapt attention.

"Most certainly!" Lucille produced her ledger and began to tally the items.

He then turned to Kaydie. "I'm going to run over to the post office before I forget and see if there's a parcel for Davey. I'll be right back, okay?"

"That's fine," Kaydie replied. "I'll just keep Lucille company while you're gone."

When Lucille closed the ledger, she met Kaydie's eyes with a gleam in her own. "Your time must be coming soon."

"Yes, the doctor says next month," Kaydie replied. "I'm going to stop by and see him before we head home just to put my mind at ease." She'd almost forgotten that she wanted to see the doctor that afternoon.

"That's a wise idea," Lucille pronounced with a somber nod of her head. "You never know what could go wrong. When I was in labor with my second son, I nearly died. It was such a horrific experience, and so long—nearly twenty hours!—and so intense that I—"

"Lucille, please," Kaydie interrupted her. She didn't want to hear the horror story Lucille was about to share.

"Oh, yes, do forgive me. I was just thinking of how I almost lost my life for that child. He almost died, too—"

"I think I'll see if Jonah is finished at the post office," Kaydie said, struggling to keep from crying. She walked to the door of the mercantile, opened it, and peered out into the street. Sure enough, Jonah was crossing the street as he approached the store.

"Well, Davey will be disappointed," he said as he climbed the porch steps. "I think he was expecting some books from his grandmother."

"Are we almost ready to go?" she asked him.

Jonah's brow creased in concern. "Are you all right, Kaydie?"

"Yes," she whispered, not wanting Lucille to know that her comments had distressed her to the point of tears.

"I'll just fetch the items, then."

"I'll wait for you here, if that's okay." She ignored his questioning look and waited while he collected the crate of goods, bid Lucille farewell, and then returned.

"I still need to stop and see the doctor," she reminded him as they exited the store.

"Reckon I almost forgot about that," Jonah said. "I have some business at the blacksmith's. I'll take you to the doctor's and then meet you there when I'm finished with Waterson."

"Thank you, Jonah."

Kaydie had hoped that going to see the doctor would put her at ease about her baby's health. But as she sat in the waiting room and tried to think about pleasant things, Lucille's frightening account filled her with fear that gave way to unsettling questions. What if something happened to her baby during labor? What if the baby died? What if Kaydie herself died in childbirth, and her baby was left with no mother or father? Close to tears again, Kaydie prayed for reassurance from the One who, she knew, had her unborn baby in His hands.

Half an hour later, Kaydie's examination was complete, and the doctor had assured her that she and the baby were doing fine. Feeling more optimistic, yet not rid entirely of her fears, Kaydie met Jonah in front of the doctor's office, and he helped her into the wagon for their trip back to the ranch.

"How was your visit?" Jonah asked as he urged the horses forward.

"Fine." Kaydie knew that her answer was unsatisfactory, but, for once, she was not in the mood for conversation.

They traveled in silence, save for the clip-clop of the horses' hooves and the rumble of the wagon wheels. It was a softer rumble than usual, though, as Jonah kept the horses at a slower pace.

Finally, after a few minutes, Jonah spoke again. "Kaydie, is something wrong?"

Kaydie shook her head. Jonah wouldn't understand. Besides, she'd shared too much with him already. On top of that, she still wasn't sure she fully trusted him, especially when it came to matters close to her heart.

Once they were outside of town, Jonah slowed the wagon to a stop at the side of the road. It seemed that talking to him would be the only way to get home. "What did the doctor say about the baby?"

Kaydie tried to speak but began to cry instead. Unable to stop the tears, she allowed them to flow freely and gave in to the choking sobs that accompanied them.

⧹⧸

"Kaydie...." Jonah leaned closer and tentatively put his hand on her shoulder, then gave it a few pats. What was a man to do with a crying woman? Should he embrace her closely, or should he move back and sit there quietly until she had stopped crying and composed herself? He decided to try the first option and put both arms around her. To his amazement, she placed her head against his chest.

"It's all right, Kaydie," he said softly, soothingly. When she didn't answer, he went on. "Is it Darius? Were you remembering something painful?"

Against his chest, he felt her head shake. He wondered what else it could be. "Did I upset you?"

Again, Kaydie shook her head and shivered slightly.

"Was it something the doctor said?"

Kaydie shook her head once more. Jonah was running out of options. He wondered if it might just be the fact that she was with child. He'd heard that the experience caused some women to be overly emotional. "Is it because of your condition?"

"It's not that," Kaydie whispered, and he thought he heard her giggle.

"What is it, then? Tell me so that I can help you."

"It's just...."

"What is it, Kaydie? You know that you can trust me."

At his words, she sat up and pulled away from him, smoothing her hair and wiping her eyes.

Jonah dropped his arms. He wished he could take back the words he'd just said. Clearly, urging her to

trust him had the opposite effect. "I didn't mean anything bad by that, Kaydie. I know you don't trust
most men, but I wanted you to know that you can
count on me for help."

Kaydie blinked her teary eyes at Jonah as if considering whether to open up to him. She chewed her
lip thoughtfully, then finally spoke. "It's just that...."

"Go on," Jonah prompted her.

Another wagon drove past, and he waved at the
driver before looking back at Kaydie.

"It was Lucille," Kaydie said as another sob shook
her shoulders.

"Lucille?"

"Yes, she—she was telling me about how horrible
her—her labor was with her second son, and—and
that she and the baby almost...almost died."

"Lucille told you that?" Jonah couldn't believe
someone would do such a thing, but then again, this
was Lucille they were talking about. Maybe he could
believe it. While Zach was rather fond of the woman,
who was almost like an aunt to him, Jonah found
his patience waning with her.

"Yes." She sniffled. "I—I don't think she was
meaning to be unkind, but—"

"She wasn't meaning to be unkind?" Jonah shook
his head. "She should never have said that to you,
Kaydie. I'm right sorry she did. I have every thought
of riding back into Pine Haven and giving that woman a piece of my mind."

"No, Jonah, please don't."

"I reckon I won't, Kaydie, but it wasn't right of her
to tell a woman in your condition such a thing. Why
would she want to frighten you like that?"

"I just don't think she gave it much thought," Kaydie said. She reached into her coat pocket and felt around, then took her hand out, still empty. "Have you seen my handkerchief?" she asked.

"Not since we were at the house," he said. "Here, you can use mine." He pulled his red handkerchief from his pocket and handed it to her.

"Thank you," Kaydie said. She dabbed the corners of her eyes, then turned away from him and quietly blew her nose.

"Kaydie, I know it's easy for me to say, but don't pay any mind to what Lucille said."

"I'm trying not to, but I keep worrying that the same thing will happen to me and my baby."

"What did the doctor say?"

"He said everything looked fine, and that I'm getting closer to my time."

"That should reassure you."

"It might have if Lucille hadn't said what she did."

"The doctor has more knowledge than Lucille. You know that."

"But the doctor never had a baby," Kaydie pointed out. "Lucille did. She has firsthand experience, and she knows what to expect."

"I reckon she does know what to expect about having *a* baby," Jonah conceded, "but she's not you, and she isn't having *your* baby. Every situation is different."

"But how can you be so sure that I won't have the same problems she did?"

"I can't be so sure about that, Kaydie. Only God knows the future."

"I sometimes wonder if I'll be too weak to have the baby," Kaydie whimpered. She began to cry.

Not again, please, Lord. Jonah reached toward her again and put his arm around her, hoping she wouldn't cower from him. "Kaydie, you are strong enough. You're a strong woman. Believe me, I don't know the first thing about babies or childbirth, but I do know one thing: God made you strong. If He hadn't, you wouldn't have been able to endure what you went through with Darius. I don't know even half of the story, but I've heard enough to understand it was bad. If you didn't have a strength about you, you wouldn't be here today."

Though she smiled faintly, Kaydie did not look convinced. "I know that the baby is healthy right now, but I sometimes worry that something will happen to her right before she's born. You see, I love her so much already. What if she's stillborn?"

"Stillborn?" Jonah said. "Does that mean, not alive when she's born?"

"Yes," Kaydie sobbed.

"Earlier today, your baby was kicking away," Jonah said, nodding to add emphasis. "Then the doctor told you she was fine. Think about those things, Kaydie. Don't think about the bad things that might happen."

"But it's hard," Kaydie protested. "When you love somebody, you don't want to lose them."

"I know." Jonah didn't know what else to say, so he closed his eyes and sent a silent prayer heavenward. *Lord, please give me the words to say to Kaydie. You know I am a mere man with no knowledge of childbirth and other such things. Please, God, give me the words to speak to her so that I can comfort her. I am dependent on You for wisdom regarding what to say and do.*

Jonah gently rubbed Kaydie's shoulder in an attempt to comfort her further. "Although I'll never carry a child, I can understand somewhat what you're saying. Let God be in control of this, Kaydie. He already knows what your little one's future holds. He created her, and He has plans for her—and for you. Don't let worry rob you of joy in these days of carrying your child."

Kaydie looked at him with a hopeful light in her eyes, and Jonah was shocked at the profound words he had uttered. He never could have come up with something like that on his own. *Thank You, Lord, for putting those words in my mouth,* he prayed.

"Thank you for your comforting words." Kaydie took a deep breath and let it out with a sigh. "I just want everything to be all right with the baby."

"I do too. And so do McKenzie, Zach, Davey, Rosemary, Asa, and all the townsfolk. There's a lot of people who care for you, and for the baby." Jonah paused. "You know, a verse from the Bible comes to mind. I believe it's from Second Corinthians. It says, *'My grace is sufficient for thee: for my strength is made perfect in weakness. Most gladly therefore will I rather glory in my infirmities, that the power of Christ may rest upon me.'* Let Christ's power be your strength in times of weakness, Kaydie."

"Second Corinthians twelve, verse nine. That is one of my favorite Scriptures." Kaydie beamed. "You're a good friend, Jonah."

"Thank you. I worked hard to earn that title." Jonah winked.

"Would you mind praying with me?"

Her request caught him off guard, and Jonah dropped his jocular manner. While he shared a close relationship with the Lord, he rarely prayed aloud, especially in front of other people. His prayer life had always been between him and the Lord, and he liked it that way. But a glimpse of Kaydie's expectant eyes, and he couldn't refuse. *Lord, please help me again with this*, he prayed silently.

"Will you please pray with me, Jonah?" Kaydie asked again.

"All right," Jonah said. He took her hand and clasped it between both of his, then closed his eyes. "Dear Lord, uh, would You please keep Kaydie and the baby healthy and safe? Would You please help Kaydie to remember that when she is weak, Your strength is made perfect during those times? Thank You and amen."

"Thank you, Jonah."

They sat there for a moment, still holding hands, which was just fine with Jonah. Kaydie's fingers were so slender and smooth, not at all rough and calloused like his.

Then, Kaydie gave his hand a squeeze and drew hers away. "I know that we haven't known each other for long, Jonah, but I don't think I've ever had a better friend than you—besides McKenzie, that is."

Unfamiliar emotions swelled in Jonah's heart. "I'm thankful for your friendship, too, Kaydie. Remember, I'm here for you whenever you need me, under one condition."

Kaydie raised her eyebrows. "And what might that be?"

"That you make me some gingerbread cookies with those little cookie cutters you got at the mercantile today."

Kaydie laughed then—a sweet, quiet laugh. "It's a deal," she said. "But you have to promise me that, this time, you won't tell everyone we polished off an entire batch of cookies—minus one."

"So, we're planning to eat another full batch?" Jonah asked.

"Indeed," Kaydie affirmed, smiling broadly.

"I promise," said Jonah. "Well, I reckon we should get home. It'll be suppertime before long."

"Thank you, Jonah, for listening and for being such a good friend."

"You're welcome," he answered with a pull on the reins. "I don't know what these horses must think. They're accustomed to a straight shot between the ranch and town, and we've stopped two times today."

Kaydie giggled. "I'm sure this is the longest trip you've ever made to town."

"I reckon so," Jonah agreed. "The most eventful, too, I might add."

Kaydie nodded. The day had been eventful, indeed. She felt exhausted just thinking about all that had transpired and knew that she would sleep well tonight. In addition to a message from her little one, a trip to the mercantile, and a visit at the doctor's office, she had made a new friend. Jonah had been there ever since Kaydie's arrival in Pine Haven, and she regretted how long it had taken her to give him a chance.

She turned for a discreet glance at Jonah. He had a nice profile, and something about the way he'd expressed care and concern for her today made him all the more attractive. But Kaydie would not allow herself to be attracted to him in a way that was more than friendly. While she was grateful for the many ways in which he'd helped her today, and while she was thankful for their blossoming friendship, their relationship would progress no further.

Everyone she had met since coming to Pine Haven had welcomed her warmly and extended the utmost kindness. As a result, she was beginning to heal from the wounds of her marriage to Darius and coming to trust others again. But there was something more about Jonah—something she did not care to dwell on. She had gone from fear to familiarity, and that scared her. Kaydie had to look out for her heart. She could not afford for it to be bruised and broken again.

CHAPTER FIVE

At breakfast the following Saturday, McKenzie invited everyone to join her and Zach in selecting a tree to bring home and decorate for Christmas.

"I wanna go!" exclaimed Davey, Zach's five-year-old adopted son, whom Kaydie had adored from the moment she'd met him.

"That does sound like a lot of fun," Kaydie agreed. She recalled Christmases from her childhood, when their butler and chauffeur, Lawrence, would always bring home a stately tree for the front parlor. She'd always wondered what it would be like to go out as a family and select one together, and now it seemed that she would finally have that experience.

After breakfast, everybody piled into the wagon—Jonah and Zach in the front seat, Kaydie and McKenzie in the back, with Davey snuggled in between them. They draped a large patchwork quilt over their legs to keep themselves warm during the journey.

The air was brisk, and clouds lined the winter sky. Unlike yesterday, which had been unseasonably warm, today seemed to promise an imminent snow-fall. All of the trees had lost their leaves, and the only greenery to be seen was that of the pine trees. "I think God created pine trees just so we would have some color during these dull winter months," Kaydie mused aloud as she pulled her hat over her ears, which were already getting cold.

"I think so, too," said Davey, pulling the blanket up to his chin, "and we're gonna find the perfect one for our Christmas tree!" He had volunteered to be the official tree scout, and he watched the woods closely as they traveled along.

"Shall we sing a Christmas carol?" McKenzie asked.

"How about 'Silent Night'?" Kaydie suggested.

Moments later, they had all joined in singing, their voices ringing through the cold, crisp air.

When they had sung the hymn to the best of their memories, stumbling over only a few words, Davey cried out, "Pa! Stop the wagon! I found our Christmas tree!" He pointed a chubby finger toward a ponderosa pine on their left as Zach slowed the horses to a stop.

"I think we can handle that. What do you think, Jonah?" Zach asked.

"Looks like Davey made a good choice," Jonah said with a nod.

Everybody climbed out of the wagon, and Jonah grabbed the two-man crosscut saw from the back of the wagon. He and Zach each took an end of the saw and began cutting down the tree Davey had chosen.

"I can't wait to decorate the tree!" Davey exclaimed. "I'm gonna make it look all pretty-like."

"You should have no shortage of decorations to choose from," McKenzie told him. "Aunt Kaydie, Grandma Rosemary, and I have been working hard on several different types of decorations, and we also have two sets of tin ornaments we purchased at the mercantile."

Kaydie thought of the decorations that she had made with the help of McKenzie and Rosemary. Many of them were cookies, shaped with the cookie cutters she had ordered from Granger Mercantile. Others were made of fabric that they had cut into shapes, such as stars and bells, then stuffed and sewn together. They had also strung garlands of dried fruit—apples and cranberries—and popcorn. McKenzie had mentioned using nuts and pieces of lace, as well. "Remember the Christmas trees we had in Boston, McKenzie?" Kaydie asked her sister.

"Of course. Weren't they a sight to behold?"

"They were lovely, even if we weren't allowed to get too close to them for Mother's fear that we'd break something," Kaydie said.

"What kind o' decorations did you have?" Davey asked her.

"Let's see...we had beautiful blown-glass orna-ments from Germany...we also had small, thin can-dles on many of the branches, and when they were lit, they gave the tree a wonderful glow. Our tree was also decorated with lots of satin ribbon, tied in bows. We would hang fresh-cut greenery, including mistle-toe, all around the house."

"We would often gather around the Christmas tree and sing carols," McKenzie put in. "Kaydie, do you remember how we would always insist on singing

'Good King Wenceslas'? That was our favorite, for some reason!"

"Who is King Wensasloth?" Davey asked, causing Kaydie and McKenzie both to erupt in giggles.

"The song about King Wenceslas," McKenzie began, pausing to catch her breath, "comes from an old story about a duke of Bohemia named Saint Wenceslaus the First, I happen to know—but that's the extent of my knowledge on that subject."

"What memories," Kaydie said. "We did have some fun times, didn't we, McKenzie?"

"We did," McKenzie agreed. "I especially enjoyed when Cook would sing along with us while we watched her prepare Christmas dinner." She paused. "I think we'll begin to make entirely new memories here, and I look forward to that."

Kaydie nodded but knew in her heart that she wouldn't be in Pine Haven long enough to create many new memories. If Mother and Father had their way, she would be spending next Christmas, and all the Christmases after that, in Boston. She sighed. As much as she cherished many of her childhood pastimes, she found herself wishing she could begin a new life here in Pine Haven instead of returning to Boston and the memories it held.

"It looks like they're almost done cutting down the tree," McKenzie observed.

"I can't wait!" Davey exclaimed. He rubbed his small, gloved hands together in anticipation. "This is gonna be the bestest Christmas ever. I just know it!"

Kaydie smiled at him, then moved closer to the tree to check the men's progress. As she watched, she was struck by Jonah's physique, shorter and huskier than Zach's tall, lean figure, but no less attractive. His thick, rust-colored hair was cut about an inch below his ears and curled up in the back in a way that made her want to touch it....

"Aunt Kaydie?" Davey asked, interrupting Kaydie's thoughts. She hoped he hadn't noticed her staring.

"Yes, Davey?"

"When the baby is born, I'll be his cousin, right?"

"You sure will," Kaydie said. She reached out her arms and gave Davey a hug. "And a wonderful cousin you'll be."

"I sure hope the baby's a boy," he declared.

Kaydie smiled. "Why is that?"

"Well, 'cause I'm gonna teach him how to fish and ride horses and do all kinds of fun things boys do," Davey said with an air of importance.

"You can still teach the baby fun things to do, even if she's a girl," Kaydie said gently.

"But it's not the same," said Davey. "I'm just hopin' it's a boy."

"I really don't mind whether it's a boy or a girl," said Kaydie. "I'm just praying God will give me a healthy baby."

She looked up to see Jonah and Zach carrying the tree toward the wagon. When Jonah met her gaze, he arched his eyebrows with a twinkle in his eyes. He must have heard her comment about the baby and wanted to remind her that he knew about her secret preference.

Kaydie returned Jonah's teasing look with one of her own, narrowing her eyes to warn him not to tell a soul that she had called the baby a "she" if it happened to be a "he."

"Whether it's a boy or a girl, we will be delighted to welcome the new baby into our family," said McKenzie as she helped Kaydie into the wagon.

When Zach and Jonah were seated up front, and Davey had reclaimed his seat between Kaydie and McKenzie—facing backward, though, to keep an eye on the tree—they began the journey back to the ranch. As they rode along, Kaydie reveled in the joy of having a freshly cut Christmas tree to decorate, and loved ones with whom to share the task. *Thank You, Lord*, she silently prayed. *Thank You for so many things, especially the people in this wagon with me.*

On Christmas Day, Kaydie was awakened in the early morning by the enthusiastic voice of a five-year-old boy. Davey had taken it upon himself to wake everyone in the house and inform them that it was Christmas. He danced around and happily shouted, "Merry Christmas to everyone!" and "Wake up! It's Jesus' birthday!"

Kaydie tried to change as quickly as she could from her nightgown into a fresh dress, but the bulk of the baby made the task difficult, and it felt like she moved more slowly than ever. When she reviewed what the day would hold, she felt almost as excited as Davey. First, they would have a reading of the story of Jesus' birth from the book of Luke, followed by the exchange of gifts and a special breakfast. Then, they would attend a church service, after which they would return home for Christmas dinner. Her nose caught the aroma of homemade cinnamon rolls, and she felt her stomach growl. "Are you as hungry as I am, little one?" Kaydie whispered.

Finally dressed, Kaydie emerged from her bedroom and stood at the top of the stairs, gazing down at the sight below her. The Christmas tree they had decorated was breathtaking against the backdrop of the window and the wintry scene outside. Davey danced around the tree, singing Christmas carols in his ever-enthusiastic voice. Seated on chairs from the kitchen table that had been moved into the living room, Rosemary and Asa chatted with Zach, McKenzie, and Jonah, all of them looking relaxed and unaffected by Davey's boisterousness. An assortment of brightly wrapped presents waited under the tree, and although the amount was nowhere near the number of gifts that had always greeted Kaydie and her sisters beneath the tree and all around the living room on Christmas mornings in Boston, she found that she didn't mind at all. It was as if her life in Boston had been a prelude to this one, and what had been important to her then mattered little or not at all to her now.

Yes, back then, her parents had made every effort to give their three daughters the gifts of their dreams. Kaydie and her sisters had lapped it up, for it was often the closest thing to an expression of love they received from Mother and Father....

❦

Everyone sat around the parlor awaiting his turn to open a gift. When it was eight-year-old Kaydie's turn, she went for a large, shiny box and smiled shyly at what she thought might be inside. As she carefully tore the wrapping paper away, her anticipation mounted to reveal the gift she'd wanted ever since she'd seen it in the window of Marney's Fine Gifts. Painstakingly, she set aside into a pile the strips of wrapping paper she'd peeled off the box.

"Hurry up, Kaydie!" McKenzie urged her. Kaydie looked up at her older sister and smiled. McKenzie always opened her gifts with such fervor that there was nary a reusable piece of wrapping paper left when she was finished. Not that they had to reuse the wrapping paper. They sometimes did, however, donate it to the less fortunate who weren't able to afford such luxuries. The wrapping papers that adorned the gifts under the Worthingtons' tree featured ornate scenes of winter landscapes, chapels, and angels. Each gift was also wrapped with colorful satin bows, which Kaydie and her sisters liked to use as hair ribbons.

The box Kaydie was opening was wrapped in paper that featured a scene of churches with tall steeples situated among snow-covered hills, with a candlelit carriage parked outside of each church. She removed another piece of paper and placed it on the pile beside her. When she had exposed the wooden box completely, she gazed down and saw, to her great delight, the very dollhouse she'd seen in the store window. Now it was hers! Kaydie squealed with glee and marveled at the miniature pieces within the house. It came complete with furniture for each of its ten rooms and a family of five dolls. "Thank you, Mother and Father!" she exclaimed. "It's just what I wanted." She got up and gave her father a big hug, who returned it with a slight squeeze before pushing her gently to arm's length.

"Who's next?" he asked, looking to McKenzie and Peyton.

On her way back to her seat, Kaydie stopped beside her mother, seated in the fancy, high-backed lavender chair. "Thank you, Mother. I love the dollhouse," she said.

"Yes, yes. Well, it was the best one we could find. I would have preferred one with more rooms, but Marney's had only two choices, and this one was superior. The other one was smaller, more plebeian. It had only six rooms and three dolls, and the furniture was poorly made."

Kaydie and her sisters continued to take turns opening their gifts. Their nanny watched from a distance, ready to assist in any way necessary at the command of either parent. In the kitchen, Kaydie could hear Cook bustling about, no doubt preparing the hot cider and cakes they would enjoy when they'd finished opening their gifts....

❧

"Kaydie, would you care to join us?" McKenzie interrupted Kaydie's reverie.

"Please excuse me," Kaydie said softly. "I was just recalling Christmases past." She walked slowly down the stairs, gripping the rough-hewn railing.

"How are you feeling today, Kaydie?" Rosemary asked her.

"I'm tired but feeling fine," she answered.

"Did you know it's Jesus' birthday today?" said Davey.

Kaydie smiled at him and ruffled his hair. "I did know that, Davey. It's the most important birthday of all."

Davey furrowed his brow for a moment, appearing to be deep in thought. "Do you know how old Jesus is?"

Everyone laughed at Davey's question. "I'm not sure, Davey, but I would have to say quite old," Kaydie replied.

"Like, maybe twenty-five years old?" asked Davey. "Because that's awful old."

"Oh, I think He's much older than that," Kaydie said with a giggle. "What's important is that He came to earth as a baby and died for our sins so we might join Him in heaven someday."

"Pa said he was gonna read us that story once ever'one got here," said Davey.

Kaydie felt herself blush. "I apologize for being late. I meant to come downstairs earlier."

"It's not a problem, dear," Rosemary reassured her. She rose to her feet. "Why don't you come sit with us?" She led Kaydie to the fancy chair by the fireplace, then returned to her own seat beside her husband.

Zach opened his Bible and began to read the story of the Savior's birth from the book of Luke.

When he finished with "*'Glory to God in the highest, and on earth peace, good will toward men,'*" Davey blurted out, "Can I go first, Pa?"

"That would be fine, Davey," Zach said, closing the Book.

Davey picked out a gift, then climbed onto his father's lap and began to peel off the brown paper. "This present is from Jonah," Davey announced.

Moments later, he had unwrapped four hand-carved wooden animals: a horse, a cow, a chicken, and a pig. "Wow! Thanks, Jonah!" Davey exclaimed.

Each person took a turn, opening humble, home-made gifts that were more meaningful than any of the expensive presents Kaydie had received as a child. Though these gifts were far from costly, Kaydie realized that they were priceless because they had been made with love. On two of her turns, Kaydie opened a set of baby clothes McKenzie and Rosemary had stitched for her, and then a picture Davey had drawn of the baby—a boy—playing with him. Her eyes filled with joyful tears. While she had received countless fine gifts, such as the intricate dollhouse, from her parents, she'd never been the recipient of a gift crafted with love by the giver. Kaydie prayed that the Lord would guide her as she strived to bestow tangible signs of love on her own child.

Toward the end of the gift exchange, Kaydie noticed that one of the gifts she had made was still under the tree, in the decorative tin hiding in the back. She asked Davey if he would mind retrieving it for her.

Davey nodded and crawled beneath the tree to fetch the tin. He read the tag and looked up at Jonah. "This is for you," he said, then handed it to him.

"Thank you, Davey." Jonah eyed the tin, which had turquoise and yellow stripes. When he opened the lid and looked inside, he grinned.

"Your very own batch of gingerbread cookies!" Kaydie said to answer everyone's curious looks. "Now, try not to eat them all in one sitting," she added in a teasing voice.

Jonah chuckled. "You're asking the impossible."

"Ah, I hear that both you and Kaydie have a fondness for gingerbread," Asa said in his thick Irish accent.

"The rumor is true," said Jonah. To Kaydie, he added, "Thank you."

He looked down admiringly at the tin for a moment, then set it on the floor and stood up. "I believe there's one more gift out in the barn," he said. "I'll be right back."

Everyone watched with puzzled looks as Jonah put on his coat and headed out the door.

"What do you suppose it is?" McKenzie asked Zach with what Kaydie thought was feigned curiosity.

He smiled and shrugged. "I reckon we'll find out real soon."

"I love surprises!" Davey squealed with a clap of his hands.

Several minutes later, there were footsteps on the front porch, followed by Jonah's voice saying, "Kaydie? Could you please close your eyes?"

Shocked that she was the recipient of his gift, Kaydie said, "Of course!" then closed her eyes and covered them with her hands so she couldn't be accused of peeking.

She heard the front door open and Jonah step into the house, followed by gasps all around. A light thud sounded near her feet.

"You can look now, Kaydie," Jonah said.

Kaydie uncovered her eyes and slowly opened them. In front of her was the most beautiful cradle she had ever seen. It was fashioned of solid wood, with a heart-shaped cutout in both the headboard and the footboard. "Jonah, it's—it's beautiful," Kaydie said, at a loss for words. She felt her eyes mist as a lump formed in her throat. "Did you—did you make this?"

"I did," said Jonah. He knelt across from Kaydie and rocked the cradle back and forth in smooth, even motions. "I made it so that you could rock the cradle with your foot, if need be. That way, you can rock your baby and knit or read at the same time."

"Jonah, I—I don't know what to say," said Kaydie.

"Well, the baby didn't have anywhere to sleep, as far as I could tell," Jonah said, thankfully filling the silence. "I've never made one before, so it was a little bit interesting, but I managed."

"He's been working on that for some time now," said McKenzie, coming over to see the finished product. "It was so hard for none of us to say anything about it to you. Jonah, it turned out lovely."

Zach nodded. "I've never seen such fine craftsmanship, Jonah. You could make cradles and sell them at the mercantile."

"Oh, I don't know about that," Jonah murmured bashfully.

"We never knew you had so many talents!" Rosemary teased.

"Ah, I think there's a lot we don't know about Jonah," said Asa, giving Jonah a playful punch in the arm.

Kaydie wiped her eyes with her handkerchief and took a deep breath. "Thank you, Jonah." How could she ever express her gratitude? She knew it must have taken him many hours, and she wondered when he'd found the time to work on it amid his time-consuming duties at the ranch. When had he started on it? And how had he known that she'd hoped for a wooden cradle ever since she'd discovered she was with child? Her eyes met his, and warmth flooded her body. How wrong she had been to fear him! Now she realized how far she had misjudged him. Jonah was a good man, a friend she could count on. He was also thoughtful. She understood why Zach and McKenzie, and all of the townsfolk, for that matter, spoke so highly of him. He was a friend she was thankful to have.

CHAPTER SIX

"I'll be fine," Kaydie reassured McKenzie the following week when her sister was preparing to go to a meeting of the quilting circle.

"Are you sure you don't want to come?" McKenzie asked, a skeptical crease in her brow. "I hate to leave you when you could give birth at any time. Rosemary and I would love for you to come along. The other women are a delightful bunch; they may have their quirks, but don't we all?"

"I would certainly like to attend a quilting circle meeting in the future, McKenzie, but I think I'll stay home today. I've been feeling rather fatigued, and I think I ought to catch up on some rest."

"All right, but promise me you'll come to the next meeting. It's a nice way to get better acquainted with the other women of Pine Haven."

"I promise. Now go, McKenzie, before you and Rosemary are late."

McKenzie started for the door, then turned around to face her sister. "Did I tell you that Zach and Davey are driving us to the meeting? Zach has some business to take care of in town, and he and Davey are going to stay there until Rosemary and I are ready to come home."

"You did," Kaydie said. "That's fine."

"Jonah and Asa are in the barn," McKenzie added, "but I've given them strict instructions to come into the house and check on you at regular intervals throughout the afternoon. I've also asked them to keep the fire going, because it's mighty cold today. I don't want you to have to tend the fire yourself. Bending over like that in your condition would not be wise. You won't try that, will you?"

"No," Kaydie assured her. "If I bend over too far in any direction, I might not achieve an upright position again."

McKenzie giggled. "How many times have I helped you to stand up from that chair?"

"More than I'd like to remember," Kaydie admitted, glancing down at the fancy blue chair she was sitting in and that had become her usual roost. Time and time again, she had found herself sitting there with no hopes of getting back on her feet without help.

"Please, don't worry about the house," McKenzie said, waving her hand to indicate the room. "I'll take care of anything that needs to be taken care of when I return home. I mean it, Kaydie. I'd much prefer that you relax and take it easy. I won't stand for anything happening to the baby because of your stubbornness."

"McKenzie," said Kaydie with a sigh, "please stop fussing over me. You sound like a bossy old hen. I will be fine, and I'm sure that Jonah will come in to check on me regularly. Now, shoo! If you're late for quilting circle, Lucille Granger is likely to come up with a story to explain why."

"All right, all right," McKenzie said with a laugh. "You know that I'm fussing over you only because I love you and care about you." She came back over and gave Kaydie a quick hug.

"Yes, I know that, McKenzie. Still, I don't know what all the fuss is about. Women have been having babies for centuries. I'll be fine. Now, off with you!"

McKenzie finished buttoning her coat and then disappeared out the door. Through the front window, Kaydie could see Zach, Davey, and Rosemary waiting in the wagon.

Alone in the house, Kaydie gazed around at her surroundings. While humbly decorated, the Sawyer house had a homey feel to it, one that Kaydie had never experienced before coming to Pine Haven. With the exception of the fancy chair Kaydie favored, the rest of the home was rustic and plain. Even the sofa her parents had sent as a wedding present for McKenzie and Zach, though formal in style, blended in with its dull, mustard-colored upholstery. Yet the home had personal touches, such as the curtains McKenzie had sewn for the windows and the artwork Davey had drawn for the walls and that McKenzie had framed. And, while the décor could in no way compete with the fine homes in Boston, Kaydie found herself feeling more at home in this space.

She felt cozy curled up in the fancy chair. The fire crackled in the fireplace, and she could hear the wind howl outside. At this time last year, she had been trying to stay warm in a dugout that Darius had found in the middle of nowhere. He'd refused to chop wood for the fireplace, so Kaydie had taken it upon herself to collect as many sticks and fallen branches as she could find to start a fire. Yet the scant pieces she'd found had burned so quickly that the warmth from the fire had lasted only a moment. Kaydie's thin, worn jacket had been her only means of staying warm, and it had helped little.

Such was not the case in the Sawyer home, where Kaydie had never felt cold. Even in the mornings when she climbed out of bed and changed from her nightgown into her clothes, she never felt the chill she'd felt so many times during her three years of marriage to Darius. However, the winter chill during those times, she reflected, was probably exacerbated by the emotional chill of her loveless marriage. Darius had chosen her as his bride only to get to her parents' money—her inheritance—and even when those funds had been depleted, he'd kept her as a prisoner. Kaydie shuddered. Lately, she'd managed to push those painful memories out of her mind, but on occasion, they still surfaced in a powerful and haunting way. She sometimes had to pinch herself to wake up from the nightmare of living in that frightening time—the time without hope.

Of course, McKenzie had changed all of that by making a self-sacrificial trip to the Montana Territory as a mail-order bride. She never would have launched such a ludicrous venture had it not been for her great love for Kaydie. McKenzie hadn't wanted to leave her comfortable home in Boston to travel to the primitive town of Pine Haven, but she had done it anyway—for Kaydie. Of course, in doing so, she had met Zach, the man who had advertised for a mail-order bride. She'd married him and fallen in love with him—in that order.

Kaydie thought of how McKenzie had always been there for her when she was growing up, caring for and protecting her—not from physical threats, of course, but from being silenced and forgotten. The Worthington girls had never feared physical harm or material lack; they'd had a nanny, a butler, a gardener, maids, and a cook, and their parents had made sure that their daughters were given every toy, article of clothing, and privilege they could afford. No, McKenzie didn't have to protect Kaydie from things of a physical nature. Instead, she had been Kaydie's voice, speaking up for her shy sister when she hadn't been able to muster her confidence. The sisters were opposite in so many ways, most obviously in that McKenzie was assertive and outspoken, while Kaydie was reserved and timid. Even when it came to looks, McKenzie and Kaydie were not alike. McKenzie had long strawberry-blonde hair and green eyes, while Kaydie had long blonde hair and brown eyes. McKenzie was tall and slender, while Kaydie was petite. Only upon close examination of their faces could one see the family resemblance between them.

McKenzie had always taken care of her sister, but she hadn't held it against her when Kaydie had exercised her self-determination for once and chosen to marry Darius Kraemer. Instead of condemning Kaydie's poor judgment and foolhardy stubbornness, McKenzie had committed herself to finding her and rescuing her from the clutches of her abusive husband. McKenzie did not give up her search for Kaydie, however daunting her whereabouts, braving the wild Montana Territory and even marrying against her will for the sake of finding her sister. And, when she'd found Kaydie, McKenzie had never said "I told you so." Instead, she had welcomed her into her home and vowed to continue taking care of her, as she always had. Kaydie found great comfort in that, and she thanked the Lord for giving her such a loving, patient, merciful sister.

Kaydie had been McKenzie's "baby" ever since she was born, even though she was only fifteen months younger. McKenzie had called her sister by this nickname until Kaydie turned seven and politely asked if she could address her by her given name. "It's embarrassing," Kaydie had said when McKenzie had protested. Although reluctant to give up her affectionate name for her sister, McKenzie finally did. However, before that day, many events transpired that further cemented the bond that was shared between the two youngest Worthington sisters.

Kaydie leaned her head back in the chair, closed her eyes, and allowed her mind to take her back in time to another memory....

⟶⟨⟨⟨⟨

"Come on, baby," McKenzie said, tying a bonnet on Kaydie's head. "Mother is going to take you for a walk."

Kaydie gave a squeal of delight, as she had heard babies do.

McKenzie tried to lift her into the baby carriage, and Kaydie helped with a bit of her own effort and climbed in. Bending the rules of make-believe was permissible when necessary, she and McKenzie had agreed. Fitting inside the baby carriage for this game was becoming more difficult as Kaydie grew, and she had to curl up in a ball with her legs bent and her head between her knees.

"Now, lie down," McKenzie instructed her. She nodded, then remembered that a baby probably wouldn't understand. "Waaa!" she wailed. That was a more convincing response.

"Now, now, baby, don't cry. Here, let Mother give you a kiss." McKenzie leaned into the baby carriage and kissed her sister on the forehead.

"Goo, goo," said Kaydie, sticking her thumb in her mouth.

"Are you cold, baby?" McKenzie asked. She went inside and returned with a blanket from the fancy parlor sofa and placed it over Kaydie. Then, she gripped the front bar and began to push the carriage.

Kaydie wished to go faster, but she realized it was probably difficult for McKenzie to push someone almost her size. Plus, if they moved too fast, they were liable to break something, and then Mother would surely find out about their game. She never would have allowed them to play with the baby carriage. However, Mother was away at a charity function and had left the girls with the new nanny, who enjoyed taking long naps on the parlor sofa in the afternoon. Kaydie and McKenzie heartily approved of this habit and took advantage of it whenever they could.

The big metal wheels groaned under Kaydie's weight as McKenzie continued to push her around the well-manicured yard. "Shall we pick some flowers for the dinner table tonight?" McKenzie asked.

"Goo, goo!" Kaydie said with a nod of her head. She realized again that a baby probably wouldn't have understood, but McKenzie didn't seem to mind.

"Very well, then. I shall pick some of these beautiful yellow ones." McKenzie skipped over to the flower garden and yanked several yellow flowers from the ground.

Kaydie gasped. "No, Mother!" she shouted, trying to retain her baby voice. "Mother, don't pick those flowers."

"Oh, now, dearie, your mother may pick these flowers, just not those," McKenzie said, pointing to a cluster of orange flowers beside the yellow ones.

"No, no, pick those," Kaydie whined.

"It's all right, baby. Besides, we must have a pretty dinner table." McKenzie kept picking flowers until she had a large handful, which she handed to Kaydie. Grinning, she began to push the baby carriage again.

"Were you just picking Mother's flowers?" Peyton's voice made Kaydie's blood run cold. She jerked her head up to see her older sister coming around the side of the house and scowling at her and McKenzie, her hands on her hips.

"Yes," McKenzie replied, "but we're allowed to pick the yellow ones."

"No, we're not."

"Yes, we are!" McKenzie insisted.

"No, we're not. The maids Nellie and Birdie may pick the orange flowers, but not the yellow ones."

McKenzie's eyes grew large, but she didn't back down. "I don't believe you," she said calmly.

"Whether you believe me or not, you'll find out the truth when I tell Mother." Peyton was eight years old, and she seemed to delight in tattling on her sisters.

"Psst," said Kaydie, signaling McKenzie as she always did when she needed to pause playing make-believe due to an "emergency."

"What is it, Kaydie?"

"Peyton's right," Kaydie whispered. "I 'member Mother saying that 'bout the yellow flowers."

"And that's not the only thing you'll be in trouble for," said Peyton. "You know better than to play with the baby carriage. Wait until Mother gets home." Peyton put her nose in the air and turned away from her sisters.

"I didn't know about the flowers," McKenzie groaned.

"We can still play, can't we?" Kaydie asked.

"Yes, baby, we can still play," McKenzie said with a smile. "Now, let Mother put your hat on better so you don't catch a cold." McKenzie reached over and tied the bonnet more securely under Kaydie's chin, then began to push the carriage again. "We'll put those flowers in a pretty vase for the dinner table. I'm sure that Mother will be pleased."

They rounded the front of the Victorian mansion, and McKenzie suddenly stopped the carriage. "Baby, do you see that butterfly in those bushes?" she asked, pointing straight ahead.

"Goo, goo," said Kaydie with a nod of her head.

"Let's go see if we can catch it," said McKenzie. Pushing even harder than before, she moved the carriage toward the flowering hedge along the front of the house.

As they neared the hedge, McKenzie slowed down, and the carriage felt sluggish under Kaydie's body. She looked out and saw that the grass was shimmering with water droplets. The gardener, Manuel, must have just watered the lawn.

They stopped, and McKenzie crouched down beside the carriage. "Oh, dear," she muttered. "I believe we're stuck in this mud."

Kaydie sat up and looked over the side of the baby carriage to see that the wheels were caked with mud. "Waaa," she wailed, pretending to cry.

"Don't cry, baby. It's nothing to be sad about. Mother will catch that butterfly for you. Will that cheer you up?"

Kaydie nodded, and McKenzie stood up and reached out toward the butterfly, which fluttered its wings slowly as it rested on a blossom. It moved just as her hand approached, and she began to jump in the air in an attempt to catch it as it floated around near the hedge. "Look, baby. It's coming near you!" McKenzie exclaimed, watching as the butterfly fluttered closer to the carriage.

"Baby get it," Kaydie said in her high-pitched voice. Without so much as a second thought, she scrambled to get to her feet in the baby carriage in order to reach the butterfly.

As she stretched toward it, she said, "Baby almost got it!"

Then, the baby carriage began to wobble, more severely so as she tried to regain her lost balance. Moments later, the carriage toppled over and dumped Kaydie in the mud.

"Baby! Are you all right?" McKenzie gasped.

"Waaaa!" Kaydie wailed, only this time the cry was real.

"Oh, no!" McKenzie ran to her sister's side. *"Are you all right?"* Dropping to her knees, she leaned over Kaydie.

"I hurt myself," Kaydie sobbed.

"Where does it hurt?"

"On my leg," Kaydie whimpered. It didn't help that her new lacy pink dress was covered in mud. Her stockings and shoes were completely soiled, as well.

"Oh, dear," McKenzie murmured, as she looked at the baby carriage.

Kaydie blinked away her tears and followed her sister's gaze. The carriage was lying on its side, and it had a hole in it from where she had fallen on top of it. The handlebar was bent. She looked at McKenzie again and noticed that she, too, was quite dirty. The bottom of her dress was steeped in mud. Gasping in horror, she began to cry again, and this time, McKenzie joined in.

"McKenzie?" she sobbed.

"We're gonna be in big trouble," said McKenzie. She wrapped her arms around Kaydie. *"Are you still hurt?"*

"Yes."

McKenzie kissed her sister on the cheek. Sitting down in the muddy grass, she held Kaydie in her lap and rocked her back and forth while they both cried, Kaydie more because of her ruined dress than the pain in her leg. She also cried for fear of what Mother and Father would say when they found out what had happened. Even if she and McKenzie were not covered from head to toe in mud, which would give away *what had happened, Peyton would be sure to inform them.*

When their mother came home, she was outraged and demanded to know where the nanny had been. McKenzie answered honestly—she hadn't known— and then Peyton filled in the details of what had happened as she smoothed away nonexistent wrinkles in her own lacy pink dress, which was spotless....

⚘

Kaydie giggled at the memory. Following the episode with the baby carriage and the flowers, their mother had fired the nanny, sent the baby carriage off to be repaired, and forbidden McKenzie and Kaydie from picking any flowers from the garden. They were also ordered never to come within four feet of the baby carriage. That had put an end to their game of "Mother and Baby."

Kaydie opened her eyes and stared again at the fireplace. She suddenly felt the urge to do something productive, and she tried to rise from the chair—to no avail. She pressed her hands into the armrests for leverage and made another attempt. Still, she could not get up from the chair. The weight of the baby was too much, and the chair was too low to the floor, for her efforts to bring the desired result. Exhausted, she rested for a minute, then tried again. "Oh, goodness!" she said, giggling in exasperation.

After about twenty minutes, Kaydie heard footsteps on the porch. Finally, someone was coming to her rescue! She looked to the door, which opened, and Jonah entered the house.

"Hello, Kaydie. I've come in to check on you," he said. Removing his coat, he hung it on the hook on the wall beside the door and glanced around. The fire looked like it was dying down, so he walked over to the wood pile beside the hearth, bent down to pick up a log, and threw it on the fire.

"Jonah?"

He began stoking the fire with a rod. "Yes, Kaydie?" he asked without turning around.

"Could you please help me out of this chair?"

"I beg your pardon?" He turned from the fireplace to face her.

"I —I'm stuck in this chair, and I could use some help getting out."

At the sight of Kaydie, her face flushed, her eyebrows knitted together in a look of perplexity, Jonah had to muster all of his effort not to laugh out loud. Her stomach took up almost the entire chair, and she was wedged in the overstuffed cushion so low that her feet were sticking straight out in front of her, unable to reach the floor.

"Perhaps you should sit there awhile longer," Jonah teased.

"Really, Jonah!" Kaydie was probably trying to sound indignant, but her voice rose only slightly higher than its usual pitch. He wondered if Kaydie had ever raised her voice.

"I've never seen a woman stuck in a chair before."

Kaydie glared at him. "Would you please be a gentleman and kindly help me out of this chair?"

There was no helping it this time. Jonah threw his head back and laughed aloud. When he looked at her again, her expression was still one of utter despair and hopelessness. She stuck out her lower lip and blew out her breath, causing the strands of hair that fell across her forehead to rise and fall.

"Of course, I'll help you out of that chair, ma'am," he drawled, tipping his hat, as if the idea of being a gentleman and rescuing her had been his all along. He extended both arms, and Kaydie reached up and clasped his hands, allowing him to pull her gently to her feet. When she was upright, she teetered slightly, and he steadied her by the arms.

"Are you all right, Kaydie?" he asked.

"Quite all right, thank you kindly," Kaydie snapped sarcastically.

"You're welcome. Anytime I can rescue you from the confines of that mean old chair, just let me know."

Kaydie tilted her head back and looked up at him. "I'll have you know that I don't make a habit of getting myself stuck in chairs. It's just because of the baby."

"Yes, I see that it's due to your condition," Jonah teased. "Now, what was so important as to make it necessary for you to be rescued from that chair?"

"I have some things I need to attend to," Kaydie said.

"I think you should be resting."

"I'll thank you kindly not to fuss over me," she declared. "Besides, I have been resting for a while now, and I have the strangest urge to busy myself with some things that need to be done."

Jonah turned to glance at the clock on the mantel. "It's only ten in the morning. Why don't you sit a spell and rest some more? Didn't the doctor say it's almost your time?"

"I want to complete the baby's quilt and the thick pads for the cradle."

"Perhaps I can fetch those things for you. I know you don't like us all fussing over you, Kaydie, but it's only because we care." Jonah looked down at her, still supported by one of his arms. He felt the urge to kiss her on the forehead to confirm his care for her but decided against it. It surprised him that Kaydie wasn't pulling away from him. He didn't want to do anything to change that, and he definitely didn't want their relationship to regress to when she kept her distance from him. Besides, having her near him felt oddly natural, not that he would admit it to anyone else.

As if she'd just noticed their closeness, Kaydie took a step back. "I have some things I need to do, Jonah," she repeated.

Hesitantly, Jonah released her. "I'll be back to check on you again soon," he told her.

Kaydie nodded, and he thought he saw her shudder.

"Are you all right?" he asked. Was she repulsed by him?

"Yes, I'm all right," she replied absently, then turned and slowly climbed the stairs.

Since Kaydie evidently did not need his help, Jonah returned to the barn to help Asa with the chores they had started earlier that morning. "Everything going all right with Kaydie?" Asa asked when he walked in.

"Yes," said Jonah, "although the oddest thing happened." He chuckled softly.

"And what might that be?"

"Well, she got stuck in the chair. Asa, I've never seen anything like it in all my life. There she was in that fancy chair that McKenzie ordered from back East. She was wedged down into the cushion with her feet sticking straight out. From the exhausted look on her face, I think she'd been trying to get up for some time before I entered the house." Jonah chuckled again at the image, still vivid in his mind.

"Did you help her?" Asa asked.

"I did." Jonah shook his head. "I think that was the one and only time I'll ever be asked to help somebody get free from a chair."

Asa chuckled, too, his brown eyes becoming mere slits beneath his graying eyebrows. "Ah, a woman stuck in a chair. You don't see one of those every day." He paused. "Speaking of Kaydie, I think she's beginning to feel more comfortable here in Pine Haven."

Jonah nodded. She had arrived in September, and it was January, which meant she had been here for more than four months. In that time, he'd noticed a significant change in her. "I agree, and I'm glad. It took her a while to feel comfortable around us, the people she lives with, let alone the townsfolk."

"It certainly took her time to feel at ease around you," Asa noted. "She's been through a lot."

"I know, and I wish I could erase all that from her memory," Jonah said. "I can't imagine any man treating a woman the way I've heard Darius treated her."

"It's likely we don't know the half of it," Asa said.

"No, I don't think we do. Once in a while, she'll open up about the past, but I think it's still pretty painful."

"Ah, you've been a good friend to her, Jonah. A woman who's been through what she has can never have too many good friends."

"I've tried to be a good friend to her, Asa, but that took a while, too. At first, she would just shrink away every time she saw me. I think she was afraid that I might be just like Darius and would hurt her."

"It's natural for one who has been hurt so deeply to need some time to heal," Asa said, patting Jonah's arm. "You don't have to tell me if I'm right or wrong, but I have the feeling that you care for Kaydie in a way that goes beyond friendship."

Jonah was taken aback. Was he really acting like he was attracted to Kaydie? "What do you mean?"

"Ah, forget I said anything," Asa said with a shrug of his stocky shoulders. "It's just...well, the way you look at her sometimes.... It's the look of a man who might have feelings for a woman."

Jonah stared at Asa, the man whose wisdom and godly advice he regularly sought. He was like a father to him, much more so than his own father, and Jonah had always valued Asa's opinion above anyone else's. He'd listened as Asa had given wise advice to Zach during the first several months of his marriage to McKenzie, which had been rather rough. And now, it wasn't that Jonah didn't want Asa's advice; it was just that he didn't feel comfortable receiving it—not when it came to matters of the heart.

"You know, Jonah, there's nothing wrong with having feelings for Kaydie," Asa said with a knowing smile.

"I'm not sure you could call them 'feelings,' Asa. I reckon I've made mention of this before: I don't intend to get married. Ever. I have no idea how to be a husband and even less of an idea how to be a father. That being the case, I have no intention of falling in love."

"You have made mention of that before," Asa said, nodding. "As I recall, it was because your pa wasn't a good example of a husband or a father."

"Yes, that's right." Jonah looked down at the barn floor and kicked at a piece of straw with the toe of his boot. "And my ma, she left when I was just a young'un. Why would I want to take the chance of marrying when my wife might leave me at the drop of a hat?"

"I think you might be getting ahead of yourself here, son," said Asa. "To have feelings for a woman doesn't necessarily mean you'll be saying wedding vows anytime soon."

"I realize that, Asa. But it seems to me that once a man lets a woman into his heart and starts courting her, he's headed toward matrimony. I can't take that chance. Not with Kaydie, not with any woman."

"It's because you don't know how to be a husband, right?" Asa asked.

"Yes, that's the main reason," Jonah said. "I wouldn't know how to love and care for a woman, seeing as I never had a good example to follow."

"It seems to me that you're doing a fine job of caring for Kaydie," Asa observed. "Rosemary and I have been admiring how you've tended to her, especially with the baby coming."

"I reckon that's what any man would do," Jonah said with a shrug.

"Perhaps, but—" Asa paused with a frown. "You know, Jonah, I won't give you any more advice, especially when you haven't asked for it."

"I do value your opinion, Asa," Jonah assured him. "And...I don't know. Maybe I do have some feelings for Kaydie. Sometimes I can't get my mind off her. She's beautiful, sweet, and silly at times. She loves the Lord, and she loves her child."

Asa nodded. "I'll give you my advice, then. You are concerned that you won't be able to love her or care for her because you never had a good example of a husband. Yet I see two examples right in front of you—Zach and, if I may say so humbly, myself. You know that Rosemary and I have been married for thirty years. We've had our arguments, to be sure, but after my love for our heavenly Father, I love Rosemary more than anything." He paused. "Actually, I can think of an even better example than those."

"Who is that?" asked Jonah.

"The example of Christ. We can consider the way He loves us, which is the ultimate example of love, and know how to love others. You know how much Jesus loves Kaydie, because that's how much He loves you, too. Love her with the love of Christ."

Jonah thought about that for a moment. "I reckon that's a good idea, since the love of Christ isn't exactly romantic. Because I don't think Kaydie feels that way about me."

"Likely she doesn't at this time. But you have to remember that she hasn't had time to heal yet. A man she thought she knew hurt her in a way you and I will never understand. Give her time, Jonah. While you are learning to love her like Christ loves her, learn to exercise patience, as the Lord does with us."

Jonah nodded as he allowed Asa's words to sink in.

"Continue to care for her as you have been doing, Jonah. Don't let a day go by without letting her know how much you care for her. Be her friend first, because a friend is what she needs most right now. If it's the Lord's will, you can court her later."

"Thanks for your advice, Asa. Promise me that you won't tell anyone about our conversation, okay?"

"I promise."

"Not even Rosemary?"

"Not even Rosemary—if you'll promise me that you will allow Christ to guide you in this matter."

"I promise," Jonah said, realizing he hadn't really prayed about his relationship with Kaydie.

As he and Asa resumed their work in the barn, he struggled to concentrate as pieces of their conversation ran through his mind. His emotions were a mess. While he had feelings for Kaydie, he knew better than to act on them. For one thing, the price of rejection was too high. For another, he doubted he could give Kaydie the love and care she deserved. Asa's words rang through his head: *Love her with the love of Christ.*

Jonah had no idea what the future held, but he knew one thing for certain: He would be the best friend Kaydie Kraemer ever had. And if that was all he would ever be to her, it would have to be enough.

CHAPTER SEVEN

Two hours later, Kaydie had finished the baby quilt and the pad for the cradle, then had prepared a lunch she'd eaten with Jonah and Asa, who had just returned to the barn to complete their work. She glanced again at the clock on the mantel to make sure she'd read it correctly. Yes, it was only a few minutes after one o'clock. How much she'd accomplished already, and yet her energy was not depleted! She found it odd that she had so much vigor, especially since she'd felt more and more exhausted as her pregnancy had progressed. Not wanting to let her energy go to waste, she set about cleaning the kitchen.

After that task was complete, she went through the house, putting away any items she found out of place. Next, she took down the latest baby clothes she had received from various women of Pine Haven, which had been hanging to dry, and folded them carefully before placing them neatly in the drawers of her bureau. "Pretty soon you'll be wearing these, little one," she said, patting her stomach.

Kaydie thought of what Doc Orville had said the last time she'd visited him. *"It won't be long now, Kaydie. You're almost in your ninth month."*

At the thought, fear struck her, and she wondered again if she would be able to make it through the labor. She gripped the side of the bureau for support. *Lord, I don't know if I can have this baby when my time comes,* she prayed. *Please, please, help me to be brave and strong. Let this tiny child be born healthy.* Kaydie squeezed her eyes shut tight. In all she had been through in the past three years, God had been there with her. *I know You're not about to leave me now, Father, but I am so scared.*

A verse she'd read earlier that day in 2 Samuel came to mind: *"The God of my rock; in him will I trust: he is my shield, and the horn of my salvation, my high tower, and my refuge, my saviour; thou savest me."* Kaydie lifted her face heavenward and breathed a sigh of relief. *Thank You, Father, that You are there.* She didn't know how much longer it would be until her baby was born, but she knew that when her little one made her entrance into the world, the Lord would be with both of them. All she had to do was remember that truth.

Kaydie sat down on the edge of her bed near where she'd placed the baby cradle and ran her hand over the smooth wood, then adjusted the fabric padding she'd sewn to line it. "Jonah made this especially for you, little one. You'll like Jonah. He's kind and thoughtful, and he's the best friend I have—besides McKenzie, of course. At first, I didn't like him all that much, but I've grown fonder of him as the months have passed. He's not at all who I thought he was when I first met him in the post office." Kaydie paused for a moment and smiled at the picture of her talking aloud to herself. "Well, why shouldn't I talk aloud to you, little one?" she reasoned. "This way, you'll know my voice when it comes time for you to be born."

She pushed herself up, left the room, and headed for the top of the stairs. Gripping the wooden handrail for support, she began her descent, taking each step slowly. With her other hand, she supported her stomach. In the living room, she picked up her Bible from a side table and made for the fancy blue chair. Remembering her episode from earlier that day, she thought better of it and sat down on the sofa, instead.

She opened to the book of Psalms, one of her favorite sources of wisdom, and began to read. When she came to the third verse of Psalm 127, she stopped and reread it several times: *"Lo, children are an heritage of the Lord: and the fruit of the womb is his reward."* She was overcome with emotion. Still relatively unschooled in the Word of God, Kaydie had never read or heard the verse before. The fact that she was with child made it all the more profound. Her little one was a gift from the Lord, in spite of the circumstances under which she had been conceived. Although Kaydie had been hurt by her family's disapproval when she'd decided to marry Darius, had suffered in a marriage full of strife, and had faced death many times in the past three years, and although she would raise her baby alone, God had still blessed her beyond measure. And He had blessed her not only with a baby, but also with her loving sister McKenzie and many others who cared for her. Kaydie read the verse once more before continuing on in the psalms, taking each new verse to heart.

About an hour later, Kaydie began to feel as though something wasn't right. Strong flashes of pain started in her back, and she tried to shift her position in the sofa to ease her discomfort. Yet the pain continued and moved to the front of her belly. She held her breath and waited for it to pass. It was an unknown pain, stronger than any she'd experienced before. After a while, the pain stopped. She picked up the Bible again and resumed reading for a few minutes before the pain returned. Gripping the arm of the sofa, Kaydie squeezed her eyes shut and waited for the pain to pass once more. It was then that she knew what was happening. Her time had come.

She attempted to stand up, but the strain only worsened her discomfort, and so she remained seated. Perhaps Jonah would come inside to check on her again soon. Each time the pain occurred, it was more severe than before, and Kaydie didn't know what to do. She needed Doc Orville, but someone would have to summon him. That meant Kaydie had to get the attention of Jonah and Asa—and soon.

She glanced at the mantel clock, which read two thirty. McKenzie and the others would not return for at least another hour. By then, the baby might have been born. Kaydie winced. What if she was all alone when she gave birth, and there were complications? What would she do? *Lord, please help me!* she prayed.

Then, she mustered all of her available energy and, in the loudest voice she could manage, shouted,

"Jonah! Asa!" She waited to see whether one of them would come inside. When several minutes passed without the appearance of either of them, Kaydie realized that they would never hear her from the barn. She would need to get closer. Again, she tried to stand up. As she did, she kicked over the crate she had been using as a footrest. Yet she could not achieve a standing position, and she sank despondently into the sofa cushion.

"Jonah! Asa!" she shouted again as another contraction seized her abdomen. Still, no one responded, so she closed her eyes and tried to be patient. Surely, Jonah would check on her again soon. Until he heard her, she would continue to call him.

⟡

Jonah set down his rag. He and Asa had almost finished cleaning the stalls, and he figured it was probably time to check on Kaydie again. "I suppose we should see how Kaydie's doing," he said.

"Would you like me to go this time?" Asa asked.

"Oh, I don't mind," Jonah assured him with a wink. "I'll be right back." He pushed open the barn door and walked to the house. As he neared the porch, he thought he heard something. He stopped on the bottom porch step and listened closely.

"Jonah! Asa!"

How long had Kaydie been calling for them? He felt paralyzed by fear that something horrible had happened, but he willed his body to move. By the time he reached the front door, he was sprinting. "Kaydie?" he called as he burst into the house.

"Jonah!" At the sight of him, Kaydie began to cry.

Jonah rushed to the sofa and got down on his knees. "Kaydie, what's wrong?" he asked frantically, grasping her hand.

"Jonah, I—I think—I think it's time," Kaydie stammered between gasps.

"You think it's time for the baby to come?" Jonah tried not to panic.

"Yes!"

"All right—I'll go fetch Doc Orville." Jonah let go of her hand and stood to his feet as he calculated in his mind how long it would take him to saddle the horse and ride to town.

"No, Jonah—wait."

Jonah looked at her, his pulse racing, his mind reeling. "What is it?" He reached for her hand again.

Kaydie gripped his hand tightly. "Please, don't leave me," she pleaded.

"But I have to go fetch the doctor. I'll be right back, I promise. I'll send Asa in to be with you while I'm gone."

"No, Jonah. Please, send Asa to fetch Doc Orville. Don't leave me!"

Surprised by her insistence, Jonah took a deep breath and held it. "All right, then, Kaydie. I'll go tell Asa to fetch Doc Orville, and then I'll be back." Jonah pulled his hand free of her grasp and rushed out the door to the barn, nearly forgetting to exhale.

"Asa!" he shouted as he pulled open the barn door.

"What is it, Jonah? Is Kaydie all right?"

"Asa, it's her time. Can you go fetch Doc Orville?"

"I will," Asa said. He flung a saddle over the nearest horse. "After I send Doc Orville, I'll stop at the quilting circle to fetch Rosemary and McKenzie. Rosemary has helped deliver many a baby."

Jonah nodded. "Thank you, Asa. Please, pray for Kaydie—and for me. I'm pretty scared, which won't calm her fears any."

"I have, and I will continue to," Asa promised. He led the horse outside, and Jonah followed him. "Trust the Lord to keep both of you calm," Asa said as he mounted. "I know it seems difficult, but I know that you can relieve some of her fear."

"I'll do my best," Jonah said, "but I've never been through anything like this before."

"Neither has Kaydie," Asa said. "Don't worry, son. You'll do fine. You have a good head on your shoulders and a compassionate spirit about you." With that, he gave the horse's flank a kick and rode off, leaving Jonah behind, alone.

Jonah went back inside the barn for a moment and fell to his knees in silent prayer. *Father, I don't know what to do. Please guide me. Please help me to comfort Kaydie. Please, let her be all right, and let her little one be healthy, too.* Even as he prayed, worries assaulted him. What if Kaydie had the baby before Doc Orville arrived? *I should've asked Asa to send over the nearest woman neighbor to stay with us while we wait for Doc Orville,* he thought. *I should've—* He stopped himself and dismissed his regrets, knowing that they were a waste of time. On his feet again, he raced out of the barn and dashed into the house.

"Jonah?" came Kaydie's tremulous voice.

"Let's take you upstairs to your bedroom," Jonah suggested in a tone that sounded braver than he felt.

"All right," Kaydie said. "But the pains—they keep coming, worse each time."

"I think that's all part of it," Jonah said, hoping to reassure her. "Here, wrap your arms around my neck, and I'll carry you upstairs."

He leaned down, slid one hand under Kaydie's knees and placed the other on her back, and lifted her off the sofa. She felt lighter than he'd expected, even with the extra weight of her baby. He carried her carefully yet steadily toward the stairs and then started up them, praying he wouldn't lose his footing.

Jonah said a silent prayer of thanks when they reached Kaydie's bedroom door without incident. He turned sideways to fit through the doorway, then gently lowered Kaydie onto the bed.

"Jonah, another pain is coming," Kaydie whimpered.

"All right. Hold on." Jonah helped Kaydie prop herself up on several pillows, and then he covered her legs with the patchwork quilt that was folded at the foot of the bed.

"Oh-h-h-h!" Kaydie moaned, clutching her stomach as tears streamed from her brown eyes.

Jonah felt helpless. "Is there anything I can do?" he asked. "Anything I can bring you?"

"Can you...."

"Yes?"

"Can you...pray with me?"

Jonah gulped. She wanted him to pray out loud *again*? He still wasn't comfortable doing it, but if it would help to put Kaydie at ease, he figured he could give it another try.

"Sure." He cleared his throat, then reached for her hand and began to pray. "Dear Lord, uh, would You please help Kaydie with the pain? Also, would

You, uh, help her with having the baby? Thank You, Lord. Amen."

"Thank you, Jonah." Kaydie sighed. "I've been so scared."

"I know." Jonah tried to think of a way to take her mind off the pain until the doctor arrived.

"Maybe you could sing to me," Kaydie suggested, as if she had heard his thoughts.

Jonah eyed her warily. While he would do just about anything for her, singing was one of his least favorite activities. He had never been able to stay on key. In church, he usually sang just loud enough to make a sound that only the Lord could hear. "Sing?"

"Yes, if you don't mind. Do you know 'Rock of Ages'? It's my favorite hymn."

Tenuously, Jonah hummed the first few notes. When he saw Kaydie's face light up, he switched to the lyrics: "Rock of Ages, cleft for me, let me hide myself in Thee...."

Kaydie joined in, a joyful expression on her face, and with every verse Jonah grew more confident. Suddenly, it didn't matter that he couldn't carry a tune. What mattered was that his singing brought comfort to her.

When they finished the hymn, Kaydie clutched her stomach for a moment, so they took a break from singing.

She soon recovered, and Jonah expected her to suggest another hymn. Instead, she said, "Jonah, can you tell me about when you were a little boy?"

Jonah shifted on the edge of the bed. In her distracted state, Kaydie must have forgotten that his childhood was not something he liked to discuss.

However, when she turned and looked at him with tired yet expectant eyes, he knew he needed to grant her request. He supposed that whatever she requested was God's way of letting him know how to relieve her fear and keep her calm.

Jonah cleared his throat. "When I was a little boy, I had a dog named Gertrude," he began.

Kaydie giggled. "Did you name her yourself?"

"Yes, I named *him*," he clarified. "You see, when we got the dog, I was only five and didn't realize it was a boy. He was a good dog, though. I taught him all kinds of tricks and how to play fetch with this ball he loved to chase. He was good at catching rabbits, too. And he caught a skunk once, which was the only time I wasn't proud of him." Jonah chuckled at the memory of Gertrude, one of the few bright spots in his dark childhood. "I sure knew right away that Gertrude caught that skunk, and I don't think he ever smelled the same after that."

Kaydie laughed again. "How old were you?"

"When Gertrude had his run-in with the skunk? I think I was about ten or eleven. Smelly or not, though, Gertrude was nice to have around for company. My pa was never home much, so I spent a lot of time on my own. I was right glad to find Gertrude. He was mangy and scraggly and looked like he hadn't eaten in days. I remember, my pa was in the saloon in town, and I was sitting outside waiting for him. That's when I saw Gertrude. He was wandering the streets on the lookout for scraps. To this day, I'm surprised my pa let me keep him. I think he figured it kept me out of his way, so that's why he agreed."

Jonah leaned over and peered out the window for any sign of Doc Orville. Surely, Asa had spoken with him by now, and he would be there soon. If he wasn't, Jonah didn't know what he'd do. He knew nothing about childbirth, and he was suddenly over-come with anxiety that he might have to deliver the baby himself. Quickly pushing that thought aside, he stood up.

"Jonah, please, don't leave me!" Kaydie pleaded in a panicked voice.

"I'm just going to fetch you a drink of water. I'll be right back, all right?"

When Kaydie nodded, Jonah left and headed downstairs. He took a pitcher from the kitchen and filled it with water from the outside well, then came back inside and filled a blue-rimmed china teacup almost to the brim. He chuckled at the fancy set of cups and saucers that now adorned most of the shelves in the Sawyer household. Before McKenzie had come to live with them, they had used mostly mismatched dishes of pewter that Zach had pur-chased at Granger Mercantile.

Jonah's musings were interrupted by a cry of agony from Kaydie, and he hastened toward the stairs, trying not to spill the cup of water. He wished that he could do more to help her. She was so frag-ile and delicate—too delicate to bear so much pain. Quickening his stride, Jonah climbed the stairs and rushed into Kaydie's room. He set the teacup on the bedside table.

"I hope Doc Orville gets here soon," Kaydie sighed as Jonah handed her the cup of water.

"He will, I'm sure. Don't worry." Jonah reached for her free hand. "Why don't you tell me about a special memory from when you were a young girl?"

Kaydie took a sip of water and closed her eyes. "Lemonade."

"Lemonade?"

Kaydie opened her eyes. "Yes, lemonade—sweet, cool, and fresh. In the summertime, we would sit on the rounded part of our porch, which wrapped around the front and sides of our home, and sip homemade lemonade. I loved that porch—it was my favorite thing about our house, which was one of the most elegant in the neighborhood. There were thick, white pillars holding up the porch, and a private balcony off my parents' room on the upper level. McKenzie and I used to play Rapunzel up there.

"I remember one day in particular. Father was at the office, and Mother was at a charitable event in the city. We had a day of freedom, and we knew that Nellie and Birdie, the maids, didn't mind our playing games as long as we cleaned up after we were finished.

"We invited Peyton to play, but she declined, as she had a tea to attend at her friend Pauline's."

Kaydie winced as another pain apparently wracked her body, but then she took a deep breath and continued.

"Peyton also told us that playing Rapunzel is only for children. She was always so stuffy! We always invited her to join us, and yet she hardly ever did. I actually pity her for all the adventures she missed out on.

"Anyway, McKenzie decided to be the handsome prince, since I had played that part the last time. That meant I had to pick out a gown to wear as Rapunzel, the princess. So, I told McKenzie that I would change clothes and then come to the balcony off our parents' bedroom.

"I ran upstairs and put on the fanciest dress I could find in my closet. It was teal, with lots of frills and a black velvet sash. Then, I walked through Mother and Father's room and opened the door to the balcony, all the while braiding my hair—you know the story, right? McKenzie would have to climb up to the balcony." Kaydie stopped and giggled before continuing. "McKenzie was standing outside beneath the balcony; she had put on one of our father's shirts and had drawn a mustache on her face with a fountain pen, as she usually did when playing the prince.

"In her best man's voice, which was actually quite hilarious, she bellowed, 'Rapunzel, Rapunzel, let down your golden hair!'"

Jonah found himself completely drawn in to the story from Kaydie's childhood. He tried to picture Kaydie as a little girl in a frilly gown playing Rapunzel with her sister.

Just then, he heard a knock on the door downstairs. "I think the doctor's here!" he said. "I'll bring him up."

He rushed out the bedroom door, into the hallway, and down the stairs to the front door. Sure enough, when he opened it, there stood Doc Orville, his black medical bag in hand.

"How is she doing?" the doctor asked as Jonah ushered him inside.

"Pretty well, in between the pains," Jonah said, then led him up the stairs.

"I tried to get here as fast as I could," the doctor explained. "Rosemary and McKenzie were right behind me." When they entered the bedroom, Doc Orville beamed at Kaydie. "Everything is going to be all right," he assured her. Then, turning to Jonah, he said, "You can go back downstairs. I'll let you know if I need anything."

Jonah turned to leave, but Kaydie's voice stopped him. "Jonah?"

"Yes?"

She smiled weakly. "Thank you for staying with me."

"You're welcome. I'll see you soon—and the baby, too, okay?"

She nodded, hesitantly at first, then with conviction.

Jonah had been downstairs for just a moment when Rosemary and McKenzie came in. They immediately went upstairs to check on Kaydie.

Several minutes later, they came back downstairs, and Jonah thought that McKenzie looked a little pale. Rosemary must have noticed, too, for she sat her down at the kitchen table and handed her a damp cloth, which she pressed to her forehead.

"Don't feel obligated to stay in the room with Kaydie, dear," Rosemary said in a soothing voice. "I'm about to boil some water, and I could use your help."

"Thank you, Rosemary," McKenzie said as she blotted her forehead with the cloth. "I do feel somewhat light-headed, and I would rather not faint. It would hardly make Kaydie feel comforted."

Jonah smiled as he recalled McKenzie's tendency to faint during stressful situations. She'd even fainted in the middle of her own wedding ceremony, right in front of the whole congregation. Poor Zach had had to say his vows two times, and Jonah had been sure that his boss would remain a bachelor.

As Rosemary set a kettle of water on the stove to boil, Asa, Zach, and Davey came in and joined Jonah in the living room. They sat in silence—even Davey, who kept unusually quiet in times of suspense—and Jonah was thankful, for he became aware that he was feeling nervous, and he was hardly in the mood for conversation. The thoughts that ran wild through his mind made him thankful to be Kaydie's friend and not the father of her baby, for how much more anxious would that have made him?

After what seemed like hours, an infant's cry echoed through the quiet house. With the exception of Rosemary, who rushed upstairs, everyone sat on the edge of his seat but remained quiet, waiting for news.

Finally, Jonah heard the bedroom door open upstairs, and Rosemary appeared at the top of the stairs. "McKenzie? You have a beautiful niece."

"How's Kaydie?" several voices chorused.

"Kaydie is fine," came Doc Orville's authoritative voice.

After a while, Rosemary invited everyone upstairs. They filed into the bedroom, where Kaydie held the baby close and cooed soft words to her. Jonah had never seen such a tiny person, and he eagerly awaited his turn as McKenzie, Zach, and Asa each held her.

"I guess this means that Rosemary and Asa are grandparents again," Kaydie said.

Wiping a tear from her eye, Rosemary smiled at her. "Although we never had children of our own, we have been blessed beyond measure with the adoptive children the Lord has given us in all of you," she said.

Still awaiting his turn, Jonah stood to the side, watching the scene unfold. He'd thanked the Lord more times than he could count for delivering Kaydie through the birthing process. When it was his turn, he approached the bedside, sat down in the chair, and took the baby in his arms, amazed by how fragile and featherlight she felt. After gazing at her for a moment, he looked up at Kaydie and smiled. "You made it through."

"Praise the Lord," said Kaydie. "There were so many times I wasn't sure...." She swallowed hard. "Thank you again for not leaving me alone. I couldn't have done this without one of my closest friends."

"You're tougher than you think, Kaydie." Jonah again looked down at the baby in his arms. "You were right about her being a girl. Guess I didn't need to be bribed to keep quiet with more gingerbread cookies, after all."

Kaydie giggled. "Isn't she beautiful?"

"Yes, she is, but I never had a doubt she wouldn't be."

"I was shocked to see that she had hair already. I didn't have hair until I was two years old, and I half expected my little one to be the same." She reached out and gently stroked the baby's thin, dark hair.

"I think she has your brown eyes," said Jonah.

Kaydie beamed.

Jonah looked once more at the baby in his arms and found himself holding back tears of emotion. She was a precious gift from the Lord, and she would be blessed beyond measure to have Kaydie as her mother. Kaydie would never leave her behind, as his ma had done to him.

Davey broke away from the other adults' conversation and peered at the baby. "What're you gonna name her, Aunt Kaydie?" he asked.

Kaydie smiled at him. "I've been thinking about Bethany Ethel."

"I think that's a right pretty name," Jonah said as Davey made a face.

"I've always loved the name Bethany," Kaydie explained. "It means 'disciple of God.' I wanted her middle name to be Ethel after the woman who cared for me after Darius's death."

"The name suits her," said Jonah. Bethany Ethel reached a small fist up in a sudden movement. "Her fingers and hands are so small."

"I hear babies don't stay small for long," Kaydie teased.

"True. I've been here on the ranch for almost four years, and I've watched Davey grow faster than a weed." Gazing down at the child in his arms, Jonah knew right away that Bethany Ethel had stolen his heart.

CHAPTER EIGHT

Geraldine Feagins accepted the hand of the stage-coach driver and stepped down from the vehicle. Gazing around, she took in the town of Pine Haven. She'd been to the Montana Territory only once before, several years ago, when Pine Haven had been a mere settlement and not yet a town. Taking a quick glance about the community, she saw that it had changed significantly, and not only in size.

While she waited on the platform beside the stage-coach for her bags to be unloaded, she stretched out one leg and gently shook her foot, then switched to stretch the other. Standing up straight, she arched her back and stretched her arms. The two-day trip had caused her muscles to ache, and she was thankful to be out of the cramped coach. She wiggled her cold toes within her boots. The foot warmer she'd been given for the duration of the trip had done little to warm her feet.

"Where would you like me to put your bags, ma'am?" the stagecoach driver asked.

"Over there would be fine," Geraldine replied, pointing to a nearby bench. "Thank you kindly."

The driver nodded and placed her two bags where she had indicated before assisting the other passengers.

"Geraldine?"

Geraldine turned and saw her dear cousin, Lucille Granger. "Lucille!" she squealed as she rushed toward her with outstretched arms. "It feels like forever since last I saw you!"

"It certainly does!" Lucille hugged Geraldine and patted her on the back. "Welcome to Pine Haven."

"It's nice to be here, even if only for a little while," Geraldine said.

"Come along, and I'll show you to where you'll be staying." Lucille motioned for Geraldine to follow her. "Don't worry about your bags. I'll send Fred out to retrieve them."

The two women hooked arms and walked down the boardwalk toward the mercantile. Along the way, Lucille introduced Geraldine to everyone they passed.

As they neared the post office, Lucille slowed her pace. "Let's stop in the post office and see if anybody's there," she said.

"That sounds fine—it's sure to be warmer in there," Geraldine replied.

Sure enough, two customers stood at the counter, but no one stood behind it. Geraldine figured that the postmaster must be retrieving a package for someone.

"Ahem, ahem." Lucille cleared her throat. "I want to introduce you all to my cousin, Geraldine Feagins," she announced. "She's come to visit me for a spell."

Geraldine smiled at the customers. "It's so nice to meet you all."

Just then, she saw a man emerge from the back room and placed a package on the counter. He looked up and met her eyes, and she saw that he was rather handsome.

"Ah, Mr. Victor—there you are!" exclaimed Lucille. "Mr. Victor, this is my cousin, Geraldine Feagins. Geraldine, this is Gerald Victor, the postmaster of Pine Haven."

Mr. Victor nodded at Geraldine. "It's a pleasure to meet you, ma'am."

"Likewise," she answered.

"Why, Geraldine! You act as though you've never seen a postmaster before," Lucille whispered.

"Oh, pardon me!" Geraldine covered her mouth with a gloved hand and hoped no one else had noticed how she'd been staring at Mr. Victor.

"Geraldine came all the way from Wilmerville, on the eastern side of the Montana Territory. She'll be staying here until March." Lucille's chest puffed out in a way that made Geraldine slightly embarrassed. It was as if Lucille considered her a celebrity. They had grown up together almost as sisters, and Lucille had always looked up to her—both because she was shorter and because she was younger and openly admired her older cousin.

"Wilmerville?" Mr. Victor asked. "I've passed the place a few times but never stopped. Is it a nice town?"

"It's a lovely town, about twice the size of Pine Haven, from what I've seen so far," Geraldine replied.

She might have said more, but she wasn't sure if Mr. Victor preferred small towns or big cities and didn't want to offend him. There was something about that man that intrigued her. Not only was he handsome, but also his eyes held a kindness that drew her to him. She wondered if he had a wife, then chided herself for being so forward in her thinking.

"Well, if you two are finished with your chitchat, I suppose we should continue to the mercantile," said Lucille in an exasperated voice. "Oh, by the way, Mr. Victor, have you received any answers to the advertisements we placed in the newspapers back East for a mail-order bride?"

Geraldine's breath caught in her throat. So, Mr. Victor wasn't married? She looked over and saw him blush. The poor man! Geraldine loved her cousin Lucille, but she was always meddling and often made people uncomfortable.

"Uh...no, Lucille," Mr. Victor stammered. "As a matter of fact, I haven't received any responses." He cleared his throat.

"Well, it's still early in the process, so don't be too worried. You're a fine man, and no woman in her right mind would fail to delight in the chance of having you for her husband." Lucille paused. "You should be hearing something soon. Until then, toodle-oo!" Lucille hooked her arm through Geraldine's and led her out of the post office.

"That Mr. Victor is the nicest man," Lucille said as they continued down the boardwalk. "It's a shame he never married. I've been trying with all the talent the good Lord gave me to find that man a wife through an advertisement for a mail-order bride. It's worked before—I found Zach Sawyer a wife last year, and they could not be happier together. Now, through Lucille's Love Connections—my new business, which I wrote to you about—I am hoping for similar success for Mr. Victor."

Geraldine nodded. Not only was Mr. Victor unmarried, but he was also actively seeking a wife! She found herself smiling at the realization, then quickly chided herself again for thinking so much about a man she'd just met.

She decided to change the subject. "Why is it, Lucille, that you call Mr. Victor by his surname? Haven't you known him for some time?"

Lucille laughed. "I don't really know the answer to that question, Geraldine. It seems we've always called him 'Mr. Victor' rather than 'Gerald.' The entire town has, for that matter. Perhaps it's because he's gaining in years."

Geraldine attempted to hide her amusement. She was fairly confident that Gerald Victor was no older than Lucille, and he might even be a few years younger.

"Here we are," said Lucille as they reached the mercantile steps. "Fred? Oh, Fred, dear?" she called as they walked through the door.

"Yes, Lucille?" came Fred's voice just before he emerged from the office. "Oh, hello, Geraldine," he said when he saw her.

"Hello, Fred."

"How was your trip?"

"Long, but I enjoyed it, for the most part," she replied.

"Fred, would you fetch Geraldine's bags from the platform?" Lucille asked.

Fred nodded, then put on a coat and left the store. Lucille turned to Geraldine. "I'll take you upstairs and show you to your room."

⌒⌒⌒

The following day, Geraldine was visiting with Lucille behind the front counter of the mercantile when the door opened and Mr. Victor walked in.

He took off his hat and strode up to the counter. "Good morning, Miss Feagins, Lucille," he said.

"Good morning, Mr. Victor," Lucille said as Geraldine smiled shyly and nodded. "What brings you out on such a snowy day? Wait, don't tell me—you received a letter from a prospective mail-order bride!" Lucille eagerly leaned over the counter, as if getting closer to Mr. Victor would produce a positive response.

"No, Lucille, the mail hasn't even arrived yet," said Mr. Victor. "I actually needed some supplies."

"Well, I'm off to the chapel to deliver some items to the reverend," Lucille said. "Perhaps Geraldine can assist you."

Geraldine smiled again with another nod, hoping to conceal her panic. Lucille had covered the basics of filling orders, but she didn't feel prepared to manage the store on her own.

"That would be fine," said Mr. Victor, who smiled at Geraldine.

"Very well, then." Lucille began to pull on her coat. "Mr. Victor has an account here, Geraldine, so just be sure to list any items on the ledger. He's always been faithful to pay what he owes each month." She opened the door. "I shall return soon!" And with that, she was gone, leaving Geraldine alone with the handsome postmaster.

"What is it I can help you with, Mr. Victor?" Her heartbeat had accelerated, and she hoped he wouldn't hear it.

"Please, call me Gerald."

"If you'll call me Geraldine."

"Geraldine it is, then."

"Thank you."

"Well, I suppose I should fetch the supplies I need."

"Shall I help you collect them?"

"No, thanks—I can manage." He walked to the far corner of the store and retrieved several items from the shelves, then returned to the counter and set them down for Geraldine to record.

"So, do you have family in Wilmerville?" he asked as she opened the ledger to a fresh page.

"No, it's just me," she said.

"Are you...uh..." he began, scratching his head.

"Yes?"

"You are?"

"I am?"

"I mean, you are?"

Geraldine laughed. "I'm not sure what you're asking, Gerald."

"Oh, I'm so glad," he sighed.

"You're glad?"

"Yes."

"I beg your pardon?" Geraldine had no idea what Gerald was talking about, and she felt sorry for having made him nervous.

Gerald chuckled then. "I guess the question I was trying to ask, though I wasn't doing a good job of it, is 'Are you married?'"

Geraldine held a hand to her mouth. "Oh my, no."

"You're not?"

"No. Are you?" she asked. Even though she knew the answer, she didn't want him to know that it was on her mind, that she was interested.

"No." He cleared his throat. "Uh, Geraldine?"

"Yes?"

"You will?"

"I beg your pardon?"

"I mean, may I take you to dinner tonight? At the café, perhaps?"

"That would be lovely." Geraldine could hardly believe her luck!

"I'll pick you up here at six thirty, if that's convenient...?"

"I'll be here," she said with a smile.

As she finished recording his purchases, he collected the items under one arm. "Until tonight, then," he said, tipping his hat with his free hand.

"Until tonight."

Around six thirty that evening, when Geraldine heard a knock on the door, she took a few deep breaths, then went to answer it.

She peeked out the small window and saw Gerald, dressed in a spiffy suit. Behind him, she could see wispy snowflakes falling. It was a magical sight, and she was thankful to find her voice when she opened the door. "Hello, Gerald."

"Good evening, Geraldine," he said, smiling warmly.

"I'm ready to go; I just need to fetch my coat. Please, won't you step inside?"

While Gerald waited in the entryway, Geraldine went upstairs and retrieved her brown coat. She pulled her arms through the sleeves, then buttoned the front as she descended the stairs. Gerald offered her his arm, and together they stepped out into the night.

Geraldine couldn't remember a time when she'd felt so anxious yet acted so composed at the same time. She'd anticipated the evening all day long and had glanced at the wall clock in the mercantile almost every minute for the past several hours. It had been so long since she'd been asked to dinner that she had worried she would not remember how to behave or what to say. One thing she was thankful for, and which contributed to her calm state, was that Lucille and Fred had other obligations that night. They had left earlier, and so they hadn't been around to ask questions of Geraldine when she was getting ready to go out with Gerald.

"It sure is a chilly night," Gerald observed.

"I'm so thankful that this snowfall waited until I reached Pine Haven," Geraldine said. "The journey was cold, but the way was clear, and for that I was grateful."

"It is a difficult season to travel, the snow being so unpredictable."

"Yes, it is. However, I wanted to take advantage of my winter vacation. The school observes a recess between mid-February and mid-March."

"Well, here we are," Gerald said, stopping beside a humble storefront. He held open the door for Geraldine.

"Hello, Mr. Victor, Miss Feagins," a plump woman greeted them cheerfully.

"Good evening, Mrs. Moore," Gerald said.

"How do you do?" said Geraldine with a quick curtsey. "And, may I ask how you knew my name? I don't believe we've met."

Mrs. Moore beamed. "Lucille's told me all about you. For weeks, your visit was all she could talk about! She described you so well that when you walked in, I just knew you must be the famous Geraldine Feagins."

"Well, I don't know about 'famous,'" Geraldine said with a laugh.

"My husband and I own this café, and your dining pleasure is our highest priority," said Mrs. Moore as she led Geraldine and Gerald to a round wooden table.

Geraldine started to sit down, but Gerald grabbed her chair and, in a display of exaggerated chivalry, pulled it back, gesturing with his arm.

"Why, thank you, Gerald!" Geraldine took her seat, then watched as he made his way to the other side of the table and lowered himself into the other chair.

"What may I bring you to drink?" Mrs. Moore asked them. "We have cider, hot chocolate, coffee, and tea."

"Hot chocolate," they both chorused.

"I guess it's unanimous, then." Mrs. Moore winked. "I'll be right back with two mugs of hot chocolate."

When she'd left their table, Geraldine giggled. "I guess we have similar tastes in beverages."

"I can't recall a time when I didn't like hot chocolate," Gerald said. "It was a special treat for my sisters and me while we were growing up in Kansas. On the bitterest of winter days, Ma needed only to put the kettle on to warm the cream, and we would come running to the kitchen. When Pa came in from the fields to get warm, we would sit around the table and sip our hot chocolate. I almost always burned my tongue, but I couldn't wait to taste it."

Geraldine could almost taste the warm liquid, herself, and she was amazed at how Gerald could turn such a simple story into something exciting.

"Here's your hot chocolate," said Mrs. Moore, setting down a cup and saucer in front of each of them. "Our special tonight is roast beef with mashed potatoes and gravy, and we have a fresh apple pie for dessert."

"That sounds wonderful on a cold night like this," said Geraldine.

"It certainly does," Gerald agreed.

"I'll be back shortly with your meals, then," said Mrs. Moore.

Gerald thanked her, then faced Geraldine. "You mentioned when we were arriving here that your school has a recess right now. Does that mean you're a teacher?"

Geraldine smiled. "Yes, but this is my last year. I'm ready to hand the reins to a new teacher so that I can concentrate on sewing, which is my favorite hobby. Folks in Wilmerville already keep me busy doing seamstress work, and while I know I'll miss teaching, it will be nice to have more time to devote to other things. Maybe I will even have more opportunities to come here and visit Lucille."

"I sense that the two of you are close," said Gerald.

"Yes, we are. We were raised almost as sisters."

"For having been raised together, you two sure are different," Gerald said with a wink.

"I know Lucille can be a bit inquisitive at times," Geraldine conceded, "but she really does have a good heart."

Gerald chuckled. "I think that when the good Lord created Lucille, He wanted to make her truly one of a kind."

Geraldine laughed. "Yes, Lucille is unique, bless her heart. I hear that she's working hard to find you a wife."

"Uh, yes."

"I'm sorry, Gerald. I'm not making fun of you. I just find it comical that Lucille has opened her own business to match up unmarried men with wives."

Gerald scratched his head. "Lucille found a wife for Zach Sawyer, so I think she believes she can find a wife for me, as well—and probably for the rest of the unmarried men in Pine Haven, too, whether they know it or not. At least, I hope I'm not the only 'lucky' recipient of her matchmaking services."

"No, I'm sure you're not," Geraldine assured him jokingly. She paused for a moment and wondered if she should ask the question that filled her mind. Because she felt so at ease with Gerald, she decided to proceed. "Have you ever been married, Gerald?"

He gave a faraway smile. "I almost was once, a long time ago. Her name was Celia. I was twenty-seven, and so was she; both of us lived in Kansas then. But I missed the chance to propose to her, and she later married someone else. I guess I was too foolish to realize that she wasn't going to wait for me forever." He paused for a moment. "Have you...uh, ever been married, Geraldine?"

She grinned. "Actually, I was almost married once, too. His name was Calvin Schosselberg. We were engaged to be married. I was twenty-one, and he was twenty-three. Calvin enlisted to fight in the Mexican War a few months before our wedding and died in battle."

"I'm sorry to hear that."

"Thank you. That seems like such a long time ago." Geraldine shook her head. "After that, I threw myself into my work, teaching in Missouri, and then in Wilmerville after I moved to the Montana Territory."

"Here're your meals," Mrs. Moore announced, setting two plates on the table. "You know, I didn't think about it before, but it sure is interesting how your names are so much alike."

"I suppose you're right," said Geraldine. "I never really gave it much thought."

"I always thought you had a good name," Gerald teased.

Mrs. Moore laughed heartily. "Well, you two enjoy your meals, now, and let me know if you need anything." Then, she moved to the next table of patrons, chuckling to herself all the while.

Glancing across the table, Geraldine felt her heart swell with an emotion she hadn't felt in many years. Her near namesake had something special about him, and she hoped he soon would feel the same way about her.

CHAPTER NINE

On a trip to the mercantile the following month, Jonah had to hold his hat in place on his head, as the March wind threatened to blow it off. He stopped in front of the post office and climbed down from the wagon, still holding on to his hat.

"Hello, Mr. Victor," he said as he stepped up to the counter.

"Well, good afternoon, Jonah! What brings you to town today?"

"I had some errands to do and thought I'd better take advantage of the weather before it snows again."

"I believe today is the first day in almost a month that we haven't had snow," said Mr. Victor.

"Davey asked me to see whether there was a parcel here for him from Boston," said Jonah.

"I'm afraid there's no parcel, but there is a letter for Kaydie." Mr. Victor thumbed through a stack of envelopes, pulled one out, and handed it to Jonah.

"Thank you," Jonah said. "I reckon this weather has kept Miss Feagins in Pine Haven a bit longer, huh?" Thanks to Lucille Granger's fondness for spreading news, it was no secret that Mr. Victor was courting her cousin.

"Yes, it has, though I must admit I'm not complaining." Mr. Victor chuckled, then paused. "Jonah, have you ever been in love?"

"Pardon?"

"Sorry," said Mr. Victor. "I reckon that's a personal question. I was just thinking about the conversation we had a while ago about Lucille trying to find me a wife."

"Have you received any responses to the advertisements she placed in the newspapers?" Jonah asked.

"I have gotten several responses, yes, but I haven't read any of them. Promise me you'll keep this between us, okay? I don't want Lucille to find out."

"I promise," said Jonah.

"I hid the letters in my desk," Mr. Victor continued. "I didn't see any real reason in opening them since...well, since I've already found someone."

"By 'someone,' you mean Miss Feagins, right?"

"How did you know?" he said with a grin.

"Let's see," Jonah said, scratching his clean-shaven chin. "Besides the fact that Lucille has informed everyone in Pine Haven of your courtship...."

"I reckon it is obvious that I have feelings for her," Mr. Victor conceded. "I know it seems sudden, but I think I love her. That's why I asked if you'd ever been in love. I was hoping to get some advice."

"I...uh, yes...I think so," said Jonah.

"That's interesting, considering how strongly you were set against anything to do with love and marriage the last time we spoke on the topic."

"I reckon I'm starting to change my mind." Jonah glanced around the post office to make sure no one else was in the building and had overheard him.

"It's odd," Mr. Victor mused aloud. "Sometimes love comes out of nowhere when you're least expecting it. That's what happened to me with Geraldine. I was content with my life as a single man, and then, all of a sudden, she shows up in Pine Haven to visit Lucille. It's the strangest thing, Jonah. From the instant I laid eyes on her beautiful face, I was in love with her. And getting better acquainted with her these past few weeks has confirmed my feelings for her. I don't think I've let one day of her visit pass without seeing her."

"Well, I reckon love can sneak up on a man sometimes," Jonah said. "So, what are you going to do when she goes back home to Wilmerville?"

"I've thought about that same question for a while, Jonah, and here's what I think: I will follow her. She's arranged to leave next week. I've decided that I would be happy to live in Wilmerville just to be with her. I'm not going to take a chance on losing her. She's a special woman, and she's worth giving up my job and leaving Pine Haven, as much as I'll miss it."

Jonah was taken aback. Mr. Victor would follow Miss Feagins to Wilmerville? He'd leave behind all of his friends and associates just for some woman? Maybe Jonah didn't know as much about love as he'd thought.

"You mentioned that you might have been in love before," said Mr. Victor. "Was that before you came to Pine Haven?"

"No," answered Jonah. "Since I came here."

"Oh." Mr. Victor looked thoughtful for a moment. "Was it a long while ago?"

"No, it's pretty recent," said Jonah. "Look, Mr. Victor, it's kind of personal."

"Come now, Jonah. I promise not to tell anyone as long as you don't tell anyone what I told you about Geraldine."

"Well, all right," Jonah finally agreed. He still felt uneasy at the prospect of someone else knowing of his feelings for Kaydie. It was bad enough that Asa already knew.

"Tell me, is it Kaydie?"

Jonah stiffened. "It is."

"I suspected as much." Mr. Victor smiled slyly.

"How did you know?"

"I've seen the way you look at her, starting on the day she first arrived in Pine Haven and came into the post office. Does she feel the same way about you?"

"No—uh, I guess I'm not sure. See, she doesn't know how I feel about her. These feelings I have for her have been recent. I don't really know how to explain it, but I look forward to seeing her each day." Jonah paused, then sighed. "It doesn't matter, though, because she believes that deep down, every man, no matter how kind and well-meaning, is just like her abusive husband was."

"Yes, I've heard terrible things about that Darius fellow," Mr. Victor said. "And everyone who knows you would say that you're nothing like that. I reckon Kaydie will realize that, too, in time."

"I don't know, Mr. Victor. For the longest time, she was scared of me. I'm thankful she's no longer fearful to be around me, and she's told me many a time how she values my friendship. I think that may be all I will ever be to her—a good friend."

"Being a friend is a fine starting point," Mr. Victor said. "I don't believe you can truly love someone without truly liking her, too."

"Maybe so," said Jonah. "Remember, Mr. Victor, this is just between you and me. If Lucille finds out, and then Kaydie finds out...." Jonah didn't even want to think of the possible consequences if that happened.

"Your secret is safe with me, Jonah," Mr. Victor assured him. "I do have some wise words of advice for you, though: don't give up on her. In time, she'll see the fine man you are." He paused. "You know, it's funny how love caught us both by surprise. You were always determined never to fall in love, and I'd just figured it was out of the question for me due to my age." Mr. Victor shook his head.

"I think there's just something about Kaydie that's changing my opinions about love," said Jonah. "I can't really explain it."

"I reckon I know exactly what you mean," said Mr. Victor. "Exactly what you mean."

⌒⌒⌒

The next day, Gerald walked across the street to the blacksmith's shop. "Good afternoon, Wayne," Gerald greeted the blacksmith.

"Good afternoon, Mr. Victor. What can I do for you?"

"I know this is short notice, but I was wondering if I could ask you a favor that would remain a secret," said Gerald.

"Sure," said Wayne. "How can I help you?"

"This has to remain a secret," insisted Gerald.

"It goes no further than me," said Wayne.

"I need an engagement ring."

"An engagement ring?"

"Yes."

"You'd be better suited to order one through the catalog at the mercantile."

"I know that," said Gerald, "and I plan to order one there at a later time, but I need a temporary one for now."

"A temporary one? I've never heard of a temporary engagement ring," said Wayne.

"I'm planning to ask Geraldine Feagins to marry me, and I need a temporary ring to give her when I propose. If she says yes, I'll order the 'real' ring." Gerald wished he didn't have to share all these details with Wayne, but he knew that unless he did, Wayne wouldn't fully understand his urgent need for a ring.

"I reckon I'm beginning to understand," said Wayne.

"I don't want to order her a ring from the mercantile because I know it won't be here in time, and I...." Gerald searched for a delicate way to phrase what he wanted to say.

"You don't want Lucille to know."

Gerald sighed in relief. "Right. I know that if Lucille finds out my intentions, she'll never be able to keep them a secret. And I'd rather ask Geraldine's hand in marriage myself rather than have her hear it from her cousin."

"I understand," said Wayne. "I think I can make you a ring, although it won't be as delicate and lightweight as a ring from the catalog, and it won't have any pretty stone in it."

"That's fine. Thank you. Would it be possible for you to make it by next Monday? Geraldine is leaving Pine Haven on Wednesday, and I'd like to have it for our dinner on Monday evening."

"I think I can do that," said Wayne. "Things have been a bit slow due to the weather, so this is the perfect time for 'special projects.'" He winked.

"Thank you, Wayne. I'll be back by on Monday to fetch it."

"I'll have it ready for you."

"And, Wayne? Please don't let on to anyone about this."

"I promise that your secret is safe with me, Mr. Victor."

As Gerald left the blacksmith shop, he fought the urge to leap into the air as he walked back across the street to the post office. His plan was coming together.

❧

After Gerald closed the post office for the day on Monday, he began to prepare for his evening with Geraldine. He pulled a small wooden table into the center of the main room and covered it with a checkered tablecloth he'd purchased at the mercantile the week before. From the back office, he carried two chairs, one at a time, out to the main room and arranged them at the table. In the center of the table, he placed the two pewter candlesticks he had brought from home, then set a tall candle in each one. A glance at the clock told him it was quarter till six. Perfect timing. He pulled on his coat and left to pick up Geraldine from the mercantile.

Humming as he walked down the nearly deserted street, Gerald was again amazed how everything had come together for this special night. Wayne Waterson had completed the temporary engagement ring with time to spare, and Gerald was pleased with the finished product. Mrs. Moore would deliver dinner to the post office before he returned with Geraldine. *Now, if only I can be brave enough to ask her the question of my heart,* Gerald thought. *Please, Lord, give me courage. I pray that if it is Your will that Geraldine and I marry, You would guide us in that direction.*

"Well, Mr. Victor! What a pleasant surprise!" Lucille flung open the door of the mercantile before Gerald even had a chance to knock.

"Hello, Lucille. I'm here for Geraldine."

"Of course. She'll be down in a minute. Won't you come in?"

"Yes, thank you," he said, stepping over the threshold. Lucille closed the door again.

"Tell me, Gerald, have you received any letters in response to the advertisement?"

In a quandary, Gerald looked blankly at Lucille. He didn't want to lie, but he also didn't want to tell Lucille about the stack of unopened responses. Besides, they wouldn't matter after tonight if everything went according to plan.

"Don't be discouraged if you haven't received any responses," Lucille told him. "After all, it's usually harder for older gentlemen. You are a fine man, Mr. Victor. If any eligible women read the advertisement and did not respond, well, it's their loss."

"Thank you, Lucille," said Gerald. He leaned over to see around Lucille's stout frame and find out if Geraldine was coming to the door.

"I have known the process to take a matter of months to a matter of years, in other cases," continued Lucille. "It all depends on who sees the advertisement. I don't want you to compare your situation to that of Zachary Sawyer. There really is no comparison, you see. But I will guarantee you one thing: Lucille's Love Connections has a reputation of success, and I intend to uphold that fine reputation by finding brides for the notable men of Pine Haven such as yourself."

"I appreciate that, Lucille," said Gerald, trying to conceal his impatience. Where was Geraldine?

"Well, now! Look. There goes Mrs. Moore with a basketful of something—probably food." Lucille opened the front door and stepped onto the porch, with Gerald following behind. "Hello, Mrs. Moore!" she called out, waving enthusiastically.

"Good evening, Lucille, Mr. Victor," said Mrs. Moore.

Gerald couldn't believe that her conspiratorial wink had escaped Lucille's notice.

"I wonder what she's doing away from the café at this time of day," said Lucille, craning her neck to follow Mrs. Moore's path. "Surely she has customers she needs to serve."

"I can't imagine," Gerald said as he positioned himself in her line of vision. What if Lucille saw her heading toward the post office?

Lucille stood on tiptoe and looked down the street. "Could you please stoop down a bit or move to the side, Mr. Victor?" she asked. "I'm trying to see where Mrs. Moore is going."

"Uh, is that Geraldine?" Gerald asked, gesturing toward the mercantile.

Fortunately, Lucille fell for the ploy and turned to see if Geraldine was coming. "I don't see her yet, but she should be ready any minute." She lowered her voice to almost a whisper. "She was acting as though tonight was a special occasion or something. Tell me, Mr. Victor, what exactly is going on? You do know that she is leaving in two days to return to Wilmerville, don't you?"

"Yes, I know that."

"You two have spent a great deal of time together recently. I suppose you'll miss her when she leaves."

"Yes, I will," Gerald answered, suddenly feeling uncomfortable under Lucille's scrutiny.

Finally, Geraldine appeared in the doorway. She looked so beautiful that he sucked in his breath, overwhelmed by his feelings for her. He hoped Lucille hadn't heard.

"Good evening, Geraldine." Moving forward, he held out his arm.

"Hello, Gerald," said Geraldine as she stepped outside.

"So, where are you two going tonight?" asked Lucille.

"I'll be back soon," Geraldine answered, taking Gerald's arm.

"Are you going to the café? Because if you are, I just saw Mrs. Moore—"

"Thank you, Lucille. I'll bring Geraldine back later this evening," Gerald interrupted her.

"All right, then," said Lucille, looking confused. "Have a good time!"

They stepped out into the night, and Geraldine smiled up at Gerald. "I'm almost as curious as my cousin. Where are we going?"

"To the post office."

"To the post office?" She furrowed her brow, then grinned. "Come to think of it, I do have a letter I need to mail."

Gerald smiled back at her. "I'm sorry, ma'am, but the post office is closed for business. Tomorrow, though, I can certainly mail that letter for you."

"Such fine service at the Pine Haven post office," said Geraldine. "I shall miss it when I leave."

"And I shall miss you," said Gerald, his voice low.

When they reached the post office, Gerald opened the door and held it for Geraldine. She walked inside and gasped with delight.

It was just as he'd pictured it. Mrs. Moore had lit the candles, set the table, and arranged two plates of food that smelled sensational. As Gerald had requested, she had filled their teacups with hot chocolate. He presumed that they would find more in the small brass kettle on the counter.

"Oh, Gerald! How lovely!" Geraldine exclaimed.

"You're lovely, Geraldine," he said, returning her warm smile. "You really look beautiful tonight."

She wiped her eyes and sniffled. "This is the nicest surprise ever!"

"There, now. No need to cry," Gerald said as he helped Geraldine out of her coat. He hung both their coats in his office, then returned and pulled out Geraldine's chair, inviting her to sit down.

After he seated himself, Gerald almost forgot about the meal, so absorbed was he by the beauty of the woman across from him. Geraldine's long, silvery-blonde hair was braided and pinned in a circular shape atop her head, as she typically wore it, but a few strands had escaped and nicely framed her lovely, heart-shaped face. Her peach calico dress made her creamy skin look even creamier, and the strand of pearls around her neck was a nice touch.

"Gerald?"

He blinked. "I apologize, Geraldine. It's just that you look so beautiful tonight."

"Thank you."

"Well, shall we have a blessing?"

⸻

When Gerald had finished his prayer, they began to eat in silence. After a few minutes, Geraldine looked up from her plate and stared at Gerald, struck by his looks as if seeing him for the first time. His hair, though mostly gray, was thick and well trimmed. Subtle wrinkles around his eyes testified to his jovial personality. His eyes conveyed kindness like none she had seen before, and his arms were lean yet muscular. Those years he'd spent doing farm work in his youth had paid off. Could it be that she was really falling in love with Gerald, a man she'd met only a month before? The thought both excited her and saddened her. In two days, she would go back to Wilmerville. How could she bear to leave behind the man who had come to mean so much to her? *Do not ruin this perfect moment with such dismal thoughts*, she told herself.

The rest of the meal was spent in lively conversation. When they had finished eating, Gerald stood up and cleared the dishes to the counter. "There's something I need to talk to you about," he said.

Geraldine turned to see him. "Is anything wrong, Gerald?"

Gerald ducked behind the counter, then stood up and walked back to the table, carrying what looked like a small wooden box. She could hardly believe her eyes when he knelt down and said, "Geraldine, I have been in love with you since the first time I saw you. Will you do me the honor of being my wife?"

"Yes—"

"I know it's soon, Geraldine, and we haven't known each other for long, but I love you, and I want more than anything to be your husband."

"Ger—"

"I promise to love you and treat you with kindness and respect, as well as to mail any letters you might need me to mail, whenever you need me to. I have waited all my life for someone like you, and I would have waited three more lifetimes just for the privilege of being your husband."

"Ger—"

"I've never felt about anyone else the way I feel about you, and I don't have to stay here. I'll move to Wilmerville, if that's what it takes to be with you. As a matter of fact, I'll move to China, if that's where you'll be. Anywhere you are, I want to be there, also. You see—"

"Gerald?" Geraldine finally managed to interrupt him.

"Yes?"

"I said yes."

"You said yes?" Gerald frowned in confusion. "To what?"

"To your marriage proposal!" Geraldine giggled.

"Oh, yes, to my proposal. You said yes?"

"Yes, Gerald. I would be honored to be your wife. And I would gladly live in Pine Haven if that's what it takes to be with you."

"I...uh, I don't know what to say," said Gerald. He fumbled with the box, then opened it and handed Geraldine a ring. "Don't worry; this is just temporary."

"Temporary?" Geraldine said. "I assure you that when I marry you, it'll be forever."

"No, I mean, it's a temporary ring. I will buy you a fancy one at the mercantile. I just didn't want Lucille to know about my plans to propose for fear she might tell you before I could ask you."

Geraldine laughed. How well he knew her cousin! "I do understand that, Gerald."

"I love you, Geraldine." Gerald stood up again and helped Geraldine to her feet. Tenderly, he wrapped his arms around her, and she met his lips for a passionate kiss. "I was hoping you'd say yes," he whispered when their lips parted.

"I was hoping you would ask."

"You were?"

"I was."

Gerald kissed her again. "Thank the Lord for His timing."

CHAPTER TEN

Kaydie kissed Bethany Ethel gently on the fore-head, then laid the sleeping baby in her cradle. It had already been a long day for her daughter, starting with church that morning. Kaydie sat down at her desk and unfolded the letter she'd received from her mother two months ago, in March. Her eyes scanned the page, which she'd already perused several times.

My dearest Kaydence,

I hope this letter finds you well. I am pleased to report that your father and I have been diligently making plans for your future. As you know, we are planning for your return to Boston this sum-mer. We have determined to permit you to stay in our home for the first several months. By then, we are confident that you will have a home of your own to share with your new husband.

Clearly, plans for your matrimony have been under way, as well. This time, your marital union shall not cause our family such upheaval

and grief as your marriage to Darius did. You'll
be pleased to know that many of our friends
and acquaintances have already expressed
their sympathy regarding the death of your
"loving husband." I hope that you have been
rehearsing the scenario I outlined for you in an
earlier letter to explain your situation as a wid-
ow with a young child.

I would also like to inform you that you should
expect a surprise to arrive in Pine Haven on
July 1. I expect you to appreciate the surprise
and to communicate to me accordingly.

Please give McKenzie our greetings and let
her know that another parcel is on its way for
Davey with more books, per her request. I do
hope those books are being put to good use.

Yours truly,
Mother

Kaydie stared at the letter. She didn't want to disappoint her parents again, but she found that with each passing day of her temporary stay in Pine Haven, her desire to remain there grew stronger. She reread the line again about the surprise that would arrive during in early July. What could it be?

"Kaydie?"

Kaydie looked up to see Jonah standing in the doorway. She was grateful to him for speaking softly so as not to wake Bethany Ethel. "Hello, Jonah."

"I was wondering if you'd like to go fishing with me," he whispered. "I have everything ready to go."

"Fishing? I've never been fishing before." Her parents never would have permitted her to partake in an activity that might soil her dress.

"I'd be happy to teach you," said Jonah. "It's one of the most relaxing pastimes, and I thought it'd be nice to catch something to cook for supper tonight. Besides, it's so beautiful by the lake this time of year. The flowers are starting to bloom, and it's always peaceful. I think that you would enjoy it."

"Spring is my favorite season," Kaydie said. She thought of the new life that abounded during that time of year.

"Mine, too," said Jonah. He looked at the letter in Kaydie's hands. "Is that the letter from your mother?"

Kaydie sighed. "Yes. She and my father are making plans for my future, and she said she mailed a surprise that I should receive on the first of July."

"I wonder what that could be?" said Jonah.

"I have no idea, but I doubt I'll like it very much."

McKenzie peeked into Kaydie's room. "I heard that you might go fishing with Jonah, and I wanted to tell you that I would be happy to keep an eye on Bethany Ethel for you."

"Thank you, McKenzie," said Kaydie. "She was so tired, and now that she's finally asleep I don't want to wake her."

"I would love to spend some time with my favorite niece," said McKenzie. "Now, you two go ahead."

"Thank you again."

"You're welcome. Have a good time!"

"It's a perfect day for fishing," Jonah declared as he handed a fishing pole to Kaydie after he'd baited the hook. He doubted she'd enjoy piercing a squirming worm using her bare hands.

"How do I use this thing?" she asked, waving the pole like a wand.

"Not like that," Jonah teased. "Here, I'll show you."

Jonah moved next to Kaydie so that she could mimic his motions. Holding his pole, he said, "Now, beginning slowly, raise the pole toward you."

"Like this?"

She moved her entire arm rather than just her wrist, and Jonah managed to stifle a laugh.

"Not exactly...here." He set down his own pole and moved closer to Kaydie, gripping the pole with his hand slightly above hers, then demonstrated the proper movement. "I think you've got it!" he said after a few tries. "Now, you'll cast the pole toward the water with a slight movement of your wrist."

Again, he helped guide her through the motion. When the line had been cast, Jonah maintained his position, gripping the pole to feel for any fish that might bite. It was then that Kaydie shivered slightly and stiffened her shoulders.

"Kaydie, are you all right?" he asked, stepping away to give her some space.

"Yes," she whispered.

"You know that I would never hurt you, don't you?"

She didn't respond but stared out at the lake with a stricken look on her face.

"Kaydie?" Jonah moved forward into her line of vision and looked into her eyes. "Kaydie, I would never do anything to harm you," he said quietly yet firmly. "I'm not like Darius."

She looked out at the lake again. "It's just that...."

"What?"

"It's just that sometimes the memory of Darius fills my mind, and I can almost hear him, *feel* him, hurting me…. He was once so charming and friendly, but he turned into someone completely different." Kaydie's voice was barely above a whisper. "When I first met Darius, he was handsome and daring. He brought me flowers all the time and told me how much he loved me. He took me all around Boston and treated me to dinner at fancy restaurants. He was a true gentleman and introduced me as the 'love of my life' to everyone we met. My wishes were his top priority. Then, after we married and moved west…." Kaydie's eyes met Jonah's again, and he saw that hers were filled with tears. "After we married and moved west, that all changed. Suddenly he no longer cared about my wishes. He often yelled and treated me violently. It seemed that my inheritance was the true love of his life, even though he spent all of it in a matter of months. He stopped caring about his appearance and allowed his hair to grow long. He rarely bathed and had two of his teeth knocked out in a saloon fight in the Dakota Territory. I feared for my life at times, not only because of his temper, but also because we had nothing to eat. No, there were no more dinners at fancy restaurants after we married."

"Kaydie, Kaydie," Jonah said, hoping to soothe her.

She dabbed at her eyes with a handkerchief. "I'm sorry, Jonah. This is more than you care to know, and I'm spoiling a perfectly lovely afternoon."

Jonah gently took the fishing pole from her and set it on the bank of the lake. Then, facing her, he slowly reached out, lifted her chin, and looked into her brown eyes. "Nothing you tell me about yourself could be more than I want to know. I care about you, Kaydie—I have since we met—and there's no way I'm going to stop caring now. When I think of the way Darius treated you, I get sick to my stomach. And I wish there was some way I could go back and change all that you've been through. But there isn't. I can't erase all that. What I can do, though, is be here for you now—and in the future."

"You're such a good friend, Jonah. I don't know what I would have done without you these past months. I've been so blessed by everyone here, and—and—" A sob choked out her words.

Jonah wrapped his arms around her, careful not to move too quickly, and he was a little surprised when she buried her head in his shoulder. Her sobs came out in spurts, and Jonah pulled her closer with each one. "Kaydie, my sweet Kaydie," he murmured, tenderly kissing the top of her head.

"I—I had to—" Kaydie pulled back slightly and reached down to pull up the bottom edge of her skirt. "I had—I had to sew—pockets—on the insides of my dresses—right inside the skirt. W-when I would bake something, like bread, for Darius, I—I would have to hide some food in the pocket for later, or—or there would be nothing for me to eat. He—he always ate it all."

Jonah's anger raged inside of him. If Darius were standing before him at this very moment, he feared he might not be able to stop himself from an admittedly un-Christlike retaliation against the man who had caused Kaydie such pain. Nausea overtook him at the thought that Kaydie had nearly starved. He recalled how thin she'd been when she'd arrived in Pine Haven. "I don't know how any man could do such a thing," Jonah said disgustedly.

"I don't know how I could have been so foolish as to believe he was a man of integrity. I was so—so foolish—to think that Darius loved me. And now...."

Jonah cupped Kaydie's face in his hands. "You did not deserve what he did to you, Kaydie. No woman should have to go through what you did. Darius treated you in a way that is beyond comprehension. And it wasn't your fault."

"But I believed he loved me."

"Some people are good at lying, like the man we read about in the newspaper who fooled hundreds of folks in Ohio. There are people like Darius in our world who convince others to believe they're something they're not. You're not the first one to believe a liar." Jonah wondered where the words he'd just spoken had come from. He wasn't accustomed to such deeply emotional conversations, yet he felt deep concern for Kaydie. He reached up and touched her cheek.

For a moment, Jonah and Kaydie stood staring at each other as Jonah tenderly stroked her cheek. "I'm here for you, Kaydie," he assured her.

Kaydie closed her eyes. "Thank you, Jonah," she murmured.

Jonah pulled her to him again, wrapping his arms around her and allowing her head to rest against his chest. He wanted to tell her that he loved her, that he would always protect her, that he cared for her more than he cared for life itself. But he knew that he couldn't. The emotions within him, and his love for her, would have to wait, as he knew she did not yet feel the same way about him.

〜

Protected in Jonah's arms, Kaydie pressed her cheek to his chest. There was something about him that made her feel safe, and she closed her eyes. She thought of his smile, and how whenever he was amused, a dimple appeared in his left cheek. She thought of how he had taken to Bethany Ethel, and how her daughter had immediately warmed to him. Kaydie wondered how things might have turned out if she'd met him before meeting Darius.

"I suppose we should try to catch a fish or two," Jonah said after a while.

"I suppose you're right." Kaydie stepped away him and reached for the fishing pole she'd used before. "Let's see if I can remember how to do this." She reviewed Jonah's instructions in her head and cast the line into the water.

Jonah did the same with his own rod. "I wonder if Mr. Victor has returned from his trip to Wilmerville. He went with Lucille and Fred Granger to help Geraldine pack up and prepare for her move to Pine Haven."

"I think it's amazing that their names are so similar. It would be like you marrying someone named Joan."

Jonah chuckled. "I'm happy for them. But poor Lucille, she tried her best to find him a mail-order bride, and he went and found a bride for himself— her own cousin!"

Kaydie giggled, thankful for the happy distraction from haunting thoughts of Darius. "I hope that Lucille isn't discouraged. She can consider herself successful, in a way, for if it hadn't been for her, Mr. Victor and Geraldine probably never would have met!"

"According to Lucille, the knower of all things in Pine Haven," Jonah said dramatically, "Mr. Victor and Geraldine have set their wedding date for October. In the meantime, Geraldine will live with Lucille and Fred."

"I think that if I ever left Pine Haven, I would miss the people so much," said Kaydie. "I would even miss Lucille, who takes pride in making everyone else's business her own."

"She is a walking newspaper," Jonah agreed. "And the only unfortunate aspect of Mr. Victor's engagement is that now Lucille will probably turn her attentions back to finding a mail-order bride for me."

"I didn't realize that you were a customer of Lucille's Love Connections," she teased.

Jonah narrowed his eyes jokingly at her. "I didn't sign up to be her customer."

"After all, Zach found McKenzie through a newspaper advertisement," Kaydie went on, stifling a giggle. "I suppose you find the process appealing and hope for similar results."

"I'll have you know, Kaydence Worthington Kraemer, that Lucille took it upon herself to find me a wife. It was never an intention of mine."

"Oh, forgive me!" Kaydie gushed melodramatically. "I would never think that it was your intention to have a wife."

"It wasn't my intention at all, which is why I suggested that she try to find Mr. Victor a wife, instead."

"You didn't!"

"I did. I felt bad diverting Lucille's attention to another man, but I figured he needed a wife more than I did, and if she succeeded, so much the better for him."

Jonah felt a tug at the end of his line. "I think I caught one!" he exclaimed as he began to reel it in. A beauty of a trout dangled at the end of the hook, and he removed it and dropped it into the bucket they'd brought along.

"That was a big fish!" Kaydie said. "How long do I have to wait to catch one?"

"Until they bite." Jonah grinned at Kaydie, who appeared rather out of place as she stood awkwardly on the bank with her fishing pole in the water. "Maybe next time."

Jonah caught three more in the course of the afternoon. Kaydie caught none, but he was pretty sure she'd enjoyed herself. "How about we try again next Sunday after church?" he suggested as they packed up their gear.

Kaydie nodded. "I'd like that very much. And I'm determined to get a catch!"

Jonah winked. "We'll just see about that."

CHAPTER ELEVEN

ood sermon, wasn't it?" Mr. Victor asked Jonah as they walked out of the crowded church after the service the following Sunday.

Jonah nodded. "Reverend Eugene sure has a gift when it comes to making the Scriptures easier to understand. Especially when he's preaching from the book of Isaiah, which sometimes confuses me with its prophecies."

"I know what you mean. Isaiah is one of my favorite books in the Bible, but it can be difficult to understand at times." Mr. Victor looked thoughtful. "I remember memorizing one of the verses Reverend Eugene spoke about today when I was just a young'un. I still remember it like it was yesterday—and I even won a peppermint stick at the county fair for knowing the most Scripture verses." Mr. Victor cleared his throat, then recited, *"'Fear thou not; for I am with thee: be not dismayed; for I am thy God: I will strengthen thee; yea, I will help thee; yea, I will uphold thee with the right hand of my righteousness.'"*

Jonah chuckled as he tried to picture Mr. Victor as a young boy, showing off his Scripture memorization skills at the county fair. "Must have been a year or two ago that you won that award," he said teasingly.

"A couple of years at the most." Mr. Victor chuckled, too. "But still, the verse sticks in my mind—the wording and meaning." He paused. "Speaking of the service today, I couldn't help but notice you and Kaydie."

"What do you mean?"

Mr. Victor smiled. "I marveled at the way you helped her with Bethany Ethel when the baby started to get fussy during the sermon. It's almost as though you're a family."

"Mr. Victor, you know my feelings on marriage and families."

"I know that, Jonah, and I say this only because we're friends, and because you've shared with me about your feelings for Kaydie. I just couldn't help but notice the camaraderie between the two of you and the love you clearly have for both Kaydie and Bethany Ethel."

Jonah shifted his feet and looked around at the townspeople who were standing in small groups and talking. His eyes found Kaydie right away. "Mr. Victor, I do care about Kaydie and Bethany Ethel, but Kaydie and I are friends, and that's how I expect it will stay."

"Reminds me of that verse we learned about today—the one I just recited."

"The one about not fearing?"

"Exactly. What are you fearing, Jonah?"

Jonah shrugged. "I fear a lot of things...that Kaydie will never feel the same way about me that I feel about her; that if I end up asking for her hand in marriage, I won't be the husband she deserves.... I fear that I wouldn't know how to be a father to Bethany Ethel, and...."

Mr. Victor put his hand on Jonah's shoulder. "And what, son?"

"I fear I'll do something to lose her trust. I've worked so hard to earn it." Jonah moved his gaze away from Kaydie and looked at Mr. Victor.

"I see," said Mr. Victor. "Well, do you suppose the Lord would help you with those fears?"

"Oh, I know He would. It's just that the price is so high to love someone like Kaydie. What she's been through, what I've been through...."

"God knows all about that, and He's bigger than broken marriages and painful childhoods."

Jonah nodded. Mr. Victor had a point.

"Well, I best be going. Geraldine and I are going for a carriage ride this afternoon."

"Thank you, Mr. Victor...for everything."

"You're welcome, Jonah." With that, Mr. Victor walked away, leaving Jonah to ponder his advice.

Soon, his gaze shifted back to Kaydie. He was too far away to overhear her conversation with Eliza Renkley but close enough to enjoy the view of the woman he had come to adore. Bethany Ethel was squirming in Kaydie's arms, and she gently set her on the ground, then resumed talking with Eliza. Jonah considered walking over and offering to watch Bethany Ethel so that Kaydie could visit, but he couldn't move. His feet were planted firmly on the ground, and his gaze was fixed firmly on Kaydie. Her long, blonde hair was tied loosely with a red ribbon, and her face glowed, her brown eyes sparkling as she talked with Eliza.

Jonah gulped. Kaydie was beautiful—too beautiful. No matter how hard he tried, he could not deny his strong attraction to her. The realization that he loved her more than just as a friend still bothered him. Even more disturbing was the fact that the idea of being married to her had cropped into his mind on more than one occasion. In the past several days, despite his attempts to deny it, he had come to realize that marriage was something he wanted in his future. With Kaydie, it would be something worthwhile. *What's wrong with you, Jonah?* he chastised himself.

He watched as Bethany Ethel scooped up some dirt in her chubby hand, and he was about to shout to alert Kaydie when he saw her bend down and gently whisk the dirt out of her daughter's hand as she spoke something softly to her. Then, she picked up her daughter and held her against her hip.

Not only is she beautiful and sweet, but she's also a wonderful mother, Jonah thought to himself. What was there not to love about Kaydie Worthington Kraemer?

At that moment, Kaydie's eyes connected with his, and he held her gaze. Soon, she blushed and averted her eyes, looking again at Eliza. Jonah would have liked to know her answer to the question that filled his mind: *And how do you feel about me, Kaydie?*

Still transfixed by Kaydie's loveliness, as well as his love for her, he prayed, *Help me not to be afraid,*

Lord. Help me not to be afraid to love her and, if it's Your will, to someday ask for her hand in marriage.

The voices of the townsfolk chattering around him were drowned out by the four simple words Jonah heard in his heart: *She's worth the risk.*

⌘

That afternoon, Jonah and Kaydie hiked to the lake to fish. Jonah carried a large quilt and the wicker picnic basket Kaydie had packed with lunch, and Kaydie carried Bethany Ethel. When they reached the lake, Kaydie spread the quilt on the ground and sat down with Bethany Ethel in her lap. Then, she opened the picnic basket and unloaded the sandwiches and gingerbread cookies.

Jonah sat down and snatched a cookie. "You should enter your gingerbread cookies in the Founder's Day baking contest next week," he suggested before taking a big bite.

Kaydie thought for a moment. "I think I might take your advice," she said. "I've never entered anything in a contest before."

"Well, unless the judges have no sense of taste, your cookies will earn a blue ribbon for sure," Jonah said as he reached for another cookie.

"I packed sandwiches, too," Kaydie reminded him.

"Yes, but they don't taste as good as the cookies. By the way, I have something for Bethany Ethel." Jonah opened a small bag he'd brought and pulled out a tin baby rattle.

"Oh, Jonah, how thoughtful!" Kaydie exclaimed.

"I ordered it from the catalogue at the mercantile," he said, holding out the toy to Bethany Ethel.

Bethany Ethel squealed with delight as she reached an unsteady hand toward the baby rattle and began to bat at it. Jonah gently placed it in her hand, and she giggled at the tinkling noise it made. "I think she likes it," said Jonah.

"You spoil her, Jonah," Kaydie teased.

"How could I not? She's pretty special." Jonah smiled fondly at Bethany Ethel. "You know that you're pretty special, don't you?"

Bethany Ethel began to babble as she tried to fit the rattle in her mouth.

"Can I hold her for a minute?" Jonah asked.

"Of course!" Kaydie handed Bethany Ethel over to him, and he held her up, her tiny, chubby legs dangling, and smiled at her. Then, leaning toward her, he rubbed his nose against hers. Bethany Ethel kept giggling and dropped the rattle. Jonah did it again, and this time Bethany Ethel squealed.

"I think she's quite fond of you, Jonah," Kaydie said.

"I'm quite fond of her," he replied. "But I'll be honest—I haven't had much experience with babies. Sure, I've watched Davey grow, but I wasn't around him when he was a baby." He continued to rub his nose against Bethany Ethel's, eliciting an endless stream of giggles. "You're looking more and more like your ma every day," he said, setting Bethany Ethel on his lap. He picked up the rattle and handed it back to her.

Kaydie smiled. She was thankful that, with her round face and brown eyes, Bethany Ethel resembled her more than Darius. "She is such a delight. I can't imagine life without her."

"The Lord sure can take something bad and turn it into something good," Jonah said.

Kaydie nodded, knowing that Jonah was referring to how God had taken Kaydie's awful marriage and brought out of it the most wonderful gift Kaydie could have asked for—her daughter. She watched as Jonah continued to play with Bethany Ethel and was struck by the realization that he truly had slipped into the role of father—easily, too. While Zach and Asa also doted on Bethany Ethel, she hadn't taken to them as she had to Jonah. For what must have been the hundredth time in the past few months, Kaydie felt grateful that Bethany Ethel would never have to know her real father. "Do you want to feed her?" she asked Jonah.

Jonah nodded eagerly and accepted the glass nursing bottle Kaydie handed to him. He propped Bethany Ethel in a reclining position and held the bottle to her lips.

She began to suckle, then wrinkled her tiny round nose and spit out the milk. "I don't think she likes my method," Jonah said.

Kaydie smiled. "I did feed her right before we left, so it's okay if she is not yet hungry again."

Jonah tried to give Bethany Ethel another sip, but she turned her head away and made a spitting motion with her lips. "We'll try again later," said Kaydie.

When they had finished eating lunch, Jonah put the bait on the end of his fishing pole. Kaydie watched with Bethany Ethel on her lap as he caught two fish almost immediately. He made it look so easy!

"If you want, I'll hold Bethany Ethel again, and you can give it a try," Jonah offered. "I know how determined you are to catch a fish."

Kaydie grinned as she stood up, then handed Bethany Ethel to Jonah and took the fishing pole from him. She cast the line into the water and waited for several minutes before feeling a tug on the line. "I think I caught one!" she yelled, hoping she hadn't startled Bethany Ethel.

"Okay, now reel it in," Jonah coached her.

"This must be a large fish," said Kaydie, struggling with the weight of whatever had latched on to the bait. She pulled on the pole with all of her strength.

"You're doing fine," said Jonah. "Just go steady."

"I don't think I can reel it in!" Kaydie said, sighing in exasperation and lessening her grip slightly.

"Sure, you can," Jonah encouraged her.

Again, mustering all of her strength, Kaydie made another attempt. She managed to pull whatever it was a bit closer. "I can't wait to see this fish—I bet it's big enough to feed all of Pine Haven! And to think I'm the one who caught it!" Kaydie laughed, giddy with excitement. "I bet Lucille talks about this fish for months!"

Kaydie pulled and pulled on the line until, suddenly, her hands slipped and she went flying backward, landing flat on her behind with a thud. The fishing pole had sprung from her hands and landed in the lake with a splash.

"Kaydie, are you all right?" With Bethany Ethel in his arms, Jonah rushed to her side.

Still on her backside, Kaydie looked up at him with exasperation. She must look a sight with her dress covered in mud. "I think I'm all right," she muttered.

Jonah had the nerve to chuckle. Bethany Ethel began to squeal, too, which made Jonah burst out laughing.

"It's really not all that funny," Kaydie said.

"Oh, I think it is." By this time, he had tears streaming down his face. "That must have been"—he chuckled and tried to catch his breath—"must have been some fish!"

"That's enough from you, Jonah Dickenson," said Kaydie. She looked toward the lake. "Where did the fishing pole go?"

"The fishing pole?" Jonah asked in disbelief. "You—you want to know where the fishing pole went?" Jonah paused for a minute and glanced down at Kaydie. She gave him a stern look, which caused him to laugh again.

"Yes, I want to know where the fishing pole went." Kaydie glared at Jonah. How dare he find humor in this situation! "For your information, Mr. Dickenson, I could have been killed!"

"I reckon I never heard of anyone getting killed trying to catch a fish and then falling over her own two feet backward into the mud!" Jonah exaggerated his Southern accent, which added to her annoyance.

"How dare you, Jonah? I didn't trip over my own feet. That fish I caught was so huge that it almost pulled me into the lake. You wouldn't be laughing so hard if you'd had to jump in and save me!" Kaydie brushed off her skirt and attempted to stand. "I suppose you're not going to help me stand up, so I'll just do it myself."

"Begging your pardon, ma'am," Jonah said, reaching out his free hand. Kaydie ignored his offer and pushed herself to her feet without his aid.

"I can't believe you, Jonah Dickenson. You stand there and watch as I struggle with all my might to catch that fish, and then, when things don't go according to plan...." Kaydie cast him another glare, and he sobered. "...When things don't go according to plan, and the fish steals the pole from me, you have the audacity to begin laughing as if you'd heard the funniest joke ever told!"

"The fish stole your fishing pole?" Jonah began to howl again.

"Jonah, you know what I mean."

"You'd better tell the sheriff about that."

"Jonah," Kaydie warned.

"Or, better yet, tell Lucille. She'll have it known across the entire Montana Territory within five minutes."

"That's it, Jonah." Kaydie put her hands on her hips. "I'm never going fishing with you again."

"Never?" Jonah stuck out his bottom lip and pretended to pout.

"Never, as long as I live."

"You know," said Jonah, adjusting Bethany Ethel in his arms, "about five minutes ago, you were saying how everyone would be so amazed that you caught this big fish, and how it was large enough to feed all of Pine Haven. Think of all the hungry people in our town. Don't you want to try catching the fish again?"

Kaydie sighed. "I did think it would be grand to catch such a big fish on only my second fishing trip."

"Forgive me for sounding like a preacher, Kaydie, but isn't there a verse?—ah, yes, I believe it's Proverbs chapter sixteen, verse eighteen: *'Pride goeth before destruction, and an haughty spirit before a fall.'*"

"I believe I'm ready to leave," Kaydie said through pursed lips.

"I've never seen you so festered up about any-thing before. It's nice to see that you have a temper," Jonah teased.

"I may be slow to boil, but when I do boil...."

"You boil over," Jonah tacked on, beginning to chuckle again.

"If you would be so kind as to help me, I'd like to pack our things and head home."

"So, you don't want to try catching that big fish again?" Jonah asked.

"No, thank you." Kaydie marched with exagger-ated steps to their picnic area and began packing up the basket. "And see if I ever make you gingerbread cookies again, Jonah Dickenson." She paused. "By the way, what is your middle name?"

"I'll never tell."

"It would be useful in times like this, when I find myself quite disturbed by your incessant teasing," Kaydie said.

"A good reason never to tell. Besides, it's not a good name."

"Please, tell me," Kaydie pleaded.

"Oh, all right, but only because I feel bad that you didn't catch your fish. It's...uh, Maynard.'"

"Maynard?" said Kaydie. "Jonah Maynard Dickenson?"

"It was my grandfather's name."

"Maynard?" Now it was Kaydie's turn to laugh. "Oh, Jonah, can you imagine if your parents had named you Maynard Jonah, instead?" She giggled uncontrollably at the thought.

"I never should have told you," Jonah said with a groan. "I knew I'd regret it."

Kaydie couldn't stop laughing as she said the name over and over in her mind. "You know, that does flow well—Jonah Maynard. Yes, Jonah Maynard Dickenson." She put on her own Southern accent, this time with a shrill pitch: "I would like y'all to meet my good friend, Jonah Maaaayneeerrrddd!"

Jonah shook his head. "Don't you dare tell a soul, Kaydie."

"It depends on whether you tell anyone about the big fish."

"All right," Jonah said reluctantly. "It's a deal. But that was a good fishing pole that just went to waste."

"Jonah," Kaydie threatened.

"All right, I promise."

Satisfied with their truce, Kaydie finished packing their things, and she and Jonah headed back toward the ranch, Bethany Ethel asleep against Jonah's shoulder. As they walked along, they took turns laughing at the afternoon's events: Jonah snickered at Kaydie and the fish that got away, and Kaydie giggled at Jonah's middle name. Even with Jonah laughing at her expense, she wondered if, despite her episode with the fish, she had ever lived a finer day.

CHAPTER TWELVE

On the morning of the annual Founder's Day celebration, Jonah and Kaydie, along with Bethany Ethel, set off toward town in one wagon, followed by Zach, McKenzie, Davey, Asa, and Rosemary in another. After driving over a deeply rutted section of road, Jonah glanced behind him to make sure that the baked goods Kaydie had packed and the quilt she had sewn were in place in the wagon bed. "Looks like there might be a blue ribbon or two back there," said Jonah with a wink at Kaydie, seated next to him.

Kaydie smiled shyly. "Between the apple pie, rhubarb pie, gingerbread cookies, and quilt, I hope that at least something wins a ribbon, even if it isn't first place. Are you anticipating the horse race?"

Jonah chuckled and held the reins in his left hand. "I anticipate it every year, and every year I've entered, I've lost to the sheriff by this much." He held his right thumb and forefinger about three inches apart. "I'm hoping this will be the year I'll walk away with the grand prize."

"I hope so, too, though I suppose it's a good sign that the sheriff usually wins," Kaydie observed. "It means he's more apt to catch any villains that try to escape."

Jonah shook his head. "He can come in second place and still be a fine sheriff."

Soon, downtown Pine Haven came into view, complete with the banner that stretched across the main street. "Look at all the decorations!" Kaydie exclaimed. "I've never been to a Founder's Day celebration before."

"Oh, it's a big event here, all right," Jonah said. "People come from miles around for just about every type of contest you can imagine. There's watermelon seed-spitting contests, three-legged races, gunny-sack races, the baking contest.... The only event that comes close to being as popular as Founder's Day is the Fourth of July celebration next month."

"Davey was telling me all about why we celebrate Founder's Day," said Kaydie. "I was impressed by his knowledge of the founder of Pine Haven, Perry Crandlemire. He explained how Mr. Crandlemire traveled here thirteen years ago from the East with a large herd of cattle and began the first settlement. Davey also told me that Mr. Crandlemire was so satisfied with the grazing land that he wrote an article for several newspapers back East inviting others to settle in the Pine Haven area."

"Davey's a smart boy. Zach just taught him all about Perry Crandlemire and the history of Pine Haven, and he remembered it exactly." Jonah paused. "It's a shame that Mr. Crandlemire passed on six years ago, and Davey never had the chance to meet him."

"Davey is certainly bright," Kaydie said. "Zach has done a good job raising him."

"I think it helps that McKenzie reads to him every night," Jonah observed.

"I think McKenzie very much enjoys being a mother," said Kaydie. "As do I." She leaned forward and kissed Bethany Ethel on the top of her head.

"Bethany Ethel is blessed to have you as a mother, Kaydie," said Jonah. "Any kid would be lucky to have a mother like you." He thought of the mother's love he'd never experienced. Not wanting to sour the happy mood of the morning, however, he forced a smile and slowed the wagon to a stop.

Mounted flags waved in the soft June breeze, and music filled the air, thanks to the volunteer musicians who had been assembled as a band. Jonah looked over at Kaydie, who looked awestruck as she gazed toward the busy square. "I've never seen Pine Haven so crowded!" she exclaimed. "It looks as though everyone is here."

"Most everyone from Pine Haven probably is, as well as plenty of folks from the nearby towns," Jonah said. "There have got to be more than two hundred and fifty people milling around over there."

He helped Kaydie down from the wagon as Zach pulled up alongside him. "I wonder where we're to enter our baked goods," said Kaydie.

"We'll find out soon enough," Jonah said as he began to unload the wagon, starting with the basket containing the pies. "Do you need me to sample the cookies once more, just to make sure they're contest material?" He winked at Kaydie, who sent him a playful frown.

McKenzie walked up with her own basket. "I believe the baked goods and quilts are being entered at the mercantile," she told Kaydie. "Shall we go find out?"

"Okay," said Kaydie.

"Would you like me to watch Bethany Ethel in the meantime?" Jonah asked her.

"Yes, if you wouldn't mind—thank you!"

Jonah regretfully added the tin of gingerbread cookies to the basket of pies and handed it to Kaydie, then took Bethany Ethel from her other arm. "Good luck!" he said to the cookies, which made Kaydie giggle. "Oh, and good luck to you, too," he said, meeting her eyes. "See you in a little while."

"Yes, see you," Kaydie said as McKenzie handed her her quilt, placed a hand on her shoulder, and led her away.

⸎

Several minutes later, Kaydie stood with McKenzie and Rosemary in a line of contestants that stretched out the front door and down the steps of Granger Mercantile and along the boardwalk. They chatted and shifted their grips on the baskets and crates containing their entries as the line moved slowly forward.

When they finally stepped inside the mercantile and arrived at the counter, Lucille Granger greeted them, notebook in hand. "Well, Kaydie, how nice to see you!" said Lucille. "I see you have a few things to enter."

Kaydie nodded and set her basket on the counter. "I have an apple pie, a rhubarb pie, and gingerbread cookies." She then laid the quilt next to the basket. "I also have the quilt I made for Bethany Ethel."

"Well, haven't you been busy?" Lucille said as she scribbled in her notebook. Then, she unloaded the tin of cookies and the pies. "I'm glad you made an apple pie, dear, but I must be frank with you: my apple pie has won for too many years to count. I don't blame you for wanting to enter, mind you, but I'll just warn you that my recipe is one of the best."

"I'm sure it is, Lucille," Kaydie said. Out of the corner of her eye, she saw McKenzie and Rosemary exchange a knowing look.

"Now, your rhubarb pie? That might have a chance at second or third," said Lucille as she inserted a numbered flag into each pie. Next, she affixed a numbered slip to the tin of cookies as another woman labeled Kaydie's quilt and carried it away.

"Well, thank you for your entry," Lucille said as Kaydie stepped past the counter. "Now, what do you have to enter, McKenzie, dear?"

Kaydie watched as her sister set her items on the counter. "Only a pecan pie and a shirt I recently sewed for Davey. I'm not nearly as ambitious as Kaydie," she teased.

Lucille nodded as she wrote in her notebook and then labeled the items. "And for you, Rosemary?" She looked up, and Kaydie thought she rather resembled a demanding schoolteacher.

"No baked goods this year," she said. "I did bring some stitching, though—some hats and scarves, two dresses, and a needlepoint sampler." Kaydie watched as Rosemary arranged her entries on the counter. She had admired them as Rosemary had worked on them and fully expected her to go home with several blue ribbons.

"You always did love to sew, didn't you?" said Lucille. "My cousin Geraldine is a fine seamstress. Please, don't feel bad if her entries score higher than yours, Rosemary. She's quite experienced, you know."

"It's all in good fun," said Rosemary, turning around to grin at Kaydie.

"It is all in good fun," Lucille agreed. "There. Now you three are all set. Best of luck to you." Lucille smiled. "Oh, did you hear the news about my cousin Geraldine and Mr. Victor? They've set a wedding date of October the fourth."

"I'm so happy for them," said Rosemary. "Mr. Victor is a fine man, and from what I know of Geraldine, she is a kindhearted woman. We shall welcome her with open arms as a permanent resident of Pine Haven."

"The three-legged race is about to start," said Asa, poking his head inside the door of the mercantile.

"We'd best be going," said McKenzie. "Thank you, Lucille."

Kaydie thanked the woman, as well, then followed McKenzie and Rosemary out of the mercantile to join Zach, Jonah, Asa, and Davey out front.

"Five minutes till the three-legged race!" Mr. Victor announced, using a megaphone to project his voice. Kaydie remembered Jonah telling her that Mr. Victor had been the master of ceremonies at the Founder's Day celebration for many years. "Find your partners and take your places at the starting line! This is an excellent opportunity to practice for the three-legged race on the Fourth of July!"

"Care to be my partner in the three-legged race?" Jonah asked Kaydie.

"Oh, I—I really couldn't," she stammered. She had never seen a three-legged race, much less run in one, and she had no idea what it involved.

"I would be happy to hold Bethany Ethel," McKenzie offered.

"I think I'll sit this one out." Kaydie felt several pairs of eyes on her and suddenly wanted to disappear.

"It's a lot of fun, Kaydie. I think you'd enjoy it," said Rosemary. "Go ahead; we'll take care of the baby."

"I don't know...." The last thing Kaydie wanted to do was make a fool of herself in front of such a large crowd of people.

"Grab your partners and line up at the starting line!" Mr. Victor ordered. "The race starts in three minutes!" Kaydie saw him climb a set of wooden stairs.

She looked back at Jonah, who clasped her hand. "What's the worst that can happen?"

"I'll fall and make a complete fool of myself."

"And the best thing that can happen is, we'll win those big blue ribbons over there, along with a free meal at the café. Come on, Kaydie, please?" Jonah persisted.

Kaydie eyed Jonah's expectant face. How many times had she wished she were braver, more courageous, and more eager to try things that other people seemed to try without thought or effort? She was conscious of Jonah's hand loosely holding hers, and the pairs of eyes that were watching her. "All right," she squeaked.

"Great! But we need to hurry. They're about to start," said Jonah.

He handed Bethany Ethel to McKenzie, then grabbed Kaydie's hand. They weaved in and out of the crowd and finally reached the starting line, where they were handed a strip of cloth. Jonah immediately tied it around his right ankle and Kaydie's left one. *What am I getting myself into?* she thought.

"Is everybody ready?" Mr. Victor asked the participants, glancing around below him. Kaydie cast a nervous glance at Jonah, but he looked determined and not at all anxious.

"On your marks, get set, go!" shouted Mr. Victor. Kaydie heard a gunshot and was simultaneously propelled forward as Jonah began to run.

"Oh dear!" Kaydie squealed as she tried to keep up with Jonah. Their movements were completely opposed, though, which made progress awkward and slow. Kaydie knew that she would fall flat on her face at any moment, taking Jonah down with her.

"You're—doing—fine," Jonah huffed, his arm firmly around Kaydie's shoulders.

"I don't—think—I can do this," Kaydie said between gasps. She put her arm around his waist and gripped his side, since reaching her arm around his shoulders was out of the question due to their eight-inch height difference.

Up ahead, another couple fell, and Kaydie moved left with Jonah's leading to avoid running into them. Moments later, Kaydie finally matched her pace with Jonah's, and they raced with almost perfectly synchronized movements toward the finish line. "We're—almost—there!" Jonah panted.

Kaydie concentrated on keeping up with Jonah as they passed couple after couple until they were in second place. She giggled at the realization that she was having fun and was glad to have entered the race. She could hear Mr. Victor's voice but couldn't understand his words, so focused was she on the race. She and Jonah moved closer and closer to the competition.

The crowd cheered enthusiastically as Jonah and Kaydie neared the finish line, still in second place. They crossed over the ribbon, which had been broken by the couple ahead of them, and Kaydie tripped and fell, taking Jonah down with her. "That was so much fun!" Kaydie exclaimed, erupting in giggles.

"And to think you didn't even want to try it," Jonah teased. He untied the strip of cloth from their ankles and helped Kaydie to her feet. "Good job, partner."

"Congratulations to our second-place team, Jonah and Kaydie!" Mr. Victor announced. He pinned a red ribbon on Jonah's shirt, then handed one to Kaydie, along with an envelope. "While the first-place winners receive a certificate for dinner at the café, I'm pleased to announce that our second-place winners receive dessert at the café. You two make a good team!"

"Thank you," chorused Kaydie and Jonah amid the cheers of the crowd.

Jonah reached around and put his arm around Kaydie. "We'll have to try that again at the Fourth of July celebration, eh, partner?"

"All right," Kaydie agreed. She fingered the red ribbon. "I still can't believe we came in second place!"

"This'll be something you'll have to share with Bethany Ethel when she gets older. She'll be so proud of her ma," said Jonah.

Kaydie felt the heat of a blush on her face. She was aware of Jonah's arm still around her shoulders but somehow felt comfortable in spite of it. "Shall we go find everyone else?" she asked.

"I spied them by the blacksmith shop when we were racing," said Jonah.

"How could you see anything while we were racing? I had to concentrate on the ground in front of us, or I would have fallen for sure!" Kaydie said with a giggle.

"You did really well, Kaydie. I think sometimes you underestimate yourself."

"When you first asked me to race with you, I thought you'd be better served entering with someone who was accustomed to such games, like Zach or Asa," she said.

Jonah steered her through the crowds toward the blacksmith shop, and Kaydie finally spotted McKenzie standing out front. "You were my first choice as a partner, Kaydie. I'm just thankful you didn't try to do any fancy backward tripping during the race," he teased.

Kaydie stopped then and elbowed him in the side. "I thought it was agreed we wouldn't bring up my fishing adventure, Jonah."

"We never agreed I wouldn't bring it up, only that I wouldn't tell anyone else about it," he reminded her.

"All right then, Maynard," Kaydie teased back.

"Understood," Jonah said as they arrived at the blacksmith shop.

Kaydie smiled. Not only had her stay in Pine Haven reunited her with her sister, but it had also provided her with the best friend she found in Jonah Maynard

Dickenson. *Thank You, Lord, for I am indeed blessed*, she prayed silently, lifting her eyes heavenward.

∽

In the moments before the horse race began, Sheriff Clyde scowled good-naturedly at Jonah. "Ready to take second place again, Dickenson?" he asked.

"I don't think so. Not this time, Sheriff," said Jonah. He tightened his grip on the reins.

"You can try to catch me, son, but you know it's no use," the sheriff joked.

"That may have been true in the past," Jonah said with a chuckle, "but this year, I'm aiming for first place."

"We'll just see about that," the sheriff answered, his eyes twinkling. "Wouldn't it be crazy if Zach, Asa, or Reverend Eugene won this year?"

Jonah laughed, knowing that Sheriff Clyde was his only true competition in the race. "It would be strange, indeed."

Mr. Victor took his place atop the wooden platform and raised a pistol in the air. "Gentlemen, prepare to begin the horse race. On your marks, get set, go!" At the sound of the gunshot, Jonah kicked his horse's flanks and launched forward, along with all the contestants in the two-mile race.

"Come on, Lightning!" Jonah urged his horse. "Remember what we practiced!" He had run Lightning through the course several times that week to make him familiar with the terrain. Lightning was the fastest horse Jonah had ever owned, and he'd always come so close to winning this race.

In the first minute or two of the race, several of the entrants were close to one another, vying for the top prize. However, that soon changed, and Jonah and the sheriff were neck and neck, leaving the others behind. "Come on, Lightning!" Jonah leaned slightly forward and stroked his horse's neck. "There's a nice, juicy apple at the finish line!"

Out of the corner of his eye, Jonah saw Sheriff Clyde riding just slightly behind him, so he urged Lightning to run even faster. He kept his eyes straight ahead, not daring to glance to the sides or behind him. One thing he had learned from past races was that he needed to remain focused. Rounding the first corner, he heard cheers from those who were standing along the course. Last year, some people had placed bets on who would win. He wondered if they'd done the same this year. Had anyone bet on him and Lightning, or had most people bet on Sheriff Clyde, assuming he would have a repeat win?

"See you later, Dickenson!" shouted the sheriff as he passed Jonah.

"Not so fast, Sheriff!" Jonah urged Lightning to a quicker pace, watching for any obstacles on the course that might impede their progress. He passed Sheriff Clyde then, his heartbeat matching his horse's rapid hoofbeats.

Moments later, Sheriff Clyde passed Jonah again, and they continued taking turns in the lead. All Jonah had to do was make sure he was ahead when they crossed the finish line.

As they rounded the final corner of the course, Jonah could see the finish line and several people standing on either side of it. He was nearly tied with

Sheriff Clyde. Lightning's black mane flew in the breeze, and Jonah was sure that his horse wanted to win almost as much as he did. "Just a little bit farther," Jonah coaxed him.

At the last minute, Lightning pulled ahead and crossed the finish line less than a second before Sheriff Clyde's horse. "Hooray!" shouted Jonah. The crowd cheered, and Jonah slowed Lightning to a trot. "We did it, Lightning! We did it!"

"We have a new winner this year: Jonah Dickenson!" Mr. Victor announced.

Jonah dismounted, and Mr. Victor handed him the cash prize. Next to the red ribbon he wore from the three-legged race, Mr. Victor pinned a blue ribbon.

"Congratulations, Dickenson," Sheriff Clyde said, shaking Jonah's hand. "I hadn't figured on you winning this year."

"Thanks, Sheriff. You sure put up a good fight. See you next year, right?"

"Of course!"

Kaydie ran up to him with Bethany Ethel in her arms. Not far behind her were McKenzie, Rosemary, and Davey. Then, Zach and Asa arrived after having dismounted their own horses.

"Congratulations, Jonah!" Kaydie cheered.

"Thanks! I've waited forever to win this race, and finally, after years of trying, I walk away with the grand prize." Jonah held up the crisp twenty-dollar bill for her to see.

"That was a great race," Zach said, patting Jonah on the back. "I always knew that one day you'd beat the sheriff. I just wasn't sure if it would be in my lifetime."

"Very funny," Jonah muttered.

"Good job, Jonah. We're proud of you," said Asa.

"We sure are," said Zach. "Everyone, I'd like you to gather around and meet this year's horse race champion, Jonah!"

Kaydie caught Jonah's eye and mouthed the words, "Jonah Maynard."

He sent her a teasing glare and mouthed, "Big fish."

⸎

Kaydie eyed the long wooden table showcasing all of the baked goods that had been entered in the contest, searching for her pies and her gingerbread cookies.

"It's time to announce the winners of the baked goods contests!" Mr. Victor announced. He looked down at the paper in his hand. "First place in the pie division goes to...Geraldine Feagins!"

Geraldine brought her hands to her mouth with a shocked expression. At the urging of the people standing near her, she moved forward to claim her blue ribbon.

"Second place in the pie division goes to... McKenzie Sawyer!"

"Congratulations, McKenzie!" Kaydie said, giving her sister a hug.

"What would Mother say if she heard of this?" giggled McKenzie. "You and I must be the first in several generations of Worthingtons to bake their own food!"

Kaydie nodded in agreement. "Perhaps we should keep the news to ourselves."

"And third place in the pie division goes to... Lucille Granger!" announced Mr. Victor.

"Well, I never!" said Lucille.

"What's wrong, Lucille?" asked Geraldine.

"I just never imagined I would win third place." Lucille accepted her ribbon with a smile that Kaydie found rather forced. This was one piece of news that she would probably want to remain within the circle of people gathered around the dessert table.

"Now, we'll move on to the cookie division," said Mr. Victor. "First place goes to Kaydie Kraemer for her delicious gingerbread cookies!"

"M-me?" Kaydie stammered in disbelief.

"You won, Kaydie!" McKenzie hugged her sister. "Do you think we could talk Peyton into entering a baking contest?" she added with a smirk.

"Congratulations, Kaydie," said Jonah. "I always knew your gingerbread cookies were the best." Their eyes met, and he held her gaze. "I'm proud of you," he added.

"Thank you, Jonah," said Kaydie, still not believing she'd heard Mr. Victor correctly.

Rosemary garnered the top award for several of her sewing accomplishments, as well as her needlepoint, Geraldine earned a blue ribbon for a dress she had sewn, and Kaydie won third place for Bethany Ethel's quilt. Zach later won the watermelon seed-spitting contest, followed by Asa in second place. Davey bobbed for the most apples and also took third place in the gunnysack race. The day passed quickly with a picnic lunch and conversations with friends mixed in with more festivities to celebrate the founding of Pine Haven.

That evening, a dance was held in the Renkleys' barn, not far from the center of town. Musical strains from harmonicas and fiddles had everyone on their feet. Kaydie leaned against the wall and watched as she cradled a sleeping Bethany Ethel in her arms. "These dances are so different from the ones we attended in Boston," Kaydie observed aloud to McKenzie, who stood beside her.

"I've been to only one other dance here, but I wholeheartedly agree that they are quite different," McKenzie said. "However, they are also a lot of fun."

Zach broke away from a group of men he was speaking with and bowed to McKenzie. "May I have this dance?" he asked.

"Why, of course!" McKenzie replied, then took his hand and followed him to the dance floor.

Kaydie shifted Bethany Ethel in her arms and leaned down to kiss her daughter's soft cheek. Although the music was loud, and the dancers even louder, Bethany Ethel was so exhausted from the busy day that any noise was unlikely to interrupt her sleep.

Tired of being on her feet, Kaydie sat down on a bale of hay and continued to watch the festivities. The last time she had danced had been at a ball she'd attended in Boston. Cedric Van Aulst, a long-time friend, had invited her. She'd worn a turquoise gown, and Nellie had woven fresh flowers through her hair. It had been a ball for Kaydie's best friend, Noleen, and Kaydie remembered it as vividly as if it had happened yesterday.

"Kaydie?"

Kaydie looked up to see Jonah, standing with his hands behind him. "I have something for you."

From behind his back, Jonah presented a hat—the peach hat with the large, wispy white ribbon around its brim that Kaydie had admired and tried on at Granger Mercantile several months ago. How had he known? She gasped with fresh admiration for the beautiful hat.

"Jonah, it's lovely," said Kaydie. "How did you know that I fancied this hat?"

Jonah smiled mischievously and sat down beside Kaydie, then gently placed the hat on her head. "You look beautiful, Kaydie," he said.

"You really shouldn't have."

"Oh, just consider it a gift for doing so well today in the three-legged race and the baking contest." Jonah smiled. "I am proud of you, Kaydie. I know it wasn't easy for you to enter those contests."

"I've always been so shy," Kaydie confessed. "However, I'm glad I did enter." She paused and reached up with one hand to touch the brim of the hat. "This hat reminds me so much of the hats we'd wear in Boston. I wasn't sure that once I moved West I'd ever see such lovely hats again."

"Do you miss Boston?" Jonah asked.

"I miss certain things about it. I miss my parents and some of my friends. I miss the gorgeous flower gardens in our yard, and I miss the ease of living in a home with servants." Kaydie thought for a moment. "But there are a lot of things I don't miss, and a lot of things I prefer here in Pine Haven: McKenzie, you, and all the other kind people here; the beauty of the Montana sky when the sun comes up over the mountains...and I enjoy fishing, too—when I'm not tumbling backwards, that is." She laughed softly.

"I'm glad you're here, Kaydie," Jonah said.

"Me, too." Kaydie glanced down at her sleeping baby. "She looks so peaceful, doesn't she?"

"She must be pretty tired to be oblivious to all this noise," said Jonah.

Rosemary joined them then. "I would be happy to hold Bethany Ethel for you if you and Jonah care to dance," she offered, winking at Kaydie.

"Would you care to dance?" Jonah asked her.

"I—I would be delighted," Kaydie said. She handed Bethany Ethel to Rosemary, set her hat on the bale of hay, and followed Jonah to the dance floor.

The fiddler began the song slowly, then the harmonica players joined in to the tune of "Oh! Susanna." Jonah intertwined his strong fingers with hers, and they began to dance. "Fancy meeting you two here!" said McKenzie as she and Zach danced closer to them.

"Brings back memories, doesn't it?" Kaydie asked her sister.

"Yes, but I think we're making even better memories now."

Kaydie nodded in agreement.

Jonah gently squeezed Kaydie's hand and twirled her around. "You're quite a good dancer, Mr. Dickenson," said Kaydie.

"I did attend a dance or two in Mississippi," Jonah said with a twinkle in his eye. "But I never danced with anyone as pretty as you."

Kaydie felt herself blush, and she smiled timidly.

The music sped up a bit, and as Kaydie and Jonah moved to the beat, another couple collided with them. Kaydie lost her balance, and Jonah let go of her hand and reached out to steady her from behind. Instinctively she wrapped her flailing arms around his neck and held on.

"Pardon us!" the other couple yelled in unison above the din of the music.

Jonah nodded. "No harm done!"

His face remained mere inches from Kaydie's, and at the awareness of how close he was, Kaydie felt something stir within her. Immediately she sought to dismiss the feeling, but to no avail. Her legs buckled, though not from the collision with the other couple. Overwhelming emotion made her weak, even as she tried to identify the nature of the emotion. Surely the odd yet pleasant fluttering in her stomach and her weakened legs were a result of her fatigue from the eventful day.

Kaydie and Jonah stood together, face-to-face, as if there was no quickening beat of the music, only the quickening beats of their hearts. As she stared into Jonah's gray eyes and remembered his steady touch and her subsequent emotions, Kaydie felt suddenly frightened. Continually aware of his arm still around her, Kaydie swallowed and directed her eyes else-where—anywhere besides Jonah's handsome face.

As if finally realizing the oddity of their being the only ones standing still, Jonah moved his hand away from Kaydie's back, reached for her free hand, and resumed dancing. They remained on the floor for two more songs before deciding they'd danced enough that night. Kaydie took Bethany Ethel back from Rosemary and wrapped her in the award-win-ning quilt, then climbed into the wagon to wait for Jonah. Minutes later, they were on their way home again, this time following the wagon Zach drove. As the wagon jostled down the dirt road, Kaydie closed her eyes, wishing she were already in bed. It had been a long day—a full, marvelous, long day. Never had Kaydie thought she would enjoy competing in a three-legged race or dancing in a barn. *Pine Haven is changing me yet*, she thought to herself.

Kaydie glanced at Jonah, his profile silhouetted by the occasional lantern inside a home they passed. She was trusting him more and more as the days passed, and she'd grown comfortable enough to share many thoughts and memories with him. At times, it almost seemed that he knew more about her than her own family did, with the exception of McKenzie. Kaydie had never had a friend like Jonah, and she thanked the Lord for placing him in her path. And to think she'd once feared him! She chided herself at the thought. Jonah was the most considerate, mild-mannered man she'd ever met. He'd stayed with her while Asa had fetched the doctor when Bethany Ethel was about to be born. He'd comforted her through many disturbing recollections of Darius. He'd encouraged her to overcome her shyness and join in the fun of the Founder's Day festivities. He'd taken to Bethany Ethel as though she was his own daughter. Most of all, he'd been her friend. Not once had Jonah judged her for the poor decision she'd made in marrying Darius. Not once had he belittled her. No, Jonah brought out the best in her. And something about that fact scared her more than anything else ever had.

Kaydie's thoughts turned to the events at the dance once again, as they had several times since the moment Jonah had steadied her and held her in his arms. She still couldn't identify the unusual emotions that had welled within her, and she willed her mind not to dwell on them. *It must have been fatigue from the eventful day,* she told herself again. *What else could it have been? After all, my feelings for Jonah are those of a friend and nothing more. Not when there is so much at stake.* As if to cement her resolve, Kaydie turned her face heavenward and prayed silently. *Father, thank You for the friend I have found in Jonah. I pray that we will always be friends, and that nothing and no one will ever come between us.*

CHAPTER THIRTEEN

The next day, Jonah walked into the post office just before closing time. "Mr. Victor, could I speak to you for a moment?" he asked.

"Sure," said Mr. Victor as he reached up and turned the sign that hung in the window from "Open" to "Closed."

"Mr. Victor! Oh, Mr. Victor!" Lucille Granger panted as she pushed on the door and rushed inside. She marched up to the counter with an envelope in hand. "I thought I wouldn't make it here before you closed!"

Jonah eyed Lucille with annoyance at the poor timing of her interruption. Had he been the postmaster of Pine Haven, he would have gently reminded Lucille that she had not made it there before closing. But Jonah knew that Mr. Victor would show grace to Lucille and allow her to mail her letter. He was like Zach in the kindness and patience he showed Lucille, and Jonah knew that he should try to do likewise. Still, her exaggerated antics drove him crazy, and it was almost impossible for him to look at them in a positive light.

"What can I do for you, Lucille?" asked Mr. Victor.

"I just have to mail this letter to my son and his wife," Lucille said, handing the envelope to Mr. Victor. "I don't know if either of you have heard the good news yet, but I'm going to be a grandmother once again!"

"Congratulations, Lucille!" Jonah and Mr. Victor chorused.

"Yes, well, as I always say whenever a new bundle of joy is about to arrive, 'Look at what Fred and I started!'"

Jonah chuckled and shook his head. *Leave it to Lucille to take credit for the birth of her grandchildren. Such a silly notion.*

Mr. Victor affixed a stamp to the envelope and placed Lucille's payment in his cash drawer. "Is there anything else I can do for you, Lucille?"

"No," she replied. She paused for a moment, then looked over at Jonah. "I was thinking about you just the other day, Jonah. I said to myself, *Now, when is that Jonah Dickenson going to come back to the mercantile and allow me to finish writing his advertisement for a mail-order bride?*"

"Uh, Lucille...." Jonah began, but he wasn't sure what to say. So far, he had successfully avoided further dealings with Lucille's Love Connections. Now was not the time to revisit Lucille's matchmaking shenanigans.

"But then, I reminded myself," Lucille went on, paying no mind to Jonah's response, "that I thought I noticed the other day an apparent fondness on your part for a certain Kaydie Worthington Kraemer."

Jonah could feel the red flooding his cheeks. He'd never been one to get embarrassed easily, but Lucille's comment, and the fact that her timing couldn't have been worse, caused him to feel incredibly awkward.

Lucille beamed at Jonah, and her smile showed a hint of pride at what she assumed was a correct guess. "So, it is true, then?"

Mr. Victor gently placed a hand on Lucille's arm. "Lucille, I believe that to be Jonah's business."

"Oh, fiddlesticks! You can share this tidbit of important information with me," said Lucille, moving closer to Jonah. "Come along, do tell!"

Jonah pondered his response. If he confirmed her suspicion, then everyone in town would know before Kaydie did, and it would not only thwart his plans but likely drive Kaydie further away from the idea of a second marriage. If he made no response, Lucille would concoct something even more outrageous than the original story. "Lucille," he finally said, his voice low, "if you promise not to tell anyone, I'll let you in on a secret."

Lucille put her hand over her chest as if to quell her racing heartbeat. "I promise, Jonah, I promise!"

"Well, as you know, Kaydie and I are close friends," Jonah began.

"Yes, yes, do go on!"

Jonah cleared his throat. "Since Kaydie and I are such good friends, we've been discussing matters in the town."

"What sort of matters?" asked Lucille.

Jonah tried to think of a way to phrase his next comment with truthfulness. "Lucille, what I am about to tell you has to remain between you, Mr. Victor, and me."

"Oh my, yes!" Lucille agreed.

"All right, then," Jonah whispered. "I'm going to run in the three-legged race on the Fourth of July."

"Really?" Lucille's eyes widened.

"Yes," said Jonah. "You know that I came close to winning the race on Founder's Day, and...well, I have plans to beat out the competition at the next race."

"Do you think you'll win?"

"There's only one way to find out," said Jonah.

"The Fourth of July is just a few weeks away," Lucille observed with excitement in her voice.

"Then, I best be sure I practice," Jonah said with a chuckle. "Now, you promise, Lucille, that you won't tell a soul the private information I just told you."

"Oh, I promise! Your secret is safe with me," Lucille assured him, beaming.

Jonah withheld the sigh of relief that begged to escape from his lungs. He was thankful that Lucille was a bit of a scatterbrain and probably never wondered what the three-legged race had to do with his feelings for Kaydie. He smiled at Lucille. *Somehow, Lucille Granger, I just know that the "secret" I just shared with you won't remain yours alone for long.*

Lucille reached up and patted her hair. "Well, I best be going, then. Jonah, Mr. Victor, it was nice to see you both."

"Always a pleasure," said Mr. Victor. "Tell Fred I said hello."

"Fred? Oh, yes, I'll tell Fred." Lucille practically ran out the door, probably eager to waste no time sharing Jonah's secret with anyone she could find.

"Now, where were we?" Mr. Victor asked. He moved around from behind the counter and locked the door.

"I was wondering if I could speak to you about a particular woman."

"Would her name happen to be Kaydie?" asked Mr. Victor.

"Uh...yes." Jonah took a deep breath and attempted to gather his wits. He needed Mr. Victor's advice, but he didn't know how or where to begin.

"Go on," Mr. Victor prompted him.

"It's just that...well, I need your opinion on something. You see, I've decided—at least, I think I've decided—to ask Kaydie to marry me."

Mr. Victor's eyes grew large. "Well, I never!"

"I know. It's not what I expected, either."

"I knew you cared for her, and we've discussed many times your hesitancy because of the past, but I'm glad that you've reached this decision," Mr. Victor said with a smile.

Jonah nodded. "I love her, Mr. Victor. I don't know when it first happened. It might have been before Bethany Ethel was born, maybe even the first time I saw her. I don't know. All I know is that I want to spend the rest of my life with her." Jonah paused. If Mr. Victor hadn't been such a close friend, he never would have been able to share his heart about something so important. "I see her every day at the ranch, sometimes several times a day. But the strange thing is, I find myself wanting to spend every moment with her."

"I think I know exactly what you mean," said Mr. Victor. "I feel the same way about Geraldine."

"Well, I just bought a plot of land—enough acres for a ranch of my own—next to Zach's. I have these plans of building a home for us, and I'd call the ranch the JDK Ranch."

"You've obviously put a lot of thought into this."

"I have. I've been lying awake at night, making plans and imaging how things will be. But that's not like me, Mr. Victor!"

"What do you mean?"

"I mean, it's not like me to think about taking a wife. It's not like me to think about settling down. I'm happy being a single man, and I'm happy working for Zach on his ranch."

"Sometimes a woman has a way of changing our minds on things," Mr. Victor said, grinning.

"Kaydie has definitely done that to me. I never thought it would be possible to love someone the way I love her." Jonah paused. Was he sharing too much? "I'm sorry, Mr. Victor. Here I am, bumbling on and on like a foolish man."

"There's nothing foolish about love, Jonah," said Mr. Victor. "If there were, I wouldn't be madly in love with a woman named Geraldine."

"But it was all so easy for you and Geraldine."

"It was?" Mr. Victor arched an eyebrow.

"You knew right away that you wanted to marry her. There was nothing bad in your past, no horrible memories, to make you fear that you might not be cut out to be a husband. And Geraldine didn't come from a marriage where she was abused by her husband. You just knew you loved her, and you acted on it."

"Whoa! Hold the team of horses a minute." Mr. Victor chuckled. "I had never imagined I would marry, either. After all, I'm no longer a young man. I'd figured I'd lost my only chance at love and marriage years ago. When Geraldine walked into my life, I was caught by surprise, just as you were."

"But you didn't wait to ask Geraldine. You had no hesitation. Here I am, dragging my feet, unsure of when, if ever, I should propose to Kaydie."

"Well, I'm glad I appear to be so confident and sure of myself!" said Mr. Victor. "I was nervous as all get-out about asking Geraldine to marry me. There I was, about to propose marriage to the most beautiful woman I've ever laid my eyes on. She could have told me no and walked away from me without looking back. I prayed many a prayer that the Lord would lead me and give me the right words to say at just the right time."

"Really? You were nervous about it?"

"More nervous than a rabbit being chased by a coyote."

"And you were hesitant?"

"Very hesitant. No one likes rejection."

"But things seemed so easy, so perfect, between the two of you."

"Far from easy, and even farther from perfect," said Mr. Victor. "As a matter of fact, Geraldine and I had our first argument just yesterday."

Jonah was shocked. From all appearances, it seemed that Mr. Victor and Geraldine got along wonderfully.

"Oh, yes. And let me tell you, I was unprepared for it."

"What did you fight about? If you don't mind my asking, I mean."

"In hindsight, it was such a silly misunderstanding, something we should have worked out long before our disagreement."

And Mr. Victor recounted his tale....

"Do we really need to decorate the church?" Mr. Victor asked.

"Yes. Yes, we do," insisted Geraldine.

"But we'll be in the church a total of ten minutes, fifteen at the most, stating our vows. Most of what happens next, including the potluck, will happen outside. That's why we decided on a nice fall day."

"No, Gerald. You decided on the nice fall day."

"As I recall, it was you who decided," Gerald murmured.

"As I recall, I wanted to get married even earlier," Geraldine insisted.

"When?"

"In September."

"You never told me you wanted to get married in September. Why didn't you mention it?"

"I did mention it, Gerald. Remember how I told you that my parents were married on September fourteenth, and how I thought that a mid-September wedding would be lovely?"

"I'm sorry, Geraldine. I don't recall your saying that, and I didn't realize you wanted to be married around the same time that your parents were."

"I really do wish you had listened, Gerald, as that is something that is—was, rather—important to me." Geraldine sighed. "I suppose it makes no difference now since we've already told everyone the date."

Gerald tried to keep his frustration out of his voice as he said, "We can change the date. It's our wedding."

"It's no matter, Gerald, really."

"Well, it sounded like it mattered to you."

"Most everyone here already knows, and my close friends from Wilmerville have made travel plans to be here on that day, anyway. There's no sense in sending another telegram."

"It's just a handful of folks coming from Wilmerville, right?" Gerald said.

"Yes. However, if we had arranged to be married in Wilmerville...."

"Did you want to get married in Wilmerville?" Gerald had taken it for granted that they would be married in Pine Haven, since that was where they'd met.

"I did."

"Why didn't you say something?" Gerald couldn't believe Geraldine hadn't told him her wishes!

"I figured it would be best to be married here, since this is where we will be living," Geraldine said.

"And I suppose you would rather that we live in Wilmerville."

"No! As I said before, I would live anywhere, Pine Haven included, to be with you," Geraldine insisted.

"You don't sound very convincing."

"Your tone of voice isn't especially gracious, either."

"Maybe we should just postpone the wedding until we have all these details worked out," suggested Gerald, his voice full of tension.

"Maybe we shouldn't get married at all," muttered Geraldine.

"Is that what you want?"

"Well, that's what you want."

"It is?" Gerald said. "Just how do you know what I want?"

"You are against decorating the church."

"Now you're changing the subject on me, Geraldine."

"That's how this whole thing started, isn't it?" Geraldine asked, folding her arms. *"My desire to dec-orate the church, and your opposition to it, since you didn't find this occasion important enough to warrant decorations."*

"Well, I never!"

"You never what?"

"I never heard of anything so ridiculous."

"Are you saying that my feelings on the subject of our wedding plans are ridiculous?" asked Geraldine.

"I never said anything of the sort. You're putting words in my mouth."

Geraldine began to cry then. *"I need to go."*

"Geraldine—"

"Leave me be, please." Geraldine pulled a hand-kerchief out of her purse and dabbed at her eyes as she headed for the door. *"This is supposed to be a happy moment, not a sad one."*

Gerald wanted to retort that it wasn't completely his fault that they were having this argument, but something made him think better of it....

⌘

"Did you and Geraldine make up?" Jonah asked. He hadn't realized they'd had an argument. He'd seen Zach and McKenzie argue a time or two and had witnessed several disagreements between Asa and Rosemary, but never Gerald and Geraldine. Their relationship seemed without fault.

"We did," answered Gerald, and he resumed his story....

Carrying the large bouquet of flowers he had picked, Gerald approached Geraldine, who sat on a large rock overlooking the river with her back to him. A quick glance around the area confirmed to Gerald that they would be alone to discuss their differences. "Geraldine?" he said, not wanting to startle her. "May I speak with you?"

After what seemed like an eternity, Geraldine finally turned around. Her face was red from crying, and her eyes were puffy. Gerald's heart broke.

"Yes?" she asked, clutching her handkerchief.

"Geraldine, we...uh, I need to talk with you." Gerald knew that his discomfort with talking about matters of the heart must be evident.

"I don't really feel like talking right now, if it's all the same to you."

Gerald sat down on the boulder beside Geraldine and handed her the bouquet. "This is for you."

Geraldine reached for the flowers and inhaled their sweet scent. "They're lovely."

"Just like you, Geraldine."

Gerald kicked a small pebble on the ground and gazed at the river. Clear, sparkling water flowed over smooth pebbles. It was a peaceful scene, and he wished that his heart could be at peace, too. "I'm sorry, Geraldine."

Geraldine turned to face him. "I'm sorry, too."

"I love you, and I don't want to upset you. If you want five thousand flowers in the church and dozens of doodly-doos, that's fine with me."

"Doodly-doos?" Geraldine started to giggle.

Gerald reached up and caressed Geraldine's cheek. "I'm not sure what they're called. I'm a humble postman in love with the most beautiful woman I've ever laid eyes on, and I only want for that beautiful woman to be happy."

"I'm sorry I grew angry with you, Gerald. I thought maybe you didn't think our wedding was important enough to have decorations. You see, I plan on this being my only wedding, and I've waited many years for this event."

"As have I," said Gerald. "And if you want to be married in mid-September, that's fine, too. I'm sorry I didn't listen when you told me that your parents were married around then."

"October is fine, Gerald."

"Do you want to be married in Wilmerville?"

"No, I really do want to be married in Pine Haven, as we planned. I've made so many wonderful friends here, besides the fact that this is where we will live."

"And that is all right with you, too? I want you to be honest with me, Geraldine."

"Of course, I want to live here. That is, unless you've changed your mind and would prefer living in London," Geraldine teased.

"I would live in a cave in the desert if I could be with the woman God has blessed me with," Gerald said.

"And I would live on the moon if I could live with the man God has blessed me with."

"The moon would definitely be a challenge...."

"I love you, Gerald."

"And I love you," Gerald said as he leaned over, took Geraldine in his arms, and kissed her passionately, as if to prove how much.

After their kiss, Gerald continued holding Geraldine. "Will you forgive me?" he asked after some time.

"If you'll forgive me."

"It's settled, then," said Gerald.

Geraldine looked up into his eyes. "Just think, Gerald. We've made it through our first fight!"

⤲⤳

"So you see, Jonah?" Mr. Victor said in closing. "Even Geraldine and I have had some challenges. Loving someone is never easy, but it's always worth it."

"You're right, Mr. Victor," said Jonah, his mind still processing all that Mr. Victor had told him.

"It's not every day that a man so opposed to marriage would change his mind. So, if you're asking my advice, I would say, ask Kaydie to marry you. Don't let her slip away."

"I won't, Mr. Victor," Jonah said, preparing to leave. "Thank you."

"You're welcome. Oh, and please don't let on to Geraldine that you know about our disagreement."

"Your secret is safe with me," said Jonah.

That night, in bed, Jonah tossed and turned. Nervousness and apprehension filled his mind as he pondered and prayed about the right time and the right way to propose to the woman he loved.

The next morning, Jonah felt strangely renewed and refreshed, despite the thoughts that had made falling asleep particularly difficult. He finally had a plan for where to propose to Kaydie. Since they had grown closer through their fishing trips, of all things, he thought that their next trip would be the perfect time to ask her to marry him. That afternoon, he would invite her to go on a special fishing trip the following Sunday. And if she agreed, he would have almost one week to practice what he would say. *Please, Lord, give me the courage to ask Kaydie to be my wife,* he prayed, *and help me to know how I should proceed so as not to scare her off.*

CHAPTER FOURTEEN

*K*aydie snuggled a sleeping Bethany Ethel on her lap as the wagon gently jostled them about. For the past week, she had looked forward to this fishing trip with great anticipation. Jonah was taking her to a place she'd never been, a few miles from town. He'd said he had a surprise for her, and she wondered what it could be. She had packed them a picnic lunch, being sure to include extra gingerbread cookies.

She was amazed at how comfortable she'd grown around Jonah. His friendship meant so much to her, and it was hard to believe that she'd ever been afraid of him. In fact, lately, her feelings for him had been more affectionate in nature. While this fondness had disturbed her at first, she now found herself embracing the possibility of their relationship progressing beyond mere friendship. She turned her head and gazed admiringly at Jonah's profile. He was handsome, yes, but, more important, loving, kind, and gentle—a godly man of integrity who kept his word.

He loved Bethany Ethel, and she hoped that, someday, he might love her, too.

"Are we almost there?" Kaydie asked, breaking the silence.

"Not quite," Jonah answered without turning his head.

Kaydie nodded. Perhaps she had heard him incorrectly. Earlier, he'd said that the fishing spot was about three miles away, and yet it felt like they had been riding in the wagon for hours. Kaydie glanced down at Bethany Ethel. Soon, she would wake up and likely be hungry.

"We may have to stop soon when Bethany Ethel wakes up," said Kaydie.

"We'll stop when we stop," muttered Jonah.

Taken aback, Kaydie laughed nervously. "I—I've never heard it put that way."

When Jonah didn't answer, Kaydie looked straight ahead. *Something isn't right*, she thought. They were nowhere near Pine Haven; she could sense it. Fear began to rise within her, and she fought the urge to worry.

Up ahead, she spotted a splintered wooden sign into which the words "Oak Winds" had been carved, along with an arrow pointing straight ahead.

"Oak Winds?" said Kaydie. "Is the fishing spot near Oak Winds?"

"You sure ask a lot of questions," said Jonah.

"I've never been to Oak Winds."

"It's about fifteen miles from Pine Haven."

"So, the fishing spot is near Oak Winds, then?"

Jonah stopped the wagon abruptly, causing Kaydie to lose her balance and nearly fall off her seat.

Something in the back of the wagon thunked, and Kaydie turned around to see what it was. She gasped to see that the wagon was loaded to its capacity with provisions—a kerosene lamp, bags of flour and sugar, and tools. There was also a large stack of linens and several other items that she didn't recognize. What she did recognize, however, was that these supplies were not the type that were useful for fishing. Still, those items weren't what her eyes focused on. No, it was the overturned picnic basket that caught her gaze. The gingerbread cookies had spilled out, and some had broken into bits and crumbs. Their sandwiches were squished under a shovel, and an apple rolled to a stop against a seed bag.

"Now see what you did?" Jonah snarled through gritted teeth.

Kaydie failed to see how she had anything to do with causing the picnic basket to spill over, but she remained silent. Being married to Darius, she'd learned that silence was often the best policy.

"You need to quit with the questions, Kaydie," Jonah growled.

She looked over at him and noticed something for the first time that frightened her beyond words. For as long as she'd known Jonah, his gray eyes had held a special kindness, a certain softness. That was just one of the things she had grown to love about him. But that was no longer the case. The gentleness in Jonah's gray eyes had been replaced with an almost dangerous-looking, cold, angry glare.

"I—I'm sorry, Jonah," Kaydie sputtered, her voice barely above a whisper. "I was just wondering where the fishing spot was."

"We're not going fishing."

"W-what?"

"I said, we're not going fishing."

Kaydie stared at Jonah, dumbfounded. Why was he being so unkind? Trying to stop herself from thinking the worst, she tried to be reasonable. Perhaps Jonah had another "surprise" in mind—a good surprise—and he was acting this way so she would not be able to guess what it was. Perhaps this was just an act, for she'd never known him to be hostile toward her.

"Are we...are we going somewhere else?" Kaydie asked.

"California."

The word caught Kaydie off guard, and it felt as if someone had punched her in the stomach. Air escaped her lungs in a whoosh. Had she heard him correctly? "California?" she asked.

"Yes, we're going to California. I hear there's a lot of good mining there, and I'm gonna be a rich man."

"But what about the ranch? What about McKenzie and Zach? What about Pine Haven?" Kaydie hadn't wanted to ask all of those questions, but she needed to know.

Jonah shrugged. "Who cares about all that?"

"I do," Kaydie whispered. "I just found McKenzie, and I love my life in Pine Haven."

"You're coming with me to California, and that's that," Jonah sneered through gritted teeth. "The way I see it, Kaydie, you can either come with me willingly, or I can force you to come. After all, we're out here in the middle of nowhere, so there's no one to help you. And if you tried to escape, you and Bethany Ethel would never make it back to town on your own—you know that as well as I do."

Kaydie held Bethany Ethel closer and looked around, panicking. Theirs seemed to be the only wagon for miles on the desolate stretch of road. Blue sky and pine trees were all she could see, and the sound of the breeze blowing through the grassy meadows was the only sound that filled the air.

"But Jonah—"

"You just don't get it, do you, Kaydie?"

"I—I beg your pardon?"

"I had you fooled, didn't I? You're a foolish woman, Kaydie."

Kaydie gulped. She'd heard those words before, more than once. Tears slid down her cheeks. Jonah wasn't the man she'd thought he was, and now it was too late.

Bethany Ethel squirmed and opened her eyes.

"I don't understand, Jonah," Kaydie said.

"You're going to be my wife, and you'll be bound to me forever!"

Bethany Ethel began to whimper.

"Be quiet!" Jonah barked at her.

Kaydie protectively wrapped her arms more tightly around her daughter. She had been foolish, so foolish. And now, not only was Kaydie going to suffer, but so was her precious daughter.

Kaydie's breath came in gasps, and her heart raced. Tears now flowed down her cheeks, and sobs filled her throat. Jonah was repeating everything that Darius had said: that she was a fool, that she was bound to him forever, that she would follow him wherever he went.

"Jonah, what happened to you? Why did you change? Please, Jonah, don't do this!" she pleaded.

Jonah shook his head. "What did you expect, Kaydie?" He leaned closer to her, and suddenly, the horror she felt was joined by confusion. Jonah's eyes were his—gray, albeit glinting hatefully—but his mouth was not. It was missing many teeth, and she'd never seen him with anything but a perfect set. Yet the teeth that remained were yellow, and his breath smelled foul.

Then, Jonah reached up with his hand to slick back his hair, only it wasn't his hair. The moment he touched his copper locks, stringy, greasy brown curls bounced back. He no longer had his own eyes and hair; he had Darius's. The realization sent a flash of terror through her veins. History was repeating itself.

With one arm firmly holding Bethany Ethel, Kaydie used her other arm to shield her eyes from the sight of Jonah. "No! Not again!" she screamed into the silence through gritted teeth. "Not again!"

The sound of a soft whimper brought Kaydie back to reality, and she jerked awake. Her eyes fluttered open, and, for a moment, confusion filled her mind. Where was the wagon? Where was Jonah? Where was Bethany Ethel? Kaydie sat up in her bed. Sunshine was beginning to stream through the curtains, and she heard the rooster crow outside. Just to the right of Kaydie's bed, Bethany Ethel was attempting to sit up in her cradle, and she whimpered softly.

Kaydie looked down and saw that her hands were shaking. Her nightgown was damp with sweat, and her pillow was wet from freshly fallen tears. Sudden relief flooded over her. *It was only a dream,* she told herself, but she almost couldn't believe it, so vivid had it been.

She leaned over and scooped Bethany Ethel up in her arms. "It was only a dream, little one," she said, planting kisses on her daughter's soft forehead. "Thank You, Lord, that it was only a dream."

Kaydie sat for a few moments, cuddling Bethany Ethel and praising God that what she'd thought to be real had been nothing more than a nightmare. However, her heart remained unsettled. She closed her eyes and relived parts of the dream—Jonah's hateful words, his deceit, her own foolishness....

Should she take it seriously? Interpret it as a warning? She shuddered to imagine what might happen if she trusted Jonah with her heart, only to have him break it by transforming into a version of Darius after marriage. She could not afford to make the same mistake that she had with her first love. Jonah Dickenson could be her friend, but nothing more. And she would have to be careful around him, just the same.

CHAPTER FIFTEEN

"Jonah, I caught one!" Kaydie exclaimed as she reeled in the fish, this time keeping both feet planted firmly on the ground.

"I knew if you practiced enough, you'd get the hang of it," he told her.

"It took me only five times before I succeeded, so I suppose that's not too bad." Kaydie added her catch to the bucket of fish Jonah had caught earlier.

Jonah peered into the bucket. "We should have enough for dinner now."

"Thank you for bringing me to this special fishing spot, and for teaching me how to fish," Kaydie said. "I had never expected to enjoy it, but it's becoming a favorite pastime."

"It was my pleasure," Jonah replied. "We have at least two good months left before the summer is over. That amounts to about eight more Sunday afternoons we can go fishing."

"At this rate, Bethany Ethel will be ready to begin learning when she's two years old," Kaydie said with a laugh.

"You're right. Before long, I'll be teaching her how to fish." Jonah handed five-month-old Bethany Ethel to her mother and began to pack up the fishing supplies.

Minutes later, they were walking back toward the ranch, the late June sun warming their backs. "This is the most perfect summer day," Kaydie sighed.

"The summers in Montana are something to treasure," Jonah agreed. "I reckon they are far shorter than the summers I was accustomed to in Mississippi, but it makes one appreciate them all the more."

"I love how the Montana sky is so blue, and with not even a cloud in it," Kaydie said. "I just imagine the Lord dipping His brush in the bluest of blue paints and using broad strokes to create the perfect sky."

"It sure is a sight to behold, and I never grow tired of it," Jonah said. "After I'd lived here only a few months, I was already able to call Montana my home." He watched for Kaydie's reaction, hoping that she would say something similar, maybe declare that Montana was her home, too. After all, he was planning to propose shortly, and he could use all the confirmation he could get that she was likely to say yes.

"I do love it here," Kaydie said. "There's more to do than I would have expected in a small Western town. Founder's Day seems like yesterday, yet the Fourth of July celebration is right around the corner."

"Yes," said Jonah. "We sure like to celebrate around here."

"Reverend Eugene's wife has asked me to contribute a basket filled with picnic items for the basket social, and I told her I would think about it. They're trying to raise money for a new school building, and I would certainly like to help with their efforts." Kaydie paused. "If I were to put together a picnic basket, would you bid on it, Jonah?"

"Of course!" Jonah replied. "You do realize that if I'm the highest bidder, you have to join me for a picnic lunch, right?" He winked at her.

"I guess I could handle that," Kaydie teased. "I've grown accustomed to our picnic lunches when we go fishing together on Sundays. Besides, if you promise to bid, I'll bake some of my delicious, award-winning gingerbread cookies for dessert, just in case you should win."

"Well, if that's the case, I promise not only to bid on the basket, but also to be the highest bidder!"

Kaydie's eyes twinkled. "Thank you, Jonah. I can't imagine standing there while Mr. Victor waits for bids on my basket and having nobody bid at all."

"You won't have to worry about that, Kaydie. There'll be plenty of bids. You've built a reputation with your gingerbread cookies. They're the best in Pine Haven and beyond." Jonah waved his hand dramatically.

Kaydie giggled. "I guess I'll tell Mrs. Eugene I'll be contributing, then, based on your promise."

They neared a grove of trees, and Jonah slowed his pace. "There's something I'd like to show you, Kaydie," he said, pointing in the general direction they would walk. He took a deep breath to steady his racing pulse. "Let's leave the picnic basket and fishing gear here. I'll carry Bethany Ethel, if you'd like, since it's a bit of a hike."

A look of curiosity crossed Kaydie's face as she handed him Bethany Ethel, who squealed with her usual delight when Jonah carried her.

"Follow me," he said, and they set off through the pine-edged forest. The beauty of the woods silenced them both, though Bethany Ethel babbled happily.

After a few minutes, Jonah spotted a mother deer and her fawn. He stopped and held out an arm to still Kaydie. "Look there," he whispered.

Kaydie followed his gaze and gasped quietly. "How precious!"

"So peaceful," said Jonah. "Do you see the fawn, Bethany Ethel?"

Bethany Ethel squealed. "Don't you ever wonder what she's saying?" Jonah whispered to Kaydie.

"All the time," she whispered back.

They watched until the deer and her fawn moved into a thicket and out of sight, then they began walking again. "It's not much farther," Jonah told Kaydie.

They hiked around a large rock formation and came alongside a river for a few paces before they reached a clearing. "We're here," Jonah said.

Kaydie gazed about her, an awestruck look on her face. Yellow flowers dotted the meadow, and a wooden fence edged the eastern side. A slight turn to the left offered a breathtaking view of the mountains. "This is lovely, Jonah."

"Do you mind if I set Bethany Ethel down?"

"Not at all. Here's her quilt." Kneeling down, Kaydie spread the quilt on a soft patch of grass.

Carefully, Jonah laid the baby on the blanket, then sat down next to Kaydie. "There's something I... uh, I need to talk to you about, Kaydie."

She glanced at him in alarm. "Is everything all right?"

"Yes, yes, everything's fine. I just...uh, I just...." Jonah paused. *Lord, please give me the courage to tell Kaydie how I feel about her,* he prayed. "This land borders Zach and McKenzie's land," he began. "When it came up for sale, I began to save money to buy it. I've always wanted my own ranch...not that I don't enjoy working for Zach, because I do. He's the best boss a man could have. I've just always wanted my own place."

"This would make a nice ranch, Jonah. You have a grand view of mountains, and the river is so close."

"Yes. This is prime grazing land. And I thought about building the house right about there," he added, pointing a short distance from where they sat. "I can see a barn next to it, and the corral over there."

"It sounds like you've done a lot of planning."

"I have. I plan to have a ranch...and I want it to be our ranch, Kaydie."

Kaydie dropped her jaw and raised her eyebrows. "Our ranch?"

"Yes, our ranch—you, me, and Bethany Ethel. Kaydie...." Jonah leaned closer to her and tenderly stroked her cheek with his thumb. "Kaydie, I love you."

"Jonah—"

"No, please, Kaydie. Let me say my piece." Jonah cleared his throat. He'd rehearsed the words in his mind over and over for the past week—ever since he'd decided to tell her how he felt about her and what he dreamed of a future together. But his practice somehow did little to ease the difficulty of expressing himself in her presence.

Nevertheless, he forged ahead, knowing that he would regret it later if he backed down. "Kaydie, I—I've loved you for a long time, and I want to spend my life with you. I can't remember exactly when it happened, but I just knew that I.... I guess what I'm trying to say is that I never wanted to even think about getting married. I mean, how was I to know what was involved in being a husband or a father? My own parents had a marriage that didn't last, and my pa couldn't stand the sight of me. For the longest time, I just figured I'd be happy being a single man all my life. There was no room in my heart for a woman—a wife—because I knew I'd probably just botch things up, just like my pa did with my ma. But then you came along, and all that changed."

Jonah leaned forward and brushed his lips against Kaydie's. Relieved that she didn't shudder or pull away from him, he put his hand gently on the side of her face and kissed her with all the love and tenderness in his heart.

❦

Kaydie didn't know what to do when Jonah began to kiss her. Part of her wanted to pull away and not let him continue, yet another part—a larger, stronger part—wanted him to continue and never stop. Her legs weakened, and her stomach was filled with an odd, fluttering sensation, as it had been at the dance. She realized that she'd never felt this way when Darius had kissed her. Fear settled in, made stronger by the memory of the nightmare she'd had recently, and she pulled away from Jonah.

"Kaydie," said Jonah, again caressing her cheek with his thumb. "I love you, and I love Bethany Ethel. With your permission, I would like to adopt her and make her my own."

"Jonah—"

"I know it's sudden, and I reckon you'll need time to think about it. But I just needed to tell you what was in my heart. I've felt this way for a long time now."

"Jonah, you are my best friend," said Kaydie. Her heart raced. She had feelings for Jonah, but the thought of acting on them unsettled her mind. Overwhelmed with panic and confusion, she wanted nothing more than to run away to a solitary place where she could sort out her feelings.

"You're my best friend, too, Kaydie. And I would give anything to have you as my wife."

"Jonah, I—I don't think I can—be your wife," Kaydie stuttered.

"Why?"

"Because—because I don't intend to marry ever again. You see, I already made one mistake with Darius. When I first met him, as you know, he was handsome and dashing and daring. He made me feel brave, which was something I hadn't often felt. I had always been the shy and reserved one in my family. It was different with Darius, and it's different with you. You make me feel brave and courageous, and I'm afraid of what will happen next."

"Kaydie...."

Jonah's face bore a pained expression that made Kaydie want to cry, yet she could not relent. She had to stand her ground. "Jonah, I just can't afford to take another chance, only to find out that you aren't who you seem to be. Darius had me fooled. He made me believe that he loved me, and that I loved him. I'll not fall for that trick again. I'm sorry."

Jonah turned away from her and stared at the ground. "Kaydie, I would never do to you what Darius did to you. I think you know that."

"I thought I knew Darius, too," Kaydie insisted. She could feel the tears that threatened to fall.

"Are you really comparing me to Darius? You're saying that I very well might allow you to starve, force you to follow me while I'm on the run from robbing banks? You're saying I would probably become violent with you, as Darius did, and spend all our money in the saloon rather than on necessities? Is that what you're saying?"

"Jonah, you don't understand."

"How well do you know me, Kaydie?" His brow furrowed in a frown that Kaydie had never seen on his face. "How well do you know me, Kaydie?" he repeated, his voice wavering slightly.

"I—I thought I knew Darius, too."

"Darius courted you for a short time before you were married. I would be willing to court you for several years, if that's what it will take to prove my constant love and devotion." Jonah's voice rose in volume. "We have been through a lot together, Kaydie. I think you know me well enough to realize that I would never do to you what Darius did."

"But I was so naïve with Darius. I just can't take that chance again. Especially now, since I have Bethany Ethel to think of, too."

"I love Bethany Ethel, and, as I said, I would like to adopt her and give her my name, if you'd let me."

"I know, Jonah. That's a thoughtful offer. But I'm scared."

"Scared?" said Jonah. "Haven't you known me long enough to know my true character? Do you honestly think Zach and McKenzie would keep me around if I were some bank-robbing brute like Darius? I don't think so."

"Jonah, I'm sorry. I know this is upsetting you." *And me, too!* Kaydie wiped a tear from her eye and looked away.

"It is upsetting me, Kaydie, because you're comparing me to Darius. Please, give me more time to show you I'm nothing like him."

"I can't."

"You can't?"

"No, Jonah, I can't. I'm sorry."

Jonah looked as if he were about to say something else, but instead, he got up from the ground and marched away, leaving Kaydie in the clearing with Bethany Ethel.

"Wait! Jonah, please wait!" She picked up Bethany Ethel and scrambled to pack up the quilt, preparing to go after him.

Jonah stopped and stood still, his back to her. "You've said your piece, Kaydie. I'm sorry I ever said mine." With that, he continued to walk away from her through the woods.

Unable to hold it in any longer, Kaydie let a sob break loose. Bethany Ethel soon joined in, crying frantically to see her mother in such a state.

Through teary eyes, Kaydie saw Jonah pause and look over his shoulder at her. When she began to follow him, he resumed walking, slow enough for her to

keep up, but far ahead enough to preclude any conversation or apologies. Kaydie cried bitterly all the
way back to the ranch.

When they reached the house, Jonah disappeared
into the barn. Kaydie rushed into the house, thankful to find it empty. Still carrying Bethany Ethel,
whose cries had subsided and given way to sleep,
she climbed the stairs as quickly as she could, entered her room, and shut the door behind her. She
set Bethany Ethel in her cradle, then collapsed on
the bed and began to sob again, hiding her face in
her hands.

She cried now with regret for having hurt Jonah so
deeply, and she wished she'd chosen different words
to express her refusal to marry him. She hadn't
meant to compare him to Darius, but the truth was,
she did fear he would become just like her former
husband. True, she had no real evidence to suggest
that he would, and from what she knew, Jonah was a
man of integrity. But his proposal had caught her by
surprise, and she had felt so frightened. He wanted
to share his life with her, adopt Bethany Ethel, and
build them a house on a neighboring ranch. Kaydie
continued to sob, her choked cries filling the room.
The things he had told her seemed too good to be
true, just like the promises Darius had made and
then broken. Yet, she had hurt Jonah in a way that
had shown all over his face and had probably pene-
trated his heart. It was for that reason that she cried
tears of shame, regret, and self-castigation.

A sob erupted from the cradle, and Kaydie realized she had awakened Bethany Ethel. "Oh, sweetie,
I am so sorry!" Kaydie wiped her eyes and rushed to

the cradle, scooping up her daughter and snuggling her close. Oh, to protect Bethany Ethel from making the same mistakes in her life! Kaydie reminded herself that her daughter was in God's hands, and that He would bring something good out of every mistake, just as He had brought Bethany Ethel—her greatest joy—out of her mistake of marrying Darius.

Kaydie glanced up and spied an envelope on her desk. She walked over to the desk, shifted Bethany Ethel to her hip, and picked up the envelope with her free hand. Reading the return address was unnecessary, for the penmanship alone told her that the letter was from her mother.

Kaydie sat down on the bed with Bethany Ethel on her lap, then opened the letter and began to read.

My dearest Kaydence,

I hope this letter arrives before your surprise on the first of July.

As you will see when you receive your surprise, your father and I have worked very hard to arrange for it to be delivered in an appropriate manner. Because we have dedicated such hard work and so great an expense to plan this surprise, we fully expect you to cooperate to your utmost ability. What I mean to say, Kaydence, is that your father and I ask that you not ruin the plans that have been put in place—plans that you will understand once you receive the surprise.

It is necessary that you look your best in the weeks ahead, and from how McKenzie appeared when I visited her, clothing in the

Montana Territory leaves much to be desired, especially compared to the finery of Boston. Therefore, I have enclosed some money for you to use toward the purchase of some new dresses. Please have them tailor-made by only the finest of seamstresses in Pine Haven; surely there is at least one such seamstress in that settlement, remote and unrefined though it be.

You must spare no expense in purchasing these dresses, and I trust that the enclosed funds will be more than sufficient to cover the cost.

Yours truly,
Mother

If her argument with Jonah hadn't been enough to ruin the day, her mother's letter certainly was. Never an "I love you" or a "How are you?" No, her mother wrote only in orders that put forth her manipulative wishes. And how was Kaydie to interpret her mother's fixation with the imminent surprise? Kaydie tossed the letter back onto the top of the desk. It was June 28. In three days, her surprise was due to arrive. Kaydie only hoped she found it to be as wonderful as her mother did.

CHAPTER SIXTEEN

Cedric Van Aulst glanced out the window at the passing scenery. He had known that the train trip from Boston to Pine Haven would be long and tiresome, but no amount of foreknowledge could have prepared him for this tedious eternity. At least Florence Worthington had been honest when she'd warned him that it would feel as if he'd been riding forever. And to discover that his trip would not be complete when the train reached its destination—for a journey by stagecoach would take him the rest of the way to Pine Haven—only added to his impatience. He sighed. Had it not been for the urgency of his situation, he would be back in Boston, working on a case and preparing for trial.

Closing his eyes, Cedric thought about the conversation he'd had with Arthur Worthington in his office before he'd left Boston....

"*Thank you for meeting with me, Cedric,*" said Arthur Worthington, seated across the desk from him. "*It is my understanding that you have hopes of becoming a partner in this firm.*"

"*Yes, sir. That's correct.*" Cedric had been in Arthur Worthington's employ for the past three years—hardly long enough to receive a promotion to partner, yet that was his dream. Actually, it had been his ambition not only to become a partner but also a part of the Worthington family. For as long as he could remember, he had fancied the youngest Worthington daughter, Kaydence. He'd often thought that she might marry him someday and thereby make him a part of the family he so longed to join.

"*You've done quite well for yourself on the past several cases,*" said Arthur, twirling the ends of his reddish mustache, as he often did while assessing something. "*As a matter of fact, it's been noted that you're building quite a reputation for yourself.*"

"*Thank you, sir.*"

"*Tell me, Cedric, have you heard the recent news about Kaydence?*" Arthur asked.

"*I believe so, sir—something about her husband passing away unexpectedly and leaving her a widow?*" Cedric's heart broke at the thought of Kaydence suffering any discomfort.

"*Yes. Darius, her late husband, had such ambition. As you may be aware, he was a young doctor from New York. His heart was heavy with the thought that so many in the uncivilized West go without quality medical care. And so, after he and Kaydence were married, they traveled to the Montana Territory, where he planned to open a practice. Sadly, he was* struck with a fatal intestinal illness. He left behind Kaydence and their young child."

"I'm sorry to hear that, sir," said Cedric. "You know how I've always fancied your daughter."

"Yes, and I know how close you were while the two of you were growing up. It saddens me that it never amounted to anything more than friendship; however, perhaps the timing merely was not right."

Cedric recalled accompanying Kaydence to many balls and other social activities. He, Kaydence, and McKenzie had shared many fun times together. Cedric, too, had often wondered why he had never courted Kaydence. He attempted to push aside the notion that it was because Kaydence thought of him only as a friend. "How is she now, sir?" he asked.

"Doing better, I believe. As you are aware, McKenzie married a poor rancher in the Montana Territory. She and her husband are allowing Kaydence and her child to stay with them temporarily, until she returns to Boston, and I was hoping to enlist your help in accompanying Kaydence back home."

Had he heard correctly? "I would be honored to accompany Kaydence to Boston," said Cedric. "However, I've never traveled farther west than Chicago."

"Florence has traveled to the Montana Territory, and she'll tell you that the journey is long and tedious. However, I hope to make it worth your while."

"How do you mean, sir?"

"Well, first off, we will cover all of your travel expenses. If you agree to go, you will arrive in Pine Haven, where Kaydence is staying, on July first. Florence and I miss our daughter terribly, and we desire that she come back to Boston to live the kind of life she had before, with the social standing she deserves." Arthur paused and lowered his voice. "It will be worth your while in that you will have another chance to woo my daughter. You have my blessing should she decide to marry you, and I have every confidence that she will. In addition, if you do marry Kaydence, you will become the newest partner of my law firm, a place I reserve only for my sons-in-law."

"Thank you, sir," said Cedric. What else could he say? Arthur Worthington was offering him the chance of a lifetime—the chance to be a partner in the largest, most reputable law firm in Boston. While Cedric's family was upstanding and wealthy in its own right, its prestige could not compare to that of the Worthington family. Not only that, but Cedric had always loved Kaydence, and this was his chance to make that known to her, once and for all.

"I'll order your tickets for the train and stagecoach and provide you with all the funds you will need," Arthur told him.

"Thank you, sir. I look forward to fulfilling my end of the bargain."

"I trust you won't let me down."

Cedric rose to his feet and shook Arthur's hand....

∽∾

The train whistle brought Cedric back to the present. Yes, he had promised Arthur Worthington to bring Kaydence back to Boston. Now, if he could only bring Kaydence to love *him* back.

∽∾

On Sunday evening, Kaydie helped McKenzie and Rosemary to clear the table after supper. Jonah had not joined them for the meal, which only made Kaydie's heart heavier than it already was because of their disagreement.

After the dishes were cleared, Kaydie took Bethany Ethel upstairs to prepare her for bed.

"Kaydie?" She looked up and saw McKenzie standing in her bedroom doorway. "May I come in?" she asked.

"Of course."

McKenzie entered the room and sat on the edge of the bed next to her. "Are you all right? You were so quiet at supper."

Kaydie gave Bethany Ethel a kiss and then turned to face McKenzie. One look at her sister's concerned expression was enough to unleash fresh tears, and she buried her face in McKenzie's shoulder. "I've ruined everything," she moaned, her voice muffled by her sister's sleeve.

"What do you mean?" McKenzie asked, wrapping her arms protectively around Kaydie.

Kaydie sat up and sniffed. "Jonah and I had a fight this afternoon."

"I wondered why he wasn't at supper," said McKenzie. "Do you mind if I ask what the fight was about?"

"He—he proposed to me," said Kaydie, stifling another sob.

"Jonah proposed to you? What did you say?"

"I couldn't say yes, McKenzie. I just couldn't. I said yes once before and barely lived to regret it."

McKenzie hugged her tighter. "I must admit, I had no idea that Jonah had marriage in mind. I could tell that he cared for you, and both of you seemed inseparable at times, but...." McKenzie shook her head.

"I do consider him my best friend—after you, of course," said Kaydie, dabbing her eyes with her sleeve. "But I don't think of him as anything more than a friend. Apparently, though, he has feelings for me. He talked of adopting Bethany Ethel and of building us a home on the piece of property he purchased."

"Did you explain why you refused him?" McKenzie asked.

"I told him that I couldn't marry him because I was scared."

"Scared?"

"Scared that he would turn out just like Darius."

McKenzie was silent for a moment. "I assume Jonah didn't take kindly to your answer...?"

"No, he didn't. McKenzie, I am overwhelmed with guilt because I hurt him so deeply. He didn't deserve to be compared to Darius, yet I compared him in every way possible, both in my mind and in my words to him."

"From what I know of Jonah, he isn't anything like Darius," McKenzie said gently.

"You remember Darius when he first began courting me?" Kaydie asked her.

"Yes, I do. I have to admit, however, that I never cared for him much, even when he was clever and charming."

"I know you didn't, McKenzie, and that was the first time I ever went against your advice. I know

Mother, Father, and Peyton all disapproved of my choice, as well. But Darius had me fooled. He was so handsome when I first met him, so dashing, daring, and brave. He seemed to know what he wanted out of life, and, for once, I was going to do something brave by following him to an unknown world. I was scared, but he assured me that he loved me, and that it would be an adventure of a lifetime. Oh, I was so foolish."

"You were foolish, Kaydie, but we're all entitled to make a mistake every now and then. You wouldn't believe the mistake I made with Zach when I first met him." McKenzie shook her head. "I was so unkind to him at first, but Zach always exhibited such patience and grace toward me. I hurt him deeply, yet he forgave me." McKenzie paused. "Kaydie, no one holds it against you that you married Darius."

"Mother and Father do."

"I take that back. Yes, Mother and Father may hold it against you, but no one here does. We've all made so many mistakes in our lives, whether big or small. Every day I strive to learn more about our heavenly Father—and still I know so little—but one thing I do know is that His mercy is limitless. He loves you, Kaydie, and He'll help you overcome the guilt you have over marrying Darius. That's in the past. Let it stay there."

Kaydie nodded. "It still doesn't change the fact that I hurt Jonah."

"Perhaps in a few days, when the pain has worn off a little, you can talk to him and tell him that while you aren't ready to get married again, you value his friendship and are sorry for hurting him."

"I don't think I'll ever be able to get married again," Kaydie said. "Not unless it's to someone I've known for years."

"You've been hurt by Darius in ways that no one should ever have to be hurt," said McKenzie. "Such wounds take time to heal."

"Thank you, McKenzie. You've always been there for me. In the years I spent trapped with Darius, I just knew that you would rescue me. And you did."

"That's what sisters are for, Kaydie. Besides, you would have done the same for me."

Kaydie chuckled. "It might have taken me a lot longer to work up the courage, but, yes, I would have done the same for you."

"You may not be entirely brave and daring, Kaydence Worthington Kraemer, but you are the best sister a girl could ask for!" McKenzie squeezed Kaydie's shoulder.

"I sometimes pity Peyton that she never experienced the closeness you and I share," said Kaydie.

"Perhaps it's because she's so much like Mother," McKenzie mused. "But, yes, I pity her, as well. Although...." McKenzie giggled. "Can you imagine for a minute...?"

"Oh, no," Kaydie moaned, feigning dread. "You aren't about to tell one of your far-fetched, made-up stories, are you?"

When they were younger, if Kaydie was feeling sad or scared, McKenzie would often make up stories to cheer her up—wild, unbelievable stories that could come only from McKenzie's imagination. They never failed to put Kaydie in a better mood. And McKenzie had always begun her stories by saying, "Can you imagine for a minute...?"

"I feel it's only appropriate to tell a story, given the circumstances," said McKenzie. "Besides, I think you need a laugh or two."

"Oh, all right." Kaydie giggled. "Go ahead."

"Can you imagine for a minute that once upon a time, there lived a young woman named Peyton Worthington Adams? Peyton was no ordinary woman. No, she was a gunfighter."

"A gunfighter?" Kaydie raised her eyebrows. "McKenzie, this really is too much—"

McKenzie held her finger to her lips to hush her sister before continuing. "After that brief interruption, we return to the story. You see, Peyton was a gunfighter and had ridden with the likes of Wild Bill Hickok—"

"Wild Bill Hickok? Oh, dear. This really is unbelievable." Kaydie forgot about her fight with Jonah for a moment and laughed at the image of Peyton handling a firearm.

"Anyway, one day, she heard that her dear sister, Kaydence, had gone missing while on the run with her scoundrel of a husband, Darius Kraemer. Peyton, Kaydence, and their lovely sister, McKenzie, had all been very close as children, and the thought of Kaydence suffering in the primitive West brought a tear to Peyton's eye. Determined to rescue the sister she loved, Peyton embarked on a journey that she would later write about in her journals."

McKenzie deepened her voice dramatically and gestured with her hands as she continued to tell the story. "With her long blonde hair flowing behind her and her overly large green eyes on the alert for any suspicious happenings, Peyton rode her horse all the way from her wealthy Boston neighborhood to the wilds of the Montana Territory. Stopping only to retrieve helpful information from her friends, the Indian scouts, Peyton pushed ahead with the goal of rescuing her sister. Finally, she came to a small town in the Montana Territory where Kaydence was being held hostage in a less-than-charming dugout."

"I really did have to live in a dugout once," said Kaydie. "And it was awful. Darius paid his friend Bulldog to keep watch over me while he took care of business in town, and Bulldog was always stalking about outside, watching my every move. I couldn't even carry a pail of water from the river without his frightening face looming over me." Kaydie shivered.

"Yes, well, Bulldog was no match for Peyton Worthington Adams," McKenzie continued. "She'd run into characters like him during her stint in the Civil War—"

"The Civil War?" Kaydie giggled. "Peyton was but a little child during the Civil War, and the soldiers weren't women."

McKenzie raised her eyebrows at her sister. "Who's telling this story? Anyway, Peyton did a stint in the Civil War, much to the chagrin of her mother, as well as Boston's upper-crust society. However, she was hailed as a hero, and her name is now in the history books. After the war, still determined to save her sister, Peyton managed to outwit Bulldog and cause his demise. Then, quicker than lightning, she dashed into the dugout to rescue Kaydence. 'Come with me, Kaydence—quickly, before Darius returns!' Peyton shouted.

"Shocked at the sight of her sister, Kaydence merely stared at her. Peyton didn't look the same as she had while they were growing up in Boston. No, the fancy satin dresses had been traded in for an ensemble of trousers, a long coat, and a black, wide-brimmed hat."

"And her mother cried herself to sleep at night knowing her eldest daughter had become a vigilante," Kaydie chimed in with a chuckle.

"Yes—that, too," McKenzie agreed. "Finally, Kaydence awakened from her state of shock and realized the necessity of escaping with her sister while she had the chance. Peyton reached for Kaydence's hand, and they ran toward the waiting horse. 'Look! There's Darius!' shouted Kaydence as she mounted the horse behind her sister.

"'No need to worry, my dear,' said Peyton, urging the horse to begin running.

"'What if he catches us?' squealed Kaydence."

"'Squealed Kaydence'? Do I squeal?" asked Kaydie, wiping tears of laughter from the corners of her eyes.

"Yes—I mean, no—I mean, in this story, you do. Now, please. You're breaking my creative flow of words here." McKenzie cleared her throat. "Kaydence and Peyton rode on the horse, which, by the way, was the fastest horse in all the United States of America, and all the territories, too. Peyton had won him in a horse race in Cincinnati."

"Cincinnati?" said Kaydie. "Really, McKenzie, has Peyton ever been to Cincinnati?"

McKenzie ignored her interruption. "They rode toward town, with Darius close behind. Unbeknownst to Darius, however, Kaydence and Peyton's marvelous sister, McKenzie, had enlisted the help of the

United States Cavalry, and they were waiting just outside of town. When Darius came over the hill, the Cavalry apprehended him. Darius was sent to a small island in the Atlantic Ocean and has never been heard from since. Kaydence was free, thanks to her sisters, Peyton and McKenzie. The end."

Kaydie was laughing so hard her sides hurt. "Do you tell these stories to Davey?" she asked.

"Sometimes," admitted McKenzie, "although they're not scary stories about daring women rescuing their sister."

"Thank you, McKenzie, for cheering me up," said Kaydie. "I am blessed beyond measure to have you as my sister."

"May I pray with you, Kaydie?" McKenzie asked.

Kaydie nodded and held hands with McKenzie. "Dear heavenly Father, please help Kaydie to mend her friendship with Jonah. I pray for Your intervention and Your peace. I also pray that You would help Kaydie to heal from the past hurts from her marriage to Darius so that she can be free from the pain and turmoil it caused. Please give Jonah a forgiving heart and allow them to be best friends again. Thank You, Father, for giving me the gift of a sister as dear as Kaydie. In Jesus' name, amen."

CHAPTER SEVENTEEN

$\mathscr{T}$he afternoon of July 1, Kaydie set a plate at each place around the table in preparation for lunch while McKenzie finished cooking the meal. She glanced down at Bethany Ethel and smiled. Time and time again, with one chubby hand behind her and a little foot in front of her, the almost six-month-old attempted to scoot on her backside across the floor. Whenever she made progress, no matter how short the distance, she would stop, giggle, and then try her unique way of crawling all over again.

Kaydie heard the front door open and glanced up to see Jonah walk in. She hadn't seen him for two days, since Sunday afternoon, and realized how much she'd missed him. Their gazes connected briefly, and Kaydie noticed that Jonah was growing the beginnings of a beard. "Hello, Jonah," she said, longing for things to be the way they once were between them.

"Kaydie," Jonah said with a brisk nod.

At that moment, Bethany Ethel squealed with excitement. Kaydie looked down and saw her raise her arms toward Jonah as she babbled happily.

Jonah walked over and knelt down beside her. "How's Bethany Ethel today?" he asked, scooping her up into his arms.

With her tiny brow furrowed, Bethany Ethel reached out and touched Jonah's unshaven cheek, then quickly pulled her hand away. Jonah chuckled, then gently rubbed his chin against her cheek. Kaydie could hear the scrape of his whiskers.

Bethany Ethel began to giggle, prompting Jonah to continue. "Does that tickle?" he asked. Bethany Ethel reached her arms around his neck and giggled even more enthusiastically as he continued.

McKenzie came to stand beside Kaydie and watched, and they both joined in laughter. "I don't think she knows what to think of your rough face, Jonah," McKenzie said with a smile.

Even as she laughed, Kaydie's heart was heavy to realize how much Jonah adored Bethany Ethel if he was willing to adopt her as his own. And she had deprived him of that wish. How disappointed he must be!

Moments later, McKenzie announced that lunch was ready. Zach and Davey joined them, and they all sat down at the table. Kaydie was grateful for the lively conversation they provided, as it covered over some of the awkwardness between her and Jonah.

After several minutes, Davey's dog, Waddles, began to bark at something outside. Davey jumped up from the table and rushed to the window to see what had Waddles so riled up. "Someone's comin'!" he exclaimed. "Someone's comin' down the road in a buggy."

Zach excused himself and walked to the window to look out. "I'm not sure who it is," he said. "I recognize the buggy—I believe it belongs to Harlan, the banker, but he's not driving it. And whoever it is apparently plans to visit us."

McKenzie cast Kaydie a curious glance, which she matched.

A knock sounded at the door, and Zach opened it. "Can I help you?" he asked.

"Yes, I'm looking for the Sawyer Ranch."

"This is the Sawyer Ranch," said Zach.

"Thank goodness. I was afraid I had gotten lost."

Kaydie knew that voice. "Cedric?"

"Kaydence?" Cedric Van Aulst peeked inside the door at her.

"Please, come in," said Zach.

Cedric entered the house, and Kaydie excused herself from the table to greet him. "Cedric, whatever are you doing here?"

Cedric tipped his hat. "Kaydence, McKenzie, it's a pleasure to see you both again."

"Did you come all the way from Boston?" asked McKenzie as she stood up.

"I did. Let me tell you, that's a lengthy journey."

"Please, come and sit down," McKenzie said, pulling an extra chair up to the table. "We were just having lunch, and there's plenty to share."

Cedric followed Kaydie to the table and sat down. "Thank goodness I was able to borrow a buggy from your banker. I understand he has two. Otherwise, I'm not sure how I would have made it from town all the way out here."

McKenzie handed Cedric a plate of food. "It seems like forever since we've seen you."

"It has been a while," Cedric acknowledged. "I've been busy working at your father's law firm for the past three years."

"How are Mother and Father?" Kaydie asked.

"They're doing well. Maxwell and Peyton are also fine," Cedric answered.

"Let me introduce you to everyone," Kaydie said. "This is Zach Sawyer, McKenzie's husband, and their son, Davey. This is Cedric Van Aulst, a longtime friend of ours."

"Pleasure to meet you," said Cedric, shaking Zach's hand.

"And this is Jonah," said Kaydie, not sure now how to introduce him. "He's...one of the ranch hands."

"Jonah," said Cedric, shaking his hand.

"And this is Bethany Ethel, my daughter," Kaydie said, gesturing to the high chair beside her.

"Well, time certainly passes fast," noted Cedric. "Seems like yesterday that we were young children, ourselves."

"No, that seems like forever ago, Cedric," McKenzie countered with a laugh. "Do you remember the time we played that trick on Peyton?"

"Of course, I remember, and I assure you that Peyton has not forgotten it, either," Cedric chuckled.

"Peyton was always so 'perfect' and proper and always managed to get Kaydie and me in trouble," McKenzie explained to Zach, Jonah, and Davey, "so it was only fitting that we play a tiny trick on her."

"I think I'm afraid to hear this," Zach said, laughing.

"Oh, it wasn't so bad," Kaydie giggled.

"Maybe not to us," Cedric said, "but for Peyton, it was...well, bad."

"Cedric found a skunk near his home and trapped it in a cage," Kaydie explained. "And then he put it in her bedroom! We climbed the trellis outside and watched through the window, waiting for her to enter her room. You should have seen the look on her face when she walked in and saw that caged skunk just lounging on her bed! It got even better when the skunk got startled and sprayed her."

"No wonder things have never been right between you two and your older sister," Zach said, shaking his head. "I'm not so sure I'd get along with sisters who put a skunk in my bedroom!"

"Peyton wasn't the only one who suffered," Cedric noted, "for I, too, was sprayed probably four times in the process of taking that skunk to the Worthingtons' house. The sacrifice was well worth it, though!"

"Good old Cedric," said Kaydie.

"Those were fine days," McKenzie recalled. "We relied on pranks like that to break the monotony of the proper, ladylike behavior that was always expected of us."

Kaydie, McKenzie, and Cedric continued to recount memories of their childhood days, and many stories made Kaydie laugh to the point of tears. Her jollity was tempered, though, by the realization that while Zach and Davey were laughing along with them, Jonah sat in silence, a sullen look on his face.

"So, Cedric, what brings you to Pine Haven?" Zach asked when their storytelling had slowed.

Without hesitation, Cedric announced, "I've come to court Kaydence."

CHAPTER EIGHTEEN

Jonah nearly choked on his bite of food. Cedric Van Aulst had come two thousand miles to court Kaydie? He glared down at his plate. Until this moment, he'd considered last Sunday the worst day of his life. He'd finally mustered the courage to propose to Kaydie, and she'd turned him down. The sting of rejection was worsened by the fact that she'd compared him to her former husband, an abusive drunk.

Now, however, he was convinced that today was even worse than Sunday. Three days after his proposal, Kaydie was about to be courted by a man with whom Jonah could never hope to compete. For why wouldn't she leap at the chance to be courted by Cedric Van Aulst? He was everything that Jonah was not—well-educated, with a successful career and great wealth; well-dressed in an expensive-looking suit with polished shoes; well-groomed with short, cropped brown hair and a clean-shaven face.... Yes, everything about him indicated a fine upbringing and a life free of manual labor or financial hardship. Any hopes Jonah might have had to yet convince Kaydie to marry him were crushed by the arrival of this dapper Bostonian.

The next day, Jonah was working in the yard when he looked up to see Cedric Van Aulst coming up the road toward the ranch in the borrowed buggy. Yesterday, Cedric had spent all day with Kaydie, and it appeared that he planned to do the same today.

"Good morning," Cedric greeted him when he'd stopped the buggy. "Would you mind watering the horses? It's so hot today, and the ride from town was hard on them." He paused. "You are one of the servants, aren't you?"

"I'm one of the ranch hands, yes," Jonah muttered. "Unless you're talking about being a servant of the Lord."

"I beg your pardon?"

"Never mind," said Jonah. "Yes, I'll water the horses for you."

"Good morning, Cedric." Kaydie emerged from the house, carrying Bethany Ethel.

"Kaydence! Aren't you a sight to behold?" Cedric exclaimed as he approached Kaydie.

Jonah glanced up from the water bucket to see Kaydie dressed in a fancy peach satin frock that he'd never seen before. It was difficult to take his eyes off of her. While he had always found her quite beautiful, today she looked radiant. Her long hair flowed down her back, and she wore the hat he had given her at the dance.

"Hello, Jonah," said Kaydie, her voice guarded.

"Kaydie," Jonah said with a nod.

"The serv—I mean, the ranch hand here was just watering the horses," Cedric said. "When he's done, we can be on our way. I thought we might go for a drive. I picked up some lunch at the café in town."

"That sounds grand," Kaydie said.

"Would you like to see if McKenzie would mind watching the child while we're gone?" Cedric asked her.

"Pardon?" asked Kaydie.

"The child," Cedric repeated. "Surely, you didn't think she would be coming with us!"

Jonah was amused by the exchange. Kaydie thought highly of Cedric, that much was clear, but how would she react to his apparent discomfort with children?

"I asked McKenzie to watch Bethany Ethel yesterday," Kaydie replied in a timid voice. "I—I would rather not impose on her again today."

"Well, what about that servant lady—Rosemary, you said her name was?" Cedric suggested.

"I would like to take Bethany Ethel along, Cedric," said Kaydie with more resolve.

"I just don't know what a child would find to enjoy about a drive through the country," said Cedric. "What if she begins to cry?"

"I think she would enjoy going for a drive," countered Kaydie, her voice still quiet.

Cedric sighed. "Fine, then. I'll compromise for you, Kaydence."

"Thank you," she said as Cedric assisted her and Bethany Ethel into the buggy.

Jonah stepped away from the horses, and Cedric climbed up into the buggy and took the reins. "So long!" he called to Jonah as they pulled away.

Kaydie turned around and met his eyes for a moment, but Jonah pretended not to have noticed and quickly looked down at the bucket he held. Time for a day of work while Cedric whisked Kaydie away for a day of pleasure.

⤳

Lost in thought, Kaydie watched Cedric's long, slender fingers as he handled the reins of the buggy. Had he honestly expected her to leave Bethany Ethel behind? She remembered that he was accustomed to the child-rearing practices of prominent families in Boston, where parents went on excursions and outings without their children, who were left in the care of their nannies. Still, something about the way he'd made the suggestion didn't sit well with her.

"I wanted to tell you, Kaydence, how sorry I am about your husband's passing," said Cedric, interrupting her thoughts. "When I heard the news, my heart broke in sympathy for you."

"Thank you," said Kaydie. She adjusted her hold on Bethany Ethel.

"I've heard that Dr. Kraemer was quite the man, and I admire his noble ambition to provide medical care to the people of the Montana Territory."

Kaydie sucked in her breath. It was finally coming together. Cedric was the surprise Mother had "sent." That was why she'd instructed Kaydie to rehearse the lie she and Kaydie's father had concocted about Darius. That was why she had told her to purchase new gowns.

"I know you must miss him," Cedric went on. "After all, relatively little time has passed since the intestinal illness claimed his life. I hope he did not suffer long." Cedric turned to look at her.

"He didn't suffer," Kaydie said truthfully.

"That's a relief. I would be loath to think that he should suffer after the bravery he demonstrated in coming to such a primitive place." Cedric cleared his throat before continuing. "I know that you have suffered, Kaydence, and I wish that had not been the case. To watch your husband die must have been dreadful. Please accept my condolences."

"Thank you, Cedric." She pushed from her mind the disturbing realization that Cedric knew a lie, while Jonah knew the truth.

"I know this is sudden, Kaydence, but there is something I need to discuss with you." Cedric pulled the buggy to a clearing and stopped. He turned toward Kaydie and reached into his pocket. "You know that I have loved you since we were young," said Cedric. "We spent many a delightful time together throughout our childhood. When we grew older, I accompanied you to balls and charity events." Cedric paused. "When I attended law school, I missed you more than you can imagine, and I never courted anyone else during our time apart. However, when I returned, you were married." He cleared his throat. "I will be honest: I am staying in Pine Haven for two weeks, and then I must return to Boston. I have a case the size of Massachusetts that requires my attention."

Bethany Ethel began to squirm, and Kaydie handed her the rattle Jonah had given her. "It's all right, sweetie," she whispered.

"Anyway, Kaydence, when I returned from law school and found that you were married to another,

I couldn't forgive myself for not making my feelings known to you when I had the chance. I suppose I figured you'd always be there, waiting until I worked up the courage to ask you to be my wife."

Kaydie swallowed hard and stared at Cedric. She could sense where he was leading with his words, and her heart beat faster.

"I'm not going to allow the opportunity to pass again, Kaydence. I love you, and I have for a good many years. Even though we have not seen each other for some time, I know you well, and you know me. You know that I am a reputable man of integrity. I have worked long and hard at your father's law firm and have secured my position as one of the most promising lawyers in the Boston area. I recently purchased a house on Lewiston Street, which, you may recall, is among the classiest areas of Boston. Anyway, I met with your father, and he has assured me of his blessing to ask for your hand in marriage."

"Cedric...." Kaydie paused, unsure of how she should feel, let alone respond.

"Please, Kaydence, let me finish before I lose my nerve." Cedric took a deep breath and continued. "With my social standing and employment status, I can give you anything you wish. I have servants, but I can hire more, if need be. I can hire a nanny for the child and, when she is older, send her to the finest boarding school for the best education money can buy."

"A nanny for Bethany Ethel isn't necessary," Kaydie insisted. She was surprised by her own firmness, yet she could not imagine leaving her daughter in someone else's care or sending her daughter away instead of raising her herself, and she needed to make that clear.

"I think you'll change your mind when you remember how busy you'll be with charity functions and teas. You've been away from Boston for several years and may not remember how different it is from where and how you live now. Not only will our life together be grand, but you'll also be reunited with your parents and with Peyton." Cedric reached forward and gently touched Kaydie's cheek. "I love you, Kaydence," he said. "I know it hasn't been long since your beloved husband died, but I am hoping that time will heal your broken heart, and that you will love me as you loved him."

Cedric leaned forward then with puckered lips, ignoring Bethany Ethel squirming between them. Kaydie thought about turning her head but decided to yield to his kiss. After what felt like a very long time, he pulled away. "I have wanted to do that for ten years," he said.

Kaydie's mind carried her back to when Jonah had kissed her, and she found herself comparing him to Cedric. While Jonah had also taken her by surprise, his kiss had stirred within her an entire spectrum of emotions she had never experienced before. Her stomach had felt strange and excited, and her legs had gone weak, as if unable to bear her weight. After Cedric's kiss, she waited for those feelings to surface, but they never did.

"As I said before, Kaydence, I know it's sudden. I know that we haven't seen each other in several years, and that you are still mourning your husband's death. However, as I also said before, I don't want to lose you again. I've already lost you once."

"Would you adopt Bethany Ethel?" Kaydie asked, shocked when the question crossed her lips. She was feeling bolder by the day.

"Adopt Bethany Ethel?" Cedric made an unpleasant face, then shrugged. "Of course, I would do whatever you asked, Kaydence—you know that. I want only to please you. However, that being said...." Cedric glanced down at Bethany Ethel. "I don't know that I could adopt the child. You see, I'm not sure if I could love another man's child."

Kaydie was speechless. While she could see herself marrying Cedric, if only because she felt safe with him and had known him for so many years, she would not marry a man who could not love her daughter as his own.

"Kaydence, will you do me the honor of being my wife?" Cedric asked. He opened the box he had pulled from his pocket and took out a diamond ring, which he held out to her.

She couldn't believe he had brought it along from Boston. "Cedric...." She stared at him, searching for words. He was handsome, she acknowledged, with his short, cropped brown hair and hazel eyes. He was likely one of the most highly sought after bachelors in Boston, and, if he continued on his career path, would soon be one of the wealthiest.

"We can have a lengthy courtship, Kaydence. We don't have to set a date for the wedding until late next year, if necessary. I figured you could return with me to Boston when I leave in a couple of weeks. In the meantime, I could arrive from town each day to spend time with you. I am renting a vacant house in Pine Haven and have been assured I may stay as long as I wish. We could spend each day together until we leave. Can you imagine how happy your parents will be at your return to Boston?"

"Cedric...." Kaydie's head began to hurt at the realization that she'd received two marriage proposals in the past week.

"Name it, Kaydence, and it's yours."

"I'm not—" How could Kaydie tell him she was afraid to marry again? He would ask her why, and then what would she say? How could she tell him she wasn't ready to entrust her life to a husband again? After all, he was oblivious to the hurts her former husband had caused her.

Kaydie chided herself. She knew Cedric—had known him for so long, and their familiarity comforted her. Perhaps after a long courtship, she would be ready to marry again.

Cedric looked impatient. "You're not—"

"May I have some time to think over your generous offer?" Kaydie interrupted him.

"Yes, yes, of course," answered Cedric. "Take as long as you wish. Keep in mind, though, that it would be far more convenient for you to decide before I return to Boston in two weeks. That way, you could travel there with me."

"I just need some time," said Kaydie, not knowing what else to say.

Cedric placed the ring back in the box and put it in his pocket. Then, he cupped Kaydie's face in his hands and kissed her again. "I love you, Kaydence. I really do."

Once more, Kaydie waited to feel something akin to what she'd experienced with Jonah. But nothing happened. Still, she did care about Cedric, she reasoned; he had always been a good friend. They shared memories from the past that she would never share with anyone else. He was kind and handsome, he would be a good provider, and he would love her. So, why did she find herself continuing to compare him to Jonah Dickenson?

CHAPTER NINETEEN

wo days later, at the Fourth of July celebration, Mr. Victor climbed atop his wooden platform and picked up his megaphone. "The annual Fourth of July parade is about to begin!" he announced, then leaned down and gave Geraldine a quick kiss on the cheek.

October 4 was not that far away, Kaydie mused, and she hoped that their whirlwind courtship would not work to Geraldine's detriment later on. She'd heard that Lucille had taken it upon herself to make all of the wedding arrangements, and that while many of the women from the quilting circle had offered to sew a dress for the bride, Geraldine had ultimately decided to make it herself.

"Kaydence, there you are!" Cedric wove through the crowd and came to stand next to her as she watched the parade with McKenzie, Zach, Jonah, Rosemary, and Asa. "I never realized that such a small town could contain so many people."

"You should have seen it at the Founder's Day celebration last month," McKenzie told him.

"Hi, Ma!" shouted Davey. He and Waddles were walking in the parade, and when Davey wasn't waving to someone he knew, he played his harmonica.

"I'm so proud of him for learning so many tunes on that thing," said Rosemary.

Bethany Ethel squealed. "She certainly knows who Davey is," Jonah observed.

"He's like a big brother to her, for sure," said Asa.

The group of townsfolk playing musical instruments moved past, followed by a cluster of people dressed in patriotic ensembles of red, white, and blue. While this parade could not compete with those Kaydie had seen in Boston, she still found it enjoyable and felt a sense of pride about the town she had come to consider home.

"Once the parade has concluded, the three-legged race will begin," Mr. Victor announced. "Participants should find their partners and meet at the far end of Main Street."

Kaydie remembered the promise she'd made to Jonah on Founder's Day about being his partner for the race today. How she wished they'd had a chance to talk about last Sunday and be reconciled! There were many unspoken words between them—words that needed to be said to repair the hurt.

"All right, Pine Haven residents! Grab your partners for the three-legged race!" said Mr. Victor.

"Jonah?" said Kaydie, glancing his way.

"Kaydie?" Jonah took a hesitant step toward her.

"What is a three-legged race?" Cedric asked, staring straight ahead. "It sounds rather primitive to me."

Kaydie ignored him and turned to Rosemary. "Would you mind holding Bethany Ethel?" she asked her.

"I never mind holding that precious baby," Rosemary declared. She reached for Bethany Ethel, who snuggled against her. "There's nothing in all the world like being a grandmother," she said, kissing the top of the baby's head.

"Grandmother?" Cedric looked at her, his brow furrowed in confusion. "Darius Kraemer was your son?"

Rosemary's eyes grew large. "Oh, no," she answered. "I am Bethany Ethel and Davey's adopted grandmother. You see, Asa and I were never blessed with children of our own."

"I see," said Cedric, still looking confused. "Kaydence?"

Kaydie and Jonah were about to head to the starting line of the three-legged race.

"She's going to enter the race," McKenzie explained. "At the Founder's Day celebration last month, she and Jonah took second place. This time, they'll surely win."

"Pardon?" said Cedric. He looked at Kaydie. "Kaydence, is it true that you mean to enter the race?"

Kaydie nodded, then turned to leave, taking Jonah's arm.

"Oh, Cedric, you're so dramatic," McKenzie teased.

"I daresay I'm not being dramatic," Kaydie heard Cedric say. "Deeply concerned would be more like it. Kaydence!"

Kaydie turned to see Cedric running to catch up with her, and she stopped. "What is it, Cedric?"

"What are you doing?"

"I'm entering the three-legged race, just like McKenzie said."

Cedric looked as if he'd seen a four-headed monster.

"What do you mean, you're entering the race?"

"That's what I mean," said Kaydie. "I'm entering the race with Jonah. We nearly won last time, and we want to try again."

"I hardly think that's becoming of a proper young lady," Cedric said, pursing his lips.

"It's fine, Cedric," Kaydie assured him.

"Kaydie, we need to be going," Jonah spoke up. "They're lining up at the start."

"Cedric, I need to go," said Kaydie, then turned and began to follow Jonah.

"What—what about your dress?" Cedric called after her. "Surely, you don't want to participate in a three-legged race while attired in fine clothing!"

Kaydie turned around once more. "Well, unfortunately, I did not bring a change of clothes, so this will have to do." Standing up for herself felt better than she'd expected it to.

"What if you fall and tear your dress?" asked Cedric. "And what would your mother say if she saw you? She'd be horrified."

"I'm sure she would be, Cedric." With that, Kaydie turned and began to run to catch up with Jonah.

At the starting line, Jonah bent down and tied a strip of cloth around their ankles. "Are you ready?" he asked her.

"I think so!" For a moment, it seemed that they both had forgotten the harsh words and hurt feelings from several days ago.

"On your marks, get set, go!" shouted Mr. Victor, who shot his gun into the air on "go."

With one arm around Jonah's waist and one hand holding up the bottom of her dress, Kaydie began to run.

She and Jonah struggled at first, their movements awkward and uncoordinated, but halfway through the race, they were able to join together in perfect rhythm, just as they had in the Founder's Day race the month before.

"We're almost there, Kaydie!" said Jonah as they passed another couple to gain the second-place position.

They sped up until they came alongside the couple in first place. The crowd cheered, and Kaydie could hear several familiar voices urging her and Jonah on to victory. She looked up at the finish line and nearly tripped.

"Are you all right?" Jonah asked, holding firmly to her shoulders to prevent her from falling.

"I'm fine," Kaydie answered, regaining her footing.

"The race is close, folks!" Mr. Victor proclaimed through the megaphone. "As you will recall from the race on Founder's Day, the couples in first and second place finished accordingly. Will history repeat itself, or will we see a new pair of winners?"

The crowd cheered even louder as the race neared its finish.

Finally, in one gigantic step, Jonah and Kaydie pulled ahead of the other couple and crossed the finish line first.

"We have a new winner!" Mr. Victor shouted over the cheers and applause of the crowd. "Jonah Dickenson and Kaydie Kraemer are the new Pine Haven three-legged race champions!"

"Did you hear that, Kaydie? We did it!" Jonah exclaimed as he untied their ankles.

"I know—I can't believe it!" she shouted.

Jonah turned to her and opened his arms for an embrace. She leaped into them, and he lifted her off the ground and twirled her around several times before setting her down. Kaydie felt dizzy, though she attributed it more to their win than to their spinning. As Mr. Victor had said after the Founder's Day race, they really did make a good team.

⁂

Cedric stood near the finish line and watched Kaydence and Jonah as they celebrated their win. He couldn't understand the big to-do about a primitive ritual in which two people tied their ankles together and looked like fools as they attempted to run across a field. But the thought of foolish-looking people running with their ankles bound wasn't what bothered Cedric most. No, what bothered him most was the look of happiness in Kaydence's eyes as Jonah picked her up and spun her around. It was more than the joy of mere camaraderie; it was a look of fondness, and Cedric didn't like it—not one bit. *I believe I may have underestimated you, ranch hand Jonah*, Cedric said to himself. *I hadn't figured on competing against you for Kaydence's hand. How blind I was.*

Cedric would have preferred not to compete for her love, but he decided that it really didn't make that big a difference. He would win her heart, no matter what. With that in mind, Cedric began to strategize and plan as if he were preparing to win an important trial. Only this time, it wasn't a trial he was preparing for; it was his future with Kaydence Worthington Kraemer.

⚬⚬⚬

The basket social followed, again with Mr. Victor as master of ceremonies. "Every year, we select a worthy cause for which to raise money," he began. "This year, the monies from our charity events are to fund the building of a new schoolhouse. As most of you have noticed, Pine Haven is growing by leaps and bounds. The population of school-age children is ever expanding, and the current school building is inadequate to accommodate all the pupils. Therefore, all proceeds from the basket social will be used to build a new school." A round of applause silenced Mr. Victor for a moment.

"For those of you who are unfamiliar with the basket social, let me explain how it works. The kind-hearted women of Pine Haven—all of them excellent cooks, I assure you—have each prepared a lunch and packed it in a basket. These baskets will be auctioned off one by one. The highest bidder not only wins the lunch inside the basket but also earns the privilege of sharing his lunch with the lovely lady who prepared it." Mr. Victor paused. "Does everyone understand how it works? Good. Let's begin." He picked up a piece of paper and glanced at it. "The first lunch basket was prepared by Lucille Granger."

Lucille marched up to stand beside Mr. Victor, lugging what looked like a heavy wicker basket. "We'll begin our bids at twenty-five cents," said Mr. Victor. "Do I hear twenty-five cents?"

Lucille smiled broadly at the crowd.

"Do I hear twenty-five cents for a delicious lunch with Lucille?"

When there was no answer, Mr. Victor turned to Lucille. "Why don't you tell us what's in your basket?"

"Well, Mr. Victor, I have roast beef sandwiches and the most delicious cinnamon rolls this side of the Mississippi," Lucille said, beaming.

"Did you hear that, fine folks of Pine Haven? Lucille has prepared roast beef sandwiches and her famous cinnamon rolls. That sounds delicious, doesn't it? And remember—all proceeds benefit a good cause," said Mr. Victor. "Twenty-five cents starts the bid on this delicious lunch."

Lucille scanned the crowd. "Fred? Where is that Fred?" she demanded.

"Pardon, Lucille?" said Mr. Victor.

"I said, where is that half-wit husband of mine?" she muttered.

"I don't rightly know, Lucille," said Mr. Victor.

"Fred!" shouted Lucille. "Where are you, Fred?"

"I'm right here, Lucille. You don't have to shout," said Fred, moving through the crowd toward the stage.

"Why aren't you bidding on my basket?"

"Your basket?"

"Yes, my basket."

"You can bid on the basket and win a lunch with your wife," Mr. Victor told him.

"Why would I want to do that?" asked Fred as he climbed the steps to the stage. "I have lunch with her every day."

"Oh, crumb cakes, Fred. It's for charity."

"Charity?" said Fred. "Well, in that case, I bid."

"How much would you like to bid?" asked Mr. Victor.

"I'll bid ten cents." Fred smiled proudly and stuck his hands in the pockets of his trousers.

"Ten cents?" asked Lucille.

"I'm sorry, Fred, but the bidding begins at twenty-five cents," Mr. Victor explained. "Would you like to bid that much?"

"I reckon so," said Fred with a sigh. "Twenty-five cents."

"Twenty-five cents for this fine basket, going once, going twice, sold to Fred Granger!" Mr. Victor announced.

As a smiling Fred and a scowling Lucille left the stage, Mr. Victor announced the next basket, which was McKenzie's. Zach was the highest bidder, naturally. After hers came baskets prepared by Rosemary, Reverend Eugene's wife, Eliza Renkley, and several other women. Soon, Kaydie was the only woman still holding her basket.

"Our final basket was prepared by Kaydie Kraemer," Mr. Victor announced.

"Here, dear, let me hold Bethany Ethel," said Rosemary.

"Thank you, Rosemary." She handed her daughter to Rosemary, then carried the basket toward the stage.

"Hello, Kaydie," said Mr. Victor. "What do we have in this basket today?"

Kaydie felt herself blush. "Some sandwiches and... gingerbread cookies," she said.

"I'm sorry, Kaydie. What was the last thing you said?"

"Gingerbread cookies," Kaydie repeated in a louder voice.

"Gingerbread cookies! Those wouldn't be your award-winning gingerbread cookies, now, would they?"

"Um, I suppose so." Kaydie shifted her weight, suddenly feeling uncomfortable in front of the crowd. She was thankful she'd made Jonah promise to bid on the basket, for she couldn't imagine having to stand there, waiting, with nobody bidding on her basket, as had happened to Lucille. But what if Jonah had decided not to bid on her basket because of the argument they'd had? She reassured herself with the thought that surely Cedric would bid on the basket if no one else did.

"We'll start the bidding at twenty-five cents," announced Mr. Victor.

"Twenty-five cents," said Jonah, stepping forward. His eyes connected with Kaydie's, and she silently thanked him.

"Twenty-five cents, going once—"

"Fifty cents," said Cedric, who also stepped forward so that he was shoulder to shoulder with Jonah.

"Fifty cents? Do I hear—"

"One dollar,"' said Jonah.

"Very well," said Mr. Victor. "One dollar it is. Do I hear—"

"Two dollars," countered Cedric.

"Three dollars," said Jonah.

By now, the crowd had fallen silent.

Kaydie saw Cedric glance over at Jonah with a look of indignation. Then he turned to Mr. Victor and stood up straight, as if he were arguing the most important case of his legal career. "Four dollars!"

"This is the priciest basket yet, folks," said Mr. Victor, shaking his head. "Would anyone else care to bid?"

The crowd remained silent.

"Well, then, we are up to four dollars. Do I hear five dollars...?"

"Five dollars," said Jonah, glaring at Cedric.

"Twenty-five dollars!" Cedric shouted with a scowl.

"Twenty-five dollars?" Mr. Victor raised his eyebrows. "This is making Pine Haven history. We've never had anyone bid that high on a basket social. Are you sure, Mr....uh...."

"Van Aulst. The name is Cedric Van Aulst." Cedric turned to face the crowd, as if expecting applause. When he received none, he shrugged and turned back toward Mr. Victor again.

"Well, Mr. Van Aulst, nice to meet you. You've made quite a bid. Thank you for your generosity toward the new school fund."

"It's my pleasure," said Cedric.

"Now, we have twenty-five dollars on the table as the top bid for this fine basket prepared by Kaydie Kraemer. It includes a lunch and her famous gingerbread cookies. Do I hear any other bids?" Mr. Victor nodded at Jonah. "Twenty-six dollars, perhaps?"

Jonah shook his head at Mr. Victor, then glanced at Kaydie. His eyes offered an unspoken apology before he stepped back into the crowd.

Trying to hide her disappointment, Kaydie smiled and awaited Mr. Victor's next words.

"Twenty-five dollars, going once, going twice, sold to Cedric Van Aulst!"

Beaming, Cedric approached the stage and shook Mr. Victor's hand.

"Congratulations, Mr. Van Aulst," said Mr. Victor.

"Thank you," Cedric replied. He took the basket from Kaydie in one hand and grasped her now empty hand with the other, then led her back through the crowd to where he had been standing. "I have to be honest with you, Kaydence," he whispered. "I can't stand the taste of gingerbread cookies."

Then why did you insist on making the highest bid on my basket? she wanted to ask him. Instead, she said, "That's fine, Cedric," then reached down into the basket and retrieved the small tin of gingerbread cookies. Glancing around, she spotted Jonah. "I'll be right back," she told Cedric.

She hurried over to Jonah. "Here," she said, handing him the tin. "These are for you. They're your favorite, and Cedric won't eat them."

"Thank you, Kaydie, but I know how much you love gingerbread cookies, too—are you sure you don't want them?"

"Believe me, I ate my fair share while I was baking them," she replied.

"I'm sorry I couldn't afford to top twenty-five dollars," Jonah said quietly. "All of my money is wrapped up in the new house."

"That's fine, Jonah. Thank you for keeping your promise. I was so afraid I'd stand up there and have no bids on my basket."

"Poor Lucille," Jonah chuckled. "I'm proud of you for being so brave, Kaydie, but I don't think you needed to worry about having no one bid on your basket. Cedric did a fine job."

"Yes, he did," Kaydie agreed. "I could picture him in a courtroom, pleading the case of his client to the judge. My father has one of the most reputable law firms in Boston, and under his tutelage, I'm sure Cedric has learned well."

Jonah nodded. "He certainly has."

Kaydie detected sadness in Jonah's gray eyes. How she wished she could take back the words she had used to compare him to Darius last week! "Jonah—"

"Kaydence? Oh, there you are, Kaydence," Cedric said, walking toward Kaydie and Jonah. "Are you ready to share that fine lunch you prepared?"

"Thank you for the cookies, Kaydie," Jonah said, holding up the tin.

"You're welcome," answered Kaydie. She turned to Cedric. "I need to get Bethany Ethel from Rosemary, and then I'll meet you over there," she said, pointing to a tree nearby.

"Surely we can have lunch without the child!" Cedric exclaimed.

"I'll be right back," said Kaydie, ignoring his comment. *If I am to even consider becoming Mrs. Van Aulst,* Kaydie thought to herself, *you, my dear Cedric, must accept Bethany Ethel and learn her name!*

❧

Cedric spread the blanket on the ground as Kaydence unpacked the picnic basket. "You know, Kaydence, that once we are married, you will never have to cook again. Last year, I hired a wonderful cook by the name of Adamina. She'll prepare all the meals, so you'll never have to make another sandwich or bake another gingerbread cookie."

"I rather like baking."

"Oh, dear." Cedric shook his head. "The sooner we remove you from Pine Haven, the better. This place has changed you into a woman I often fail to recognize."

"Cedric, I'm not sure I want to leave Pine Haven."

"Don't be ridiculous, Kaydence." Cedric bristled at the memory of Kaydence and Jonah's embrace after the three-legged race, as well as at Jonah's attempt to outbid him. "I know you're still mourning your beloved husband's death, and I respect that. I will give you all the time you need. However, you don't belong here. And I think you know that."

"Shh, it's all right, sweetie," Kaydence crooned to the child, who squirmed and fussed in her lap.

Cedric rolled his eyes "That's another thing, Kaydence," he continued. "A nanny is in proper order for the child. I know we've discussed this before, but it will be easier once we're married and the child has someone to care for her. As it is, I don't feel like I can spend any time alone with you."

"I don't want a nanny for Bethany Ethel," Kaydence protested rather uncharacteristically.

Cedric was taken aback by her assertiveness. "Well, that's fine, Kaydence. I didn't realize you felt so strongly about it. I only want what's best for us all. If you don't want the child to have a nanny, I understand. I only want to please you and give you the life you deserve."

Kaydence glanced up at something in the distance, and Cedric followed her gaze. He saw Jonah tossing a ball with the child of McKenzie's husband. Cedric cleared his throat. "Do you have feelings for the ranch hand, Kaydence?"

"Pardon?" she asked, her eyes shifting quickly to him.

"The ranch hand—do you have feelings for him?"

"Jonah is a good friend of mine," she said.

"A good friend?" Cedric scoffed. "It's odd for a single woman to have a good friend who is an unmarried man. It doesn't seem proper."

"Things are different here, Cedric," said Kaydence. "Jonah has always been there for me. He helped me when I was expecting Bethany Ethel, and he even made a cradle for her."

"A cradle for the child?" said Cedric. "After we are married, she will have the finest bassinet in the state of Massachusetts." Cedric paused. "I'm only relieved you don't have feelings for the ranch hand."

Kaydence remained silent and stared blankly ahead.

"Kaydence? Oh, Kaydence?"

She blinked at him. "Yes?"

"You're staring off as if daydreaming. Are you all right?" he asked her.

"I'm fine, thank you, Cedric," said Kaydie. She took a bite of her sandwich and then fed a tiny piece to the child.

A sense of uneasiness welled within Cedric. In just over a week, he would return to Boston. By then, he hoped that Kaydence would accept his marriage proposal. Although he was not yet a well-seasoned lawyer, he had a gift for reading people. And if his hunch was correct, Kaydence had been thinking about the ranch hand. That hunch didn't sit well with him. *It's time to show Mr. Ranch Hand Jonah just who has won Kaydence's heart*, Cedric said to himself. And he knew just the way to show it.

CHAPTER TWENTY

The next afternoon, Kaydie carried Bethany Ethel to a small meadow not far from the Sawyer home. She spread her daughter's quilt on the ground, and they sat together in the early July sunshine. She needed some time to herself—time to pray and think about the events that had transpired in the past week.

Kaydie heard the purling river in the distance and was reminded of her Sunday afternoon fishing trips with Jonah. They would not be fishing this Sunday, however, for the tension between them had not fully faded.

Kaydie missed the close friendship they had shared. "What should I do?" she asked aloud, prompting Bethany Ethel to look up from the flower she'd been studying and stare at her mother. Kaydie folded her hands and prayed silently. *Lord, I am in need of Your guidance. I am not sure what to do.* She felt the tears begin to fall and, not caring that it was unladylike, wiped them with the back of her hand.

Father, I have created such a mess for myself. How will things ever be the way they should be? Please, Lord, help me to see Your will in all of this.

"Kaydie?"

Kaydie turned to see Rosemary walking by the meadow and carrying a bouquet of flowers. "Hello, Rosemary," she sniffed.

"I was just picking some wildflowers for the dinner table." Rosemary came closer to the quilt. "Are you all right, Kaydie? You look as though you've been crying."

"I—I—oh, Rosemary, I have made a terrible mess of things," Kaydie sobbed, then buried her face in her hands.

"Now, now," said Rosemary. She lowered herself onto the quilt beside Kaydie and wrapped her arms around her shoulders. "What's the matter, dear?"

Kaydie looked up into Rosemary's face. Over the past nine months, she had grown so fond of this woman, whose motherly kindness had touched Kaydie's heart more times than she could count. She felt blessed to consider Rosemary a grandmother to her daughter.

"Is it Jonah?" Rosemary asked.

"Yes, and Cedric, too," Kaydie moaned.

"Would you care to talk about it?"

"I think I would like that," answered Kaydie. "I'm just not sure where to begin."

"Why not start at the beginning?" Rosemary suggested. "My afternoon is yours."

Kaydie managed a smile. "Thank you, Rosemary." Kaydie paused. "Jonah and I have been close friends. Last Sunday, he asked me to marry him."

Rosemary smiled in a way that said she'd expected as much. "And I take it that you said no."

"I am so scared of marriage. After Darius, I told myself I would never marry again. I made the mistake of comparing Jonah to Darius. I—I was so afraid that if I said yes to Jonah and married him, he would turn out as Darius had. When I first met Darius, he was handsome and kind, and he showered me with expensive gifts. He told me he loved me. But after we married, he changed completely. He squandered all of my inheritance, and it wasn't long before we were on the run from the law for the many bank robberies he was committing. I was blind and so foolish. I vowed I would never make such an absurd decision again. Not only had I gotten hurt, but I'd disappointed and disgraced my parents, as well."

"We are all entitled to make mistakes in life," Rosemary said with a smile and a gentle pat to Kaydie's shoulder. "It is my understanding that after Darius died, you came to know the Lord."

"Yes, a sweet elderly woman named Ethel took me in and taught me all about Jesus. I was with her such a short time, but I learned so much. I became hungry for the wisdom in the Bible."

"God used that difficult time to bring you to Him," said Rosemary. "He showed you that you can depend on Him." She glanced at Bethany Ethel. "She is the blessing that came from your marriage to Darius."

"I know," Kaydie said, allowing the tears to fall. "I am so grateful for her, and I would go through it all again a million times over if I had to in order to have such a precious daughter."

Rosemary nodded. "I take it that Jonah didn't appreciate being compared to Darius."

"No, he didn't take it well at all, and I don't blame him. He seemed heartbroken. And if that wasn't bad enough, Cedric shows up out of nowhere and proposes to me, too."

"What was your answer?"

"I told him I had to think about it," said Kaydie. "And now I find myself comparing Jonah and Cedric. I've known Cedric most of my life, so I know his character, and I trust that he will never become like Darius. However, I don't have feelings of love for him. Jonah, on the other hand...I don't know him that well, although I've seen him almost every day since I arrived in Pine Haven. Still, I feel that I can't be sure that he won't turn out like Darius."

"Darius's duplicity seems rather rare," Rosemary said, her voice gentle. "It might be a bit unfair to assume that Jonah will exhibit the same behavior."

"I know," said Kaydie. "I'm just so scared."

"Do you love Jonah?"

"I do," Kaydie affirmed. There! She'd finally admitted it—to herself, as well as to Rosemary. "When I'm with him, I feel something that I've never felt before—not with Darius, and not with Cedric. And it's more than just a feeling. I enjoy being with him, and he's kind and loves Bethany Ethel so much." Kaydie's voice wavered. "I know that Cedric can provide for me in a way that I was raised to appreciate. He is wealthy and has a secure position in my father's law firm. No doubt he'll soon be a partner. But I would hope that he could someday grow to love Bethany Ethel. I know he has spent so little time with her, since he's been in Pine Haven for only a week, but...." Kaydie sighed. "I keep thinking that if I marry him, I can return to my family and for once please my parents and show them I'm not still making foolish mistakes. Maybe Cedric can become the father that Bethany Ethel needs and the husband God has planned for me." As reasonable as that sounded, Kaydie found herself sobbing again.

"I believe that Cedric could grow to love Bethany Ethel," said Rosemary. "From what I know of him, he's a kind and considerate man. Besides, it certainly wouldn't take much to love Bethany Ethel. She's a precious child."

"I know that he would provide for all her needs," said Kaydie. "He would see to it that she never had a want in the world. She would attend the finest schools and have all the privileges I had as a child. Still...."

"She needs a father who loves her," said Rosemary.

"Yes," answered Kaydie. "I know that to you, it probably seems easy to make this decision, but for me, it's very difficult. My parents are insisting I marry Cedric, yet my heart tells me I should do otherwise."

"Have you been in prayer about it?" asked Rosemary.

"Yes, quite a lot," said Kaydie.

"One of my favorite Scriptures is Proverbs three, verses five and six: *'Trust in the LORD with all thine heart; and lean not unto thine own understanding. In all thy ways acknowledge Him, and He shall direct thy paths.'* If you put your trust in the Lord and allow Him to handle this situation, He will guide you in the way you should go. He will make it clear to you."

Kaydie sniffled, and Rosemary hugged her again. "May I pray for you, dear?" she asked.

"Yes, please."

"Dear heavenly Father, sometimes we struggle to find the correct path we should take. I pray that You would guide and direct Kaydie in this important decision. I pray that she will put her trust in You and allow Your will to be done. I pray that it would be clear to her what she should do. I pray for wisdom, guidance, and peace for her. I also pray for a forgiving heart in Jonah. Thank You, Father, that You are always there to hear our concerns. In Jesus' name, amen."

"Thank you, Rosemary," said Kaydie.

"I am always here for you, Kaydie. I think of you as one of the daughters I never had. Both you and McKenzie are so dear to me."

"We feel the same about you," said Kaydie.

Rosemary smiled. "Now, then. I'm going to go back to the house so that you can spend some time with the Lord. Let me know if you need me."

"I will," Kaydie assured her.

Rosemary stood to her feet and gathered the bouquet of flowers she had picked. "I'll be praying for you."

Kaydie nodded and stared at the blue Montana sky. A sense of peace engulfed her, and she heard the Lord speak to her heart with familiar words from Psalm 46: *"Be still, and know that I am God."*

⸻

On Tuesday, Cedric spent the entire day at the Sawyer Ranch with Kaydence. He had only a few days left in Pine Haven, and it was imperative that he find every way possible to convince Kaydence to accompany him back to Boston. At the evening meal, Cedric planned to secure his place in her heart and remove any doubt from his mind that Ranch Hand Jonah had any chance with the woman Cedric had loved for so many years.

Cedric lounged in the main room while Kaydence, McKenzie, and Rosemary began to prepare the meal. "Cedric?" said Kaydence, interrupting his thoughts. "Would you mind keeping an eye on Bethany Ethel?"

"I beg your pardon?" asked Cedric.

"Would you mind keeping an eye on Bethany Ethel while I help McKenzie and Rosemary in the kitchen?" Kaydence asked.

Begrudgingly, Cedric stood up and looked at Kaydence, who was holding a stack of plates. "You do realize that once you've returned to Boston, you'll no longer have to partake in such menial tasks fit only for servants, don't you?" He stepped closer and kissed her on the cheek. "Yes, Kaydence—once we're married, your days of cooking and cleaning and setting the table will be over."

Kaydence didn't respond but looked past him. "Bethany Ethel?"

Cedric turned around and saw the child stop crawling and turn around to look at her mother. "Ma-ma-ma-ma!" she babbled, then turned and began to crawl away.

"Cedric, would you please make sure she doesn't go near the woodstove?" Kaydence asked.

"Oh, yes, the child," said Cedric with a roll of his eyes. It never ceased to amaze him how that baby could manage to interfere. "I'll keep an eye on her."

Walking toward where the child was playing, he called to her. "Come here," he said softly.

Bethany Ethel stopped again, turned, and stared up at Cedric. A glance behind him told him that Kaydence was still watching. This would be a good time to work on winning her affections. He knew how much she cared for her child. Perhaps if he tried to care, too, it would help his case. "Come here, child," he called, his voice calm. He walked closer to Bethany Ethel with his arms outstretched. Kneeling down, he picked her up in his arms, feeling uncomfortable and out of place.

Bethany Ethel began to scream, and her face turned red. "All right, all right," said Cedric, setting her back down on the floor again. He shook his head. He'd never spent much time around children and didn't intend to start. He was an only child and had been raised by nannies. Throughout his life, Cedric had spent most of his time with adults, with the exception of when he had been permitted to play with the Worthington girls.

Just then, the front door opened, and Davey rushed in, followed by Zach, Asa, and Jonah. "Is Bethany Ethel all right?" Davey asked. "We heard her crying."

"She's fine," said Kaydence. "But, Davey? Would mind keeping an eye on her for me until suppertime?"

"Sure," answered Davey. He walked into the kitchen and grabbed a pot and a wooden spoon. "Here, Bethany Ethel. Try this." With the fondness of a doting big brother, Davey sat down on the floor next to Bethany Ethel. He turned the pot upside down and began to hit it with the spoon. *What a terrible racket!*

Cedric thought. But the child was clearly delighted at the dinging sound, for she began to squeal and reached for the spoon.

Cedric collapsed onto the sofa, his nerves frayed from the cacophony and his heart pounding at the thought of the plan he meant to unfold during the evening meal. Never would he be happier to return to Boston. In two short days, he would be boarding the stagecoach, then the train, with Kaydence on his arm. He grinned at the thought and was thankful that she would soon be his wife.

He managed to remain lost in thought as the meal was prepared, and it was Davey's "Suppertime!" that finally roused him.

When everyone had taken a place at the table, Zach said, "Asa, would you mind leading us in prayer?"

Asa nodded and bowed his head. "Dear heavenly Father, we thank You for this glorious day You have given us and for the bountiful food You continually provide. Please protect our health and allow Cedric to return home safely to Boston. In Jesus' name, amen."

When the commotion of passing platters of potatoes and corn on the cob had settled, Cedric stood to his feet. "I have an announcement to make," he declared, clinking his fork against his water glass.

The room fell silent, and all eyes were fixed on Cedric. He cleared his throat and straightened his posture, smoothing any wrinkles from his suit as if he were about to address the judge in a court case. "As you all know," he began, "I came to Pine Haven to court Kaydence." He smiled down at her and patted her gently on the shoulder. "Kaydence and I have known each other for over fifteen years. In that time, we have shared many good memories. I have always loved her and desired for us to spend our lives together.

"When Kaydence's parents, Arthur and Florence, told me the terrible news that their youngest daughter had lost her beloved husband, Darius, to a severe intestinal illness that befell him while he was pursuing his courageous plan to bring medical care to the people of the Montana Territory, my heart broke for her. I know how deeply my Kaydence loves, and so, as someone who knows her almost as well as her own parents, I share that grief with her."

A frown crossed Jonah's face. Cedric figured it to be a sign of frustration, an acknowledgment of defeat. His plan was working. Cedric looked at Kaydence, but she kept her eyes on her plate and poked at her food with her fork. Why did she look so uncomfortable? Never mind. He decided to go on.

"I would like you all to know," he continued, looking from one person to the next around the dinner table, "that I have every intention of making Kaydence my wife. We have discussed this matter at length during my visit and have made arrangements for our upcoming wedding and where we shall live. When we are married, Kaydence will have everything her heart desires and more—lovely gowns, fine china, diamond jewelry. It will be my pleasure to provide her with the type of life she led before she followed her dear husband to the Montana Territory." Cedric noticed the looks of shock around the dinner table and smiled. He must have impressed them with all that he had to offer. "I know that there may be others who believe they can give Kaydence a suitable life"—Cedric paused and made eye contact with Jonah—"however, they are sorely mistaken. She deserves far better than even the best that someone in Pine Haven could ever give her. Further, she is in no position to marry beneath her status."

Jonah stood up and excused himself from the table, then walked out of the house, letting the front door close behind him with a bang. Cedric was mildly disappointed that the ranch hand would miss his proposal, but he supposed it didn't matter that much.

Reaching into his pocket, Cedric turned to face his future bride. "Kaydence Worthington Kraemer, will you marry me?"

What was Kaydence doing with her eyes on the front door, instead? "I can see that you are in shock at my glorious proposal," Cedric said with a nervous chuckle. He reached down and grabbed her left hand, then pushed the large diamond ring onto her ring finger. "I will love you forever, Kaydence," he declared.

"Cedric?" Kaydence nearly whispered.

"It's all right to say yes; after all, you know these people," Cedric said, waving a hand toward the kitchen table.

"Cedric, I can't marry you," said Kaydie.

"I beg your pardon?"

"I can't marry you." Kaydence pulled the ring off her finger and handed it back to him. "I'm sorry."

"But why?" he asked. He looked at McKenzie. "You've known me for just as long as Kaydence has. Can you think of a good reason why she shouldn't marry me?"

⧤⧥

Was Cedric really that dense? "Please excuse me," said Kaydie, getting up from her seat. "McKenzie, would you watch Bethany Ethel?"

McKenzie nodded, and Kaydie rushed out the front door, searching for where Jonah had gone. From the porch, she saw him in the distance, riding Lightning toward town at what appeared to be a faster speed than he'd ridden in the Founder's Day race.

An uneasy feeling stirred within her, and she opened the front door and leaned inside. "Zach? Would you please take me into town?"

He nodded and pushed his chair back from the table. "I'll saddle up the horse."

"I don't understand," said Cedric. "What's going on?" He looked about in confusion, and Kaydie almost felt sorry for him.

When Zach led his horse from the barn, Kaydie rushed over to him. "I need to follow Jonah," she told him.

Zach nodded and hoisted Kaydie into the saddle, then climbed up in front of her and prompted the horse toward town.

⧤⧥

Jonah rode Lightning toward downtown Pine Haven, his shoulders feeling the weight of heartache, disappointment, anger, and discouragement. He didn't know where he was going, only that he needed to get away—away from the happily betrothed couple and the embarrassment of thinking Kaydie might marry him when she could have someone like Cedric, instead. He'd been ignoring the possibility of Cedric proposing and Kaydie accepting. While he'd known that Cedric was courting her, he'd figured that Cedric would go back to Boston, and that things in Pine Haven would return to normal. But now, Kaydie was leaving Pine Haven, too, and he would probably never see her again. *You're such a fool,* he thought to himself. *A fool for thinking that someone like Kaydie would ever fall in love with you. After all, how could you hope to compete with the likes of Cedric? Compared to him, you have nothing to offer. You're even more of a fool for allowing yourself to fall in love and consider marriage when you know all along that nothing good can come of it. You've seen that firsthand.*

The landscape rushed by in a blur as Jonah prompted Lightning down the road. Had he ridden in the Founder's Day race as he rode now, he would have won by a wide margin, crossing the finish line full minutes before Sheriff Clyde.

But none of that mattered now. Nothing did. For so long, his mind had been filled with thoughts of Kaydie—of spending time with her, of caring for her, of convincing her that he was nothing like Darius. And now, those thoughts had been in vain, for she would marry another.

He recalled their conversation on that fateful Sunday, when Kaydie had said that she feared he would turn out like Darius. That was probably one reason she was marrying Cedric—she could be comfortably certain that Cedric was nothing like Darius and would never be. She hadn't known Jonah long enough to feel the same certainty about him. Her open distrust of him cut through his heart, and he begged his memory to forget.

As Jonah neared downtown Pine Haven, he slowed Lightning's pace. The streets were empty, and all was quiet, except for the saloon and its usual commotion. *The saloon.* Jonah's eyes settled on the establishment, the likes of which he had once frequented, although he had never stepped inside a bar since moving to Pine Haven. He pulled on Lightning's reins and stopped the horse near the entrance, then climbed down and tied him to a hitching post.

Jonah peered through an open front window and saw several men at the bar. The smell of cigarette smoke filled his nostrils, and he choked at the odor. He turned toward the street and stood with his back against the front of the building. *Maybe just one drink, and all your problems will disappear,* he thought to himself. *It always helped you back in Mississippi....* He thought of the countless times he'd heard his pa yell at him merely for being in his presence. "Yer ma gone off and left ye with me!" his father would shout. "Now look at what she done. She leaves me with yer sorry self to raise while she goes off and makes a life for 'erself. It ain't fair!" His father would then punch the wall in anger. "'Course, jest a couple more years, and ye'll be gone. Then I kin have my life back again without the likes of some worthless kid always hangin' around!"

Jonah would flinch each time his father hit the wall, knowing that each blow was meant for him. He'd always wondered why his mother had left and not taken him with her. Had he been that bad of a child? He'd been only three when she'd left. Yet the question he'd mulled his whole life remained unanswered, as it likely always would.

Jonah closed his eyes. It had been the memories of those times of neglect and rejection that had caused him to seek refuge in the saloon. He would drink until the bartender refused to serve him anything more. Sure enough, he would forget all his problems, albeit temporarily. He would step drunkenly out of the saloon and almost always find himself in a fight. Every payday, it was the same routine: head to the saloon and spend his wad of cash to forget his problems. Jonah had struggled to save money, since he would spend almost every dime on drinks. His life had swirled out of control, yet no one had cared. He was so young—too young to be hanging around the likes of the characters who frequented the saloon. But that hadn't mattered to him, nor had it mattered to the bartenders who served him. He had money, and it was always welcome wherever whiskey could be purchased.

Jonah took a deep breath and turned around to face the saloon. He peered through the window once more. What was the harm of wallowing in self-pity just for a few minutes? He dug around in his pockets for money and pulled out a couple of coins. Hearing hoofbeats, he turned and saw Kaydie and Zach together on horseback, riding into town. He shook his head. They were probably here to order stagecoach tickets for Kaydie and Cedric's upcoming trip.

Jonah approached the door of the saloon, his hand already poised on the handle. "Hey, we see you out there, Dickenson!" he heard the bartender yell. "Why don'cha come on in?"

"Dickenson, as in Jonah Dickenson?" came another voice. "Ain't never seen the likes of him in this here establishment!"

Chuckles arose from the other patrons. "Yeah, come on in, Dickenson. Your money's good here!" yelled the bartender.

"Jonah?"

Jonah whirled around and saw Kaydie, still on horseback with Zach.

"What are you doing here?" Jonah asked.

"You're not thinking of going in there, are you?" Zach asked.

"Hey, Sawyer! Is that you out there?" shouted the bartender.

"Dickenson and Sawyer? Don't think I've ever seen them hangin' 'round here 'afore," said a voice.

"You can come in, too, Sawyer. Your money is as good as Dickenson's," the bartender insisted. "Why don'cha both come on in? I'll fix y'up real good. Bring that li'l lady on in with you, too."

"No, thank you," Zach replied. He gave Jonah a stern look. "Come on, Jonah."

Jonah shook his head. "This isn't any of your business, Zach," he said. "Not any of your business, and not any of Kaydie's business," he added through clenched teeth.

"Tell you what," called the bartender. "First drink's on me. How does that sound?"

Jonah turned and watched the bartender fill a glass and place it on the counter in front of an empty stool. "See here, Dickenson? First drink's on me. Come on in and join the fun."

Jonah reached up once more for the door handle. "Jonah?" Kaydie said again. "Jonah, please don't go in there."

Lord, please, help me resist this temptation, Jonah prayed silently. He only wanted to escape the pain of losing Kaydie, yet he knew how easily he might slip back into the cycle that had trapped him when he'd lived in Mississippi.

"Don't listen to the woman, Dickenson!" the bartender called out. "Come on in and have some whiskey."

"Please, Jonah, no," Kaydie pleaded.

Jonah could not make himself take his hand off the door handle. "I'm sorry, Kaydie," he muttered, then pushed open the door.

"This is just what Darius did," Kaydie said, her voice monotone.

Jonah stopped then and stood still. *"This is just what Darius did."* The words echoed through his soul and made him shudder. He took a step back onto the sidewalk and let go of the door, letting it slam shut.

"Aw, come on, Dickenson!" someone shouted from inside the saloon. "Don't listen to 'er. Don'cha wanna come in and have a drink?"

"No, thanks," Jonah said, turning around. Kaydie opened her arms wide, and he stepped forward to embrace her, burying his face in her hair. "I'm sorry, Kaydie," he whispered. "I'm so sorry."

CHAPTER TWENTY-ONE

I'm going to head back to the ranch," said Zach, patting Jonah on the back. "I think you and Kaydie have some things you need to discuss."

"Thank you, Zach," said Jonah. He turned to Kaydie. "Do you mind if we walk home?"

"That's fine," she said. "It's a beautiful night."

He untied Lightning from the hitching post, and they started walking. "Kaydie, I'm sorry about what happened back there," Jonah began. "When I heard that you and Cedric were getting married, I knew I needed to get away and sort through my thoughts. I never meant to set foot inside the saloon. When I rode into town, I heard the noises from the saloon, and those old temptations returned." Jonah paused. "I know I frightened you, and I'm sorry. I've told you before how, when I lived in Mississippi, I used to drown my sorrows with whiskey, and how my life changed and I no longer needed it when Jamal Winthrop introduced me to the Lord." He sighed. "I can't believe how close I came to seeking refuge in whiskey once again rather than taking my sorrow to the foot of the cross. It's a mistake I pray I'll never make again."

Kaydie took Jonah's free hand in hers. "I'm glad you didn't go in the saloon."

"When you said that I was being just like Darius, I—I knew I was making a mistake. I'm sorry I hurt you."

"I have some apologizing of my own to do," said Kaydie. She stared down at the ground as they walked. "It was unfair of me to compare you to Darius. I was just so scared that I would fall in love with you, and—and that you would become someone else, like he did. Only after we were married did I meet the real Darius. There was so much I didn't know about him, and I figured you could easily be the same way. I know that I hurt you, Jonah, and I am truly sorry."

Jonah squeezed her hand. "I know you haven't told me everything Darius did to you, Kaydie, but I assure you again that I would never hurt you the way he did. A man should never treat a woman the way he treated you." Jonah paused. "I'm surprised you came after me, considering your betrothal to Cedric. I figured it wouldn't be proper. You are a faithful friend."

"Jonah, I'm not marrying Cedric."

"You aren't?" Jonah stopped in his tracks and felt his pulse quicken.

"I did consider it," Kaydie said, turning to face him. "After all, I've known him for so many years, and I felt sure that he would take care of me. I also wanted to please my parents, since they were so disappointed in me for marrying Darius. I know that Mother and Father were behind Cedric coming to Pine Haven in the first place."

"But Cedric said that you—"

"I know what he said." Kaydie sighed. "I think he honestly believed I would follow him back to Boston if he made it sound good enough. But a life of ease no longer appeals to me. So, no, I am not marrying Cedric." She paused. "I don't love Cedric, either."

"No?"

"No. I—I love someone else."

"Do I know him?" Jonah asked. His heart began to beat even faster.

"You might." Kaydie smiled slyly. "He's about so tall"—she indicated Jonah's height with her hand—"and has gray eyes, and he's handsome and kind."

"Whoever he is, he's a lucky man to have won your affection," said Jonah. "You should introduce me to him so I can offer my congratulations."

Kaydie giggled, then became serious. "You know, Jonah, I prayed so often that I would make the right decision. I knew that I couldn't marry someone who couldn't love Bethany Ethel with the love of a father. Perhaps Cedric could have eventually, but perhaps not. But I know that Bethany Ethel loves you, and that you love her. I also didn't think I could marry someone who didn't know the truth about Darius. My parents concocted a story about Darius to tell to everybody in Boston, including Cedric. That's why he believed that Darius was a doctor—and a loving husband. But you, Jonah—you know the truth, and I find great comfort in that."

Jonah took a step forward and stroked Kaydie's cheek with his thumb. "Thank you, Kaydie, for choosing me," he said. Then he kissed her with all the passion he'd felt since the day he'd realized he loved her.

When they paused, Kaydie took a step back. "There's another reason I decided to accept your proposal and not Cedric's."

"What is that?"

Kaydie grinned, and Jonah noticed the blush that brightened her cheeks. "I have never felt with anyone else the way I feel when you...kiss me."

Jonah chuckled. "Ah, my precious Kaydie, becoming bolder by the minute." He put his arm around her shoulders. "It may comfort you to know that I have never been in love until now." He kissed her again, and then knelt down on one knee. "Kaydie, will you marry me?"

Kaydie gazed at him tenderly. "I would be honored to marry you, Jonah," she said quietly yet firmly.

Overwhelmed with excitement, Jonah jumped up and threw his hat in the air, which prompted Lightning to neigh in alarm. "Did you hear that, Lightning?" he asked. "Kaydie agreed to marry me!" He grinned at Kaydie. "Thank you for saying yes this time. I wouldn't want to have to ask a third time."

Kaydie smiled and placed her hand in his. "For once, I think I've made a good decision—probably the best decision of my life," she said.

Jonah picked up his hat and put it back on his head. He led Lightning and put one arm around Kaydie's shoulders as they resumed their walk. Who would have guessed that Jonah Dickenson, committed bachelor, would fall in love? *Thank You, Lord, for guiding me tonight when I could have made so many mistakes*, he prayed. *And thank You especially for changing my mind about marriage and for bringing Kaydie into my life.*

Cedric handed his luggage to the stagecoach driver and then turned to address those who had come to see him off on his journey back to Boston. "Thank you for your hospitality," he said to Zach and McKenzie. "It has been an experience I shall never forget."

"It was nice to see you again after so many years, Cedric," said McKenzie. "Have a safe trip home."

Cedric nodded and turned to Kaydence. "Although this trip did not turn out as I had planned, I do wish you all the best, Kaydence." He kissed her hand and felt anew the despair in his heart over her decision not to marry him. Yet, he knew that the pain would heal someday. He then addressed Jonah. "May I speak to you in private for a minute?" he asked, then stepped several feet away and waited for Jonah to join him.

"I could always tell from the way Kaydence looked at you that she had feelings for you," Cedric confessed. "I didn't want to admit it to myself, of course, and I thought that if I just tried hard enough, she would love me. But I know that it was not to be."

"I'm sorry, Cedric," said Jonah.

"I see that you are the one she loves, and that you will treat her right and make her happy. That's all I've ever wanted for Kaydence. I shall miss her beyond belief and shall continue to nurse my broken heart for some time, but I want you to know that I harbor no hard feelings against you."

Jonah reached out and shook Cedric's hand. "Thank you," he said.

"One other thing before I forget," said Cedric. "I know that you are fond of the child, and that after you and Kaydence are married, you plan to adopt her."

"Yes," said Jonah. "I love her and plan to raise her as my own."

"That's another thing I wasn't able to give Kaydence, I'm afraid," said Cedric. "Anyhow, I want you to know that when the time comes for you to adopt the child, I would be honored to draw up the adoption papers."

"Thank you, Cedric. I appreciate that."

"I plan to do it at no charge, as a wedding gift of sorts," he added.

"Thank you again, Cedric. And don't worry about Kaydie."

"I won't," Cedric assured him. "I will have some explaining to do once I return to Boston without Kaydence and have to face her parents, which I'm not looking forward to, but no, I won't worry about her. I know she's in good hands."

"All aboard!" shouted the stagecoach driver.

"I guess that means me," said Cedric. He started toward the stagecoach.

"So long, Cedric," said Kaydence.

"So long, Kaydence," Cedric answered. He waved, then looked away. It would do his heart no good to dwell on her beautiful face.

CHAPTER TWENTY-TWO

*K*aydie put down her pen and reread the letter
she had written to her parents.

Dearest Mother and Father,

*Please allow me to begin by saying how grate-
ful I am that you cared enough to send Cedric
for me. I appreciate the time and funds that
were expended on my behalf and your desire
to bring me home again. By now, Cedric has
returned to Boston, and you have surely heard
that I have decided not to marry him.*

*While Cedric is a kind man and a dear friend
of many years, I find that I have given my heart
to another. During the time that I have resided
with McKenzie and Zach, I have fallen in love
with Jonah Dickenson, a warm and handsome
man who works on the ranch with Zach. Mother, you may remember him from your visit to
Pine Haven last year.*

*Jonah proposed to me even before Cedric did,
and I have decided to marry him and remain*

in Pine Haven. Please do not be disappointed in me, as I know after much prayer that this decision is the Lord's will. Jonah will legally adopt Bethany Ethel, and we will live in the new home he is building on a ranch that borders McKenzie and Zach's.

Jonah and I will be married on September 29 at five o'clock at the Pine Haven Chapel. The date is significant, as it will be one year since the day I first met Jonah at the post office when I arrived here. It is my greatest wish that you both would attend. Please know that you are always welcome at my home, as well as McKenzie's, and that we look forward to seeing you whenever your schedule permits you to visit.

Again, thank you for caring about me and offering to help me start a new life in Boston. I wish you the best and look forward to seeing you in the near future.

Fondly,
Kaydence

Satisfied with the letter, Kaydie folded it and placed it in the envelope. She then clasped her hands together and bowed her head. "Father, I pray that You would soften Mother and Father's hearts to receive this letter. Please allow them to understand my decision and to respect it, although I don't expect they will agree with it. Lord, I pray that You would go ahead of me and lead me into a future that is pleasing to You. Thank You, Father, for the many blessings You have bestowed on me. In Jesus' name, amen."

Seeing that Bethany Ethel was still napping, Kaydie rose to her feet and mentally ran through the list of items she needed to do before her wedding in two short months. Accomplishing every task involved would require nothing short of a miracle.

⤛⤜

As Asa walked her down the aisle of Pine Haven Chapel, Kaydie kept her vision straight ahead toward the front of the church, where Jonah stood with Reverend Eugene. She feared that if she allowed her eyes to deviate from Jonah, she might turn and run from the church. She'd never felt comfortable in front of large audiences, and never had she felt shyer than she did now. Of course, she would never change her mind about marrying Jonah. She still chastised herself now and then for being so foolish the first time he'd proposed. He knew her better than anyone, except for McKenzie—and the Lord, of course. He had been there for her from the first time they'd met, and he would continue to be there for as long as the Lord allowed them to share their lives. Taking a deep breath, Kaydie prayed for peace and calm and continued down the aisle.

⤛⤜

Jonah watched with anticipation as Kaydie walked toward him on Asa's arm. Just when he'd thought she could never look prettier, he found himself mesmerized by her beauty, and it nearly took his breath away. He loved her with a love so strong that it almost scared him. *Lord, please, let me be the kind of husband You desire me to be*, he prayed. *As You know, I'm pretty clueless when it comes to being a husband, as well as a father. Please, Lord, guide me and give me the wisdom I seek. I know that by Your grace I can be the kind of husband Kaydie deserves and the kind of father You want me to be to Bethany Ethel. Father, enable me to love Kaydie the way You love the church, and let me love Bethany Ethel the way You love Your children.* He smiled at Kaydie as she and Asa stepped closer. In a matter of minutes, Kaydie would be his wife! *Thank You, Lord, and amen,* Jonah hastily concluded.

Asa embraced Kaydie and gave Jonah a pat on the back before taking his seat in the front row next to Rosemary. He gave his wife a quick kiss on the cheek, and Jonah wondered how he could have gone so many years thinking that marriage was nothing special. Those two were an obvious example to the contrary, and he hoped that he and Kaydie would have just as much love and joy in their marriage.

৩৩

Kaydie faced Jonah as Reverend Eugene spoke, and while she could hear his voice, she heard not a word. Her stomach was aflutter with nerves—or was it with excitement to marry Jonah?

"Just sit anywhere," a familiar voice said. Kaydie turned her head to see her mother standing in the middle of the aisle with a boy who could be none other than Peyton's ten-year-old son, Maxwell Nathaniel Jr.

"Mother?"' she gasped.

"Oh, hello, Kaydence. Sorry we're late. We'll just find a place to sit, and then we'll be ready to watch the ceremony." Her mother smoothed the creases from her dress and then sat in the nearest pew, sliding down to make room for Nate.

Kaydie stared for a minute at her mother, still unable to believe she had traveled to Pine Haven for the wedding. Had she arrived ten minutes later, she would have missed the entire ceremony.

Hearing the reverend resume, Kaydie turned once more to face Jonah, the man she had grown to love first as a friend, then as a fiancé.

"If there are any objections to this union, please state so now, or forever hold your peace," said Reverend Eugene. He glanced at the guests, and, for a moment, Kaydie held her breath, hoping her mother would not stand up and speak. Relief washed over her when everyone remained silent.

Reverend Eugene went on with the vows, and Kaydie again found herself hearing yet not totally comprehending. She snapped to attention, though, when he turned to her and said, "And do you, Kaydence Worthington Kraemer, take this man, Jonah M. Dickenson, to be your lawfully wedded husband, to live together after God's ordinance in the holy estate of matrimony? Will you love him, comfort him, honor and keep him, for better, for worse; for richer, for poorer; in sickness and in health; and, forsaking all others, be faithful only to him from this day forward, until death do you part?"

Kaydie almost began to giggle at the memory of how adamantly Jonah had insisted that Reverend Eugene not announce his middle name during the vows. Smiling, she answered in a quiet yet firm voice, "I do."

After Jonah slid the wedding ring onto her finger, Reverend Eugene beamed. "I introduce to you

Mr. and Mrs. Jonah Dickenson," he announced. "You may kiss the bride," he added with a wink.

Jonah gently took her face in his hands and kissed her tenderly. She only wished that it could have lasted longer.

When they separated to the sounds of cheers and applause, Jonah whispered, "Your mother is here?"

"Yes—I know, I can't believe it!" Kaydie whispered back.

They processed up the aisle and out the doors, where they greeted the guests as they exited the chapel.

"Congratulations, Kaydence," her mother said as she stopped—the last one in the line. "I suppose it's all I really can say, considering the circumstances."

"Thank you, Mother," said Kaydie. "I would like you to meet Jonah, my husband."

"I do recall him from my last visit here," her mother said. "Nice to meet you once again, Jonah. I must say that while your lack of wealth is evident, I do appreciate that my Kaydence has chosen a handsome man to marry."

"I'm so glad you could make it," said Kaydie, hoping to change the subject before Jonah could get offended.

"Yes, well, traveling here was not first on my list of things to do, but I did not think it proper for you to get married without at least one parent present. By the way," she said, turning to Jonah, "this is my grandson, Maxwell Nathaniel Adams Junior. I was not about to travel so great a distance on my own again, and since Kaydence's father cannot travel, I decided to take young Maxwell Junior with me. He's far better company than our chauffeur, Lawrence, and it was time he saw the uncivilized West."

"It's a pleasure to meet you, Maxwell," said Jonah, extending his arm for a handshake.

"You can call me Nate." He looked around. "This place isn't so bad. You made it sound like the pits of the earth, Grandmother."

"Pish posh," her mother said. "It is the pits of the earth, as far as I'm concerned."

"I don't think so," said Nate. "I think I'd like to live here someday."

"And you can say that after spending a mere thirty minutes in this place?" she asked, raising an eyebrow at her grandson.

Nate nodded. "I sure can, Grandmother. You'll see. Someday I'm going to live here. I like it because the folks are nice, and it's not crowded like Boston. I can see it now, Grandmother—living out in the Wild West, with my own ranch, a buggy, and a team of horses, and—"

"Nonsense, child," her mother cut in.

"I even like this church," Nate continued, as if she hadn't interrupted.

Kaydie watched as Nate walked back up the front steps and down the aisle to the well-worn wooden podium. "Hello, and thank you for coming today," he said with deepened voice. "Would you please turn to page one forty-five in your hymnals?" He looked down and picked up the tattered hymnal that Reverend Eugene had handed to Jonah for him and Kaydie to share during the wedding ceremony. As he ran his fingers along the edges of the book, Kaydie wondered how often he had used one. Unless things had changed dramatically, his family attended church on occasion, out of a sense of duty and social obligation. Kaydie said a silent prayer that he would one day give his life to Christ—and that his parents, Maxwell and her sister Peyton, would do so, as well.

"Maxwell Nathaniel Adams Junior! Come down from there this instant!" Kaydie's mother demanded.

Nate glanced up as his grandmother walked briskly toward him. "I really would like to live here someday, Grandmother," he repeated.

"There will be no more talk of that, young man. I've already lost two daughters to this uncivilized place. I'm not about to lose a grandson to it, too!"

Nate shrugged and stepped down from the podium. Coming back outside with his grandmother, he asked, "Aunt Kaydie, where's Davey? I've heard so much about him."

"He's right over there with Aunt McKenzie," Kaydie said, pointing.

"Still a precocious child, I'm sure," her mother said drily. "Now, about this marriage: you'll note that I did not stand up and object during the ceremony, although I seriously considered doing so." Kaydie wished that her mother would move along instead of monopolizing her and Jonah. She smiled at the guests who waved from the churchyard. "You must know that your father is at home nursing a broken heart. You may not realize that he had every intention of you marrying Cedric."

"Yes, Mother, I do know that," said Kaydie. "And I'm thankful that you and Father have taken my decision to marry Jonah better than I first thought you would."

"I wouldn't say that your father and I have taken this decision well, as that is not the case at all. I'm not at all sure what happened to your common sense, or the common sense of McKenzie, for that matter, but your father and I must accept your choice of a husband, no matter how undesirable that choice may be. You see, you father and I had it all planned that you would marry Cedric, who would provide a home for you in Boston. Your past would be forgotten, and all would be well. Cedric would be a partner in your father's law firm, and you again would help uphold the reputation of the Worthington family. Instead...." She waved her arm toward Jonah. "You have chosen to marry a man who makes his living tending to animals and who lives in a place that is far less advantageous than Boston."

"Mother, Jonah is the kindest man you will ever meet, and I love him. I didn't love Cedric," said Kaydie. She was embarrassed by her mother's loud voice, but a glance at the wedding guests told her that most of them were absorbed in their own conversations and had not overheard.

"I'm sure you've heard me say before that I don't know what love has to do with anything. I didn't love your father when I first married him. Love takes time to grow. Besides, it isn't necessarily what makes for a good marriage and a beneficial partnership."

"It's important to me, Mother," said Kaydie.

Her mother rolled her eyes. "I fear, Kaydence, that you have spent far too much time with your sister McKenzie. What happened to my shy and reticent youngest daughter?"

"Mother, I appreciate your concern, but the choice in husbands is really mine to make," said Kaydie.

"As it was when you made the choice to marry Darius?" Her mother narrowed her eyes.

"Mrs. Worthington, Darius is in the past," Jonah put in. "Let's leave him there." He draped an arm protectively around Kaydie's shoulders, for which she was thankful.

"I see," said her mother. "Well, the deed is done, and there is nothing I can do about it." She dabbed the corner of her eye with a lace handkerchief. "I suppose we must make the best of it." She paused to regain her composure. "I must be moving on, anyhow. I have yet to greet my other daughter." With that, she turned and made her way toward McKenzie.

"Don't worry about it, Kaydie," said Jonah, giving her shoulders a squeeze. "We won't let her ruin this happy day, and we can be thankful for the fact that we can pray for her."

"You're right, Jonah," said Kaydie. "I know that there's only One who can change Mother, and it certainly is not I."

⌖

Jonah carried her over the threshold of their beautiful new ranch home and kissed her before gently setting her down.

"For all of the planning we did, this day has been full of surprises," Jonah said. "Especially your mother arriving in Pine Haven for the wedding."

"That was certainly unexpected," Kaydie agreed. "But the biggest surprise was probably when Father found out from Cedric that he and I were not getting married."

Jonah nodded. "I'm still surprised you said yes to me," he said. "I might add that I'm mighty thankful, too. I love you, Kaydie."

"I love you, too, Jonah." Yes, life was full of surprises, and nothing, absolutely nothing, could ruin this wonderful day God had blessed her with, nor the wonderful life she was starting with her husband. Nothing.

A Preview of

Hailee

Book Three in the Montana Skies Series

By Penny Zeller
Coming Fall 2011

CHAPTER ONE

*H*ailee Annigan removed the discolored sheet of paper from the community board in the train depot. Time and weather had faded the words, so they were barely readable, but she had them memorized:

> *Looking for Philip and Reuben Annigan.*
> *If you have any information, kindly respond to*
> *Hailee Annigan, c/o*
> *Dot Pangbourn's Boardinghouse,*
> *West Eberlee Street, Cincinnati, Ohio*

She crumpled the paper in her hand and stuffed it into her purse. In its place, she posted the notice she'd written that morning, then stepped back to make sure it would be noticeable to people passing by or preparing to board a train.

> *Looking for Philip and Reuben Annigan.*
> *If you have any information, kindly respond to*
> *Hailee Annigan, c/o Pine Haven School,*
> *Pine Haven, Montana*

For the past several years, she had replaced the posting every month, two times in order to alter the address where she could be located if someone knew of her brothers' whereabouts.

Hailee swallowed hard to hold back her tears. She didn't want to leave Cincinnati and diminish her chances of finding her younger brothers. However, she knew that a change in location would do her heart good, and that she was following God's prompting to fulfill the dream she'd had in her heart since she was a young girl.

Tomorrow, Hailee would travel nearly two thousand miles to a place she'd never been, where she had been hired as the town's new teacher. Yes, such a change would help her to leave the past behind and start life anew.

She turned and walked the short distance from the train depot to Austin Street. Her feet ached from all the walking she'd done in the past few hours, replacing each of the seven postings in varied locations around the city. Now she had one more place to visit before leaving Ohio—one more person to see.

Hailee sat on the wooden bench and waited for the horse-drawn hansom cab to round the corner during one of its many scheduled stops. Hoping she had read the schedule for the cab correctly, she counted the money in her coin purse. She'd ridden in a hansom only a handful of times due to the cost, but today was an exception. Today was the day she needed to travel to a distant part of the city to say a final good-bye to an important part of her life. Yes, she needed to put a period at the end of the sentence that had affected her more than anything else in her nineteen years.

Within minutes, Hailee spied the carriage. She rose to her feet as the hansom cab slowed to a stop.

A short, husky man with a mustache that was black peppered with gray and that curled up in swirly loops at the ends stepped down from the back of the carriage. He removed his top hat and, with a bow, greeted her. "Good afternoon, ma'am. Ambrose at your service. Where may I take you today?"

"Hello, Ambrose. My name is Hailee Annigan. Would you please take me to The Sanctuary of Promise?" Hailee smiled at the driver.

"My! A ways away, is it not?" said Ambrose. "But, yes, Miss Annigan, I can take you there." He extended a white-gloved hand and helped Hailee into the cab. "If you need anything, anything at all, please don't hesitate to let me know. I can hear you through the open window in the roof."

Hailee nodded and glanced up at the small window with a hinged cover that was open. As she settled into her seat, Ambrose prepared to close the door. "Are you comfortable?" he asked.

"Yes, thank you."

"Very well, then. We shall be on our way." He bowed again, placed his hat back on his head, and closed the door. Moments later, they lurched forward with the clatter of horses' hooves.

"Are you from Cincinnati, miss?" Ambrose asked sometime later.

"Yes, I've lived here all my life," Hailee replied. She appreciated the driver's small talk. It took her mind off of the nervousness she felt.

"As have I," said Ambrose. "Do you have family here?"

Hailee wasn't sure how to answer that question. Were her brothers still in Cincinnati? Or, had they traveled far from the city that held so many memories? "My parents have gone to be with the Lord, but I do have two brothers," she finally answered.

"I'm sorry to hear about your parents, miss." Ambrose paused. "It sure is a lovely time of year, isn't it, with the flowers blooming and the trees with all their leaves? I have to admit, I enjoy every season, but winter gets a mite cold at times driving the cab."

Hailee smiled and nodded. She could only imagine how a cold Cincinnati winter might affect cab drivers. She wondered about the winters in Montana. Were they similar to those she had experienced her entire life in Ohio? Would she still love summer the best of all the seasons once she was settled in her new home? She watched in silence as they passed by the tall buildings, some dating back to the turn of the century, and dozens of other buggies traversing the crowded avenue. Would Pine Haven match the hustle and bustle of Cincinnati? Would it have streets lined with storefronts offering a wide variety of goods? Somehow, she doubted it. From what she had heard, Montana was rugged and wild, Pine Haven nothing like a big city. *A change will do you good, Hailee*, she reminded herself. *Even if that change is a drastic one.*

"We're almost there," Ambrose announced. "It's been a while since I've traveled out this way. I'd forgotten how beautiful this road looks, lined with trees as it is."

"It is beautiful," Hailee agreed. The buildings became fewer and farther apart, while the buckeye trees grew more numerous. They folded out their branches as if to welcome Hailee to the place she would never forget, a place where God had molded her into the type of woman He desired her to become.

In the circular driveway in front of The Sanctuary of Promise, the cab slowed to a stop. The door opened, and Ambrose peered in. "Here we are, Miss Annigan." He held out an arm to assist her out of the cab.

"Thank you, Ambrose." Hailee climbed out, handing him her hard-earned money for the fare. She bid him farewell as he climbed back onto the cab and picked up the reins.

As he drove away, she waved good-bye, then turned around and surveyed the mammoth building before her. The brick structure had four stories and two wings, the third- and fourth-floor windows of which were covered with curtains, and a covered porch held up by four faded white pillars. The building was surrounded by a well-manicured lawn, and Hailee spied the familiar tiered birdbath under an oak tree. To the left of the tree was the fenced-in garden where she had learned much about farming.

Looking back at the building, Hailee could see the heads of students inside the first floor windows and recalled the many hours she'd spent in the classroom. A little girl turned her head and peered out at Hailee with a look of curiosity.

Hailee smiled at her and urged her feet to move toward the front door. Had there really been a time when she'd spent almost every waking moment in this looming fortress of a building? It felt as if she'd stepped back in time; while everything around her had changed through the years, and while hundreds of children from entirely different backgrounds had lived in its walls and played on its grounds, The Sanctuary of Promise had undergone no observable alterations, at least on its exterior.

On the porch now, Hailee sucked in her breath and turned the doorknob. As she stepped inside the vast entryway, a mix of emotions stirred within her.

"I'll be right with you," a woman called from an adjacent room.

Hailee recognized the voice and smiled. "Miss Ella?"

"Hailee Annigan, is that you?" Ella Fanshaw rushed through the door toward Hailee and wrapped her arms around the much younger woman. "It's been the better of three months since we last saw each other. How have you been?"

"I've been well, thank you."

"Please, come into the dining area," Ella invited her.

Hailee followed Ella and sat down at the long, worn wooden table—quite possibly for the last time in her life, she realized—where she had once taken every meal. Gazing around the room, she recalled the first day she'd entered The Sanctuary of Promise, at fourteen years of age....

⚬⚬⚬

"I don't belong here!" Hailee shouted at Officer Ulmer, who had taken her inside the large, frightening building.

"The judge ordered for you to come to The Sanctuary of Promise, so that is where you'll stay," Officer Ulmer said firmly. "Had you not done what you did, you

wouldn't have found yourself in this predicament." He paused and shook his head. "Just about every child I remand to The Sanctuary of Promise makes the same claim about not belonging here. When will you street children come to learn that crime doesn't pay? It never has and never will."

"But I don't belong here!" Hailee stamped her feet.

"If you don't belong here, then why do you have a reputation for thievery among the storefront owners in East Cincinnati?"

"A reputation?"

"Yes, a reputation. There's nary a storekeeper who hasn't fallen victim to your thieving ways and lying tongue."

Hailee ignored the officer's insinuations. Yes, she had stolen; yes, she had lied; and, yes, she had deceived. What of it? It had been out of necessity that she had done such things. Had she not needed to provide for her younger brothers, she wouldn't have dreamed of lying, stealing, and deceiving.

"You don't understand. I need to be with my brothers!" Without forethought, Hailee pushed past the man, rushed out the door, and raced across the vast lawn. Spurred on by the rhythmic thumping of her heart within her chest, she ran with all her might, willing her eyes to adjust to the darkness of night so that she could make out her path.

"You come back here, young lady!"

Hailee stole a glance over her shoulder and saw Officer Ulmer running after her, but the thickset man was no match for her speed. "Stop that girl!" he yelled as the gap between them continued to widen. "Stop her!"

As Hailee rounded the corner of East Seventh Street and Holmes, a strong hand grabbed her arm and stopped her in mid-stride. "Not so fast," the officer said sternly.

"Let me go!" Hailee wailed as she tried to wriggle out of the officer's grasp.

"Not this time," he said. "Another runaway?"

Hailee looked around. Officer Ulmer was stumbling toward them, gasping for breath.

"Yes," he managed, still panting. "Ten years ago, I could have caught her"—he expelled a loud breath—"but my best years of chasing street urchins are behind me."

The other officer chuckled. "That's true of a lot of us, Quincy."

"That's why I requested this post, delivering wayward juveniles to The Sanctuary of Promise," Officer Ulmer continued. "It's supposed to be easier and less eventful. But then, spitfires like this Hailee Annigan come along and make my job almost impossible." He breathed in and out, in and out. "Still, children like Hailee give me reason to pray even harder. Yes, I lift every lost child I meet to my Father's throne, asking Him to take care of their needs, and—"

Out of desperation, Hailee leaned forward and bit the officer who held her on the arm. Yelling in pain, he immediately released his grip. Hailee stepped back and was ready to run, but Officer Ulmer grabbed her arms and held her fast. "She really doesn't think she belongs in The Sanctuary of Promise, Officer Edwards," he said.

"Hmph. Do any of them?" Officer Edwards scowled and rubbed his arm where Hailee had bitten him.

She glanced around, hoping for another way to escape her captors. She would not give in and be taken to The Sanctuary of Promise. Sure, it was a big brick mansion, but it was just a fancy jail. Besides, she had her brothers to care for. Why couldn't these officers see that?

"You don't understand," she whined. "My brother Philip, he has to walk with a crutch." She pasted a sad look on her face in hopes of eliciting their pity. One thing she had learned on the streets was how to manipulate others through emotional appeals.

"Right. And I'm the president of the United States," Officer Ulmer said with a chuckle. "Let's get moving." He started walking and pulled her along.

"I'm telling the truth," Hailee insisted, trying to keep her voice low and her tone mournful.

"Are you aware of the alternative of going to The Sanctuary of Promise?" Officer Ulmer asked.

"What?" Hailee demanded.

"You would be put in jail."

"The Sanctuary of Promise is a jail—just a fancy one," she retorted. "Nothing good ever comes from being in a place like that."

"I think you'll find The Sanctuary of Promise quite different from the jail where you were held until the judge heard your case."

"I don't want to be in any jail. I want to be free!" Hailee gritted her teeth and again tried to wriggle out of his grasp, but Officer Edwards held fast to her shoulder as he walked alongside. She was no match for two grown men.

"You know, most kids at The Sanctuary are released after about a year and a half," mused Officer

Ulmer. "With the little shenanigan you just pulled, you're likely to spend more time there, though."

"I won't stay there," Hailee insisted. "I'll just escape. I have to. My brothers are depending on me. Who'll make them dinner? Who'll tell little Philip the story about baby Moses in the basket?"

"I'm sure someone will see to it that they're taken care of," Officer Edwards muttered. "If they even exist."

"You don't believe that I have brothers?" Hailee couldn't believe what she was hearing. Why would she make that up?

"You wouldn't believe the stories we hear," Officer Ulmer chuckled. "Do you think you're the first wayward juvenile to insist she has younger siblings to care for? And we've heard the brother-with-a-crutch story one too many times."

"But it's the truth! One of Philip's feet is turned the wrong way. He was born like that. And it makes it hard for him to walk, so he has to use a crutch."

"And just how old is this Philip?" Officer Ulmer asked as they entered The Sanctuary of Promise grounds.

"He's only six."

"What about your other brother? I'm sure he can care for him just fine," Officer Edwards said dryly.

"Reuben?" Hailee was getting angry. "Reuben can't care for him—not like I can. He's only twelve. And, sometimes, Reuben is...well...grouchy."

"And where do these brothers live?" asked Officer Ulmer.

"Over on Gardner St—wait, why?"

"Gardner Street?" asked Officer Ulmer.

"No, not Gardner Street," Hailee said. "I meant to say Garrison Avenue."

"Either way, we'll find them," said Officer Edwards. "Again, assuming they exist."

"Why doesn't anybody believe me?" Hailee demanded.

"With the crimes you've committed and the lies you've told, it is a bit difficult to believe you," Officer Ulmer reasoned. He reached out with his free hand and opened the front door of The Sanctuary. "Good evening Miss Torenz," he said as they stepped inside and were greeted by a young woman. "We've got one who insists on escaping."

"Don't worry, she won't be escaping," the woman assured him. "Please bring her upstairs to the Yellow Flower Room."

Still fighting to be released, Hailee kicked and wriggled as the officers dragged her up the stairs. Miss Torenz opened a door, and the officers shoved Hailee inside and quickly shut the door.

"Let me out!" she shouted, beating on the door with her fists. She had to get out of here—her brothers' lives depended on it! No doubt, little Philip was hungry right now. It was bad enough that she'd spent last night in jail and left Philip and Reuben all alone. But two nights in a row? Hailee cringed at the thought.

"It'll do you no good to pound on the door," said Miss Torenz through the door, her voice firm. "We'll bring you some breakfast in the morning."

"No, wait! You can't leave me here!" Hailee resumed pounding again on the door. After a while, her fists sore, she turned to assess her whereabouts. A tiny window on the far wall allowed a minute amount of moonlight into the room. With the exception of a bed with a faded quilt, the closet-sized room was empty. Hailee squinted. Was the wallpaper yellow with large sunflowers? It was difficult to tell in the dim light, but she supposed it was, which would account for the name of the room.

One last time, Hailee pounded on the door and screamed until her throat hurt. Finally, she gave up, turned, and leaned back against the door. She slid down into a seated position, buried her face in her hands, and began to sob. While she'd never been one to give up, no matter how harsh the circumstances life had dealt to her, this was the exception. She was trapped, and there was nothing she could do about it....

ABOUT THE AUTHOR

Penny Zeller is the author of several books and numerous magazine articles in national and regional publications. She is also the author of the humor blog "A Day in the Life of a Mom, Wife, and Author" (www.pennyzeller.wordpress.com). She is an active volunteer in her community, serving as a women's Bible study small-group leader and co-organizing a women's prayer group. Her passion is to use the gift of the written word that God has given her to glorify Him and to benefit His kingdom. *Kaydie* follows *McKenzie* in Montana Skies, her first series with Whitaker House.

When she's not writing, Penny enjoys spending time with her family and camping, hiking, canoeing, and playing volleyball. She and her husband, Lon, reside in Wyoming with their two children. Penny loves to hear from her readers at her Web site, www.pennyzeller.com.

McKenzie
Penny Zeller

Desperation to save her younger sister from an abusive husband prompts McKenzie Worthington to run away from the comforts of her Boston home as a mail-order bride for a rancher in the Montana Territory. She takes comfort in knowing she can have the marriage annulled when she rescues her sister. Desperation is also what prompted Zachary Sawyer to post the ad, and he eagerly awaits the woman God has chosen as his wife. When they meet, McKenzie tries to keep her distance, but she can't help feeling attracted to Zach and his selfless, godly ways. What will become of her plan?

ISBN: 978-1-60374-216-0 • Trade • 320 pages

WHITAKER
HOUSE